HEAVY METAL

Murder

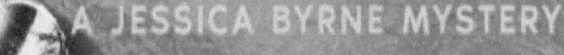

A JESSICA BYRNE MYSTERY

KRISTEN ANDREWS

One

Vlad Boyko is a big, scary ex-con who owns a garage in the shadow of the dump near the outskirts of town. He's a former member of the Ukrainian army and once stuck a screwdriver in a guy's forehead during a vodka-infused argument over the Philadelphia Eagles. Vlad's a big Eagles fan. Someone's been stealing catalytic converters from his lot full of old junkers, and that's how Vlad and I became acquainted. He's my client. The local cops weren't too concerned with his catalytic converter problem, so he hired me to check into it.

The county has recently issued me, Jessica Byrne a brand-new private investigator's license. I'm in business with my best friend, Sam DiAngelo, and we rent an office in downtown Pottstown, above Tito's Tacos Mexican Restaurant. Sam's not a private investigator. She's a different kind of PI. The kind that hunts things that go bump in the night. I chase cheating spouses, and Sam hunts ghosts and cryptids. The deal is, we help each other out on cases. For me, that means trying not to swallow my tongue from laughing as Sam attempts to communicate with someone's dearly departed papaw. Sam's a true believer and I'm a debunker. Or bunker. Whatever the term is for major nonbeliever.

The temperature was hovering just below freezing on a late January night and my body was covered in black thermals and a heavy winter jacket. Tonight I was conducting surveillance for Vlad. I jumped in my car, picked

Sam up at her condo across town, and we headed over to Boyko Motors. Sam's wavy brown hair was covered by a pink ski hat with a fake fur puff on top of it, and she wore a matching pink puffer jacket. Sam's curvy and gorgeous. She was briefly employed as a professional belly dancer before she threw her back out and was forced to hang up her bedazzled bikini top. In contrast, I'm what the world refers to as "petite." I'm barely five foot four, most of which is legs, and my long red hair was currently stuffed under a ratty, old baseball cap. At least once a month, usually at a gas station, some skeevy guy will wink at me and say, "Red in the head, hot in the bed." Old ladies in the grocery store like to touch my hair. I've learned to roll with it.

We arrived at Vlad's garage in an aging industrial area of West Pottsgrove Township, and I pulled into Doogal's Lawn and Tree Service parking lot across the street from Vlad's. I tucked my car behind a low hedgerow and killed the engine.

"It's real spooky back here, Jess." Sam thinks everything is spooky, possessed, or from another dimension. "There's no cars parked at the other businesses."

"Yeah, I noticed that too. No second shifts, I guess."

Sam opened the Maryanne's Moist Muffins and More box that she brought with her, and set it on the dashboard.

I opened the lid and checked the contents. "Four chocolate chip muffins. Excellent." Quality snacks are a must-have when pulling surveillance.

Sam took a muffin from the box and peeled off the paper. "You know, we're only a mile from the old landfill. That deserted old trash mountain has real potential for paranormal activity. Who knows what kind of mutant creatures live out there? If I'm going to expand the paranormal side of our business, I need to become a subject matter expert on cryptids. You and I should go up there sometime and have a look around, you know?"

I gave her the side-eye and selected a muffin from the box. This wasn't the oddest conversation we've had since we started the business. Not even close. "Sure, Sam. Sometime."

"We could conduct some real scientific research, and take some videos of my investigation. We can put it up on TikTok and YouTube. I could become a paranormal influencer and make some real bank."

"How about I just tag along and hold the camera for you?" I drew a hard line at me, the paranormal, and social media exposure.

Sam finished her muffin, settled back in her seat and closed her eyes. A few minutes later, her snores filled the car. Every so often, I started the car up and blasted the heater so we wouldn't freeze solid. After two hours of watching nothing, my ass was asleep and I'd depleted the remaining muffins. I was ready to call it a night when a pickup truck rolled up to the curb outside Boyko Motors. Sam was still dozing. I poked her awake and pointed to the street. She yawned, picked up her digital camera and began snapping photos. Two guys dressed in all black jumped from the pickup, glanced around, then removed some tools from the back.

"Those fools are dressed up like ninjas from an old karate movie," Sam said, adjusting the lens. "Head to toe black, with only their eyes showing. What's that one guy holding, bolt-cutters?"

I picked up my binoculars and adjusted them. "Looks like it. Do you see any guns on them?"

Sam zoomed in. "No. But you know what assuming does."

The men approached the eight-foot-high chain-link fence surrounding Vlad's side lot. One guy took the bolt cutters to the lock, and the other shoved the gate open. A motion light blinked on, illuminating the lot. It didn't seem to faze them. The men propped up a dented minivan with a scissor jack and slid under it on their backs with their legs sticking out. The sound of saws grinding on metal continued for a minute or two, then they slid back out with the catalytic converter. Sam's camera clicked away.

"Jeez, Sam. That was quick."

"Quick way to lose a limb. If that flimsy-ass jack falls, those idiots could be squashed like bugs."

"Vlad told me that there's precious metals inside catalytic converters. That's why people steal them."

"Whatever the hell is in them, they aren't worth being crushed, arrested, or both."

"Agreed."

The thieves moved to a sideswiped SUV and repeated the same process.

"Just call the cops and let them handle it, Jess. Then we can go home. I'm freezing my ass off. Your heater sucks."

"There's nothing wrong with my heater. And Vlad doesn't want me to call the cops. He said he wants to deal with the thieves himself. Whatever that means."

"It means a free lobotomy with a rusty screwdriver."

"Whatever, Sam. When you zoom in, can you see the license plate on their pickup?"

She shook her head. "No. Not from this angle."

By the time the thieves were done boosting the third catalytic converter, I was pissed. I waited until they scooted under the next derelict car, set the binoculars down and shoved my phone into my pocket. "Wait here, Sam."

She put the camera on her lap. "What are you doing?"

I opened the door and jumped out of the car. I sprinted down Doogal's driveway, crossed the street to the ninjas' pickup and hunkered down by the front tire. I pulled my phone from my pocket and texted Sam. *Did they see me*?

A second later she replied, *Not yet! WTF*? with an angry face emoji.

I scooted to the back of the pickup truck, snapped a photo, and dashed back toward my car. The men began shouting. Shit. I was busted. A gunshot blasted the pavement a foot away from me. I froze.

Sam stuck her head out the passenger window and screamed, "You bastards are lucky I don't have my boyfriend's gun with me! I'd shoot you right in the nards!"

"Yeah, yeah," one the men shouted back.

A second shot whizzed past me and blew out the Doogal's Lawn and Tree Service sign, and I dove for the pavement.

"Get up! Get up!" Sam shouted. "Run!"

I scrambled up and raced for the car, bent over with my arms covering my head. Another shot ricocheted off Doogal's driveway and ended up who knows where. Sam shrieked unintelligibly, dashed around the back of my car, and jumped in the driver's seat. She leaned across and shoved the passenger door open. I slid across the hood of the car Dukes of Hazzard style, turned, and jumped headfirst into the passenger seat as the car began moving. When my ass found the seat, Sam mashed the gas pedal and peeled out of the driveway. I flailed around and pulled the car door shut as Sam floored it down the street. Sirens sounded off in the distance.

Sam punched me in the arm.

"Ow! What the hell was that for?"

"Do you have a friggin' death wish or something?"

Another shot went off. My car took a direct hit to the ass end. We ducked, the car swerved, and we narrowly missed slamming into a fire hydrant. We both felt around to make sure we didn't have any bullet holes in us.

"Are you good, Sam?"

"Never better!" She blew a stop sign and yanked my car onto High Street.

I fastened my seatbelt. "Dammit. I hate it when my car gets shot. That's the second time now."

"That's gonna hurt your resale value."

Two

It's not easy falling asleep right after you've been shot at. Personally, I need time to decompress and reevaluate my life choices. It took me a few hours to convince myself that I was a normal, well-adjusted person who makes good decisions. I think I got about four hours asleep before Bruce, my super-sized orange tabby cat, woke me up after eight with his butt in my face. Bleary-eyed, I turned him around to face me and told him what happened the night before. He listened to me, purring.

"Getting the thieves' license plate number was a step in the right direction, Bruce, but the new bullet hole in my car is a pain in the ass."

I acquired the first bullet hole in my car from my very first divorce case a few months ago. The skanky girlfriend I was surveilling pulled a pea shooter out of her fake Marc Jacobs bag and shot a hole in my bumper. Sam tossed her milkshake through the woman's sunroof as we sped away, so I'd call it even. I'd made a halfhearted attempt to fix the hole with some crap I bought at AutoZone, but the result wasn't pretty.

Bruce blinked at me. He was only interested in breakfast.

I crawled out of bed, stretched out the knots in my back, eased into the shower and let the hot water pound my shoulders. I dried and fluffed my hair, applied some lip stick, and dressed in my standard winter attire of jeans, boots, and a pullover sweater. One benefit of self-employment is that you can dress however the hell you want, which for me is utilitarian meets comfortable.

I headed downstairs. My mom, Valentina, was in the kitchen making coffee in her pink zip-up robe and Bruce was at his bowl eating his crunchies.

"Hi, Mom."

Mom moved in with me after she retired from her job as a nurse at St. Agnes Hospital a few years ago and broke her leg learning to snowboard at age sixty-five. I liked the help with the mortgage and she liked the company, so she never moved out. I'm the youngest of three and I think I'm the oops kid, but Mom denies this claim. My sister Margaret, the middle child, lives in upstate New York, and my brother Michael lives in San Diego. She's an artist and knows a lot of big words, and he's a tech nerd. It's possible that I'm the oops kid *and* the underachiever in the family.

"Good morning, Jess." She poured herself a cup, stirred in creamer and sugar, and sat down at the kitchen table.

I crossed my fingers that she hadn't laid eyes on the bumper bullet hole on her trip down the driveway to get the newspaper, which she reads daily for the yard sale announcements, obituaries and the crossword puzzle. "What are you up to today?"

"Harry and I are swinging by the Otter Club. The party planning committee is organizing the next benefit dance."

Harry and Mom have been engaged for over twenty years. Harry wants to marry my mom, but she likes the arrangement the way it is. Harry's been a member of the Loyal and Vigilant Order of the Otters since forever, and Mom joined the club when they began admitting women as full members five years ago. Right now, she's head of the party planning committee, a dysfunctional group of postmenopausal women who get in fights about things like the color of streamers and what brand of decaf coffee to serve.

"The theme is the eighties, and it's going to be a hoot," she said. "You really should join the club, Jess."

"Pass."

"Come on, Jess. You'd meet people and maybe even pick up some new clients."

The Otter Club has been part of the downtown social scene since the nineteen forties, probably around the time the last actual otters packed up and vacated Pottstown's stretch of the Schuylkill River. The Otters started out as a businessmen's social club but over time has devolved into a coed drinking club for retirees. Besides consuming alcohol, the Otters work on a few charity events throughout the year. The club occupies a stately Victorian home downtown, and sometimes I visit as a guest with Mom and Harry. They have good bar food, cheap drinks, and free entertainment in the form of drunk old people.

"I don't have time to make the meetings, Mom. You know my job has weird hours." The truth is, I'm not joining the Otter Club for at least another thirty years. Maybe not even then.

I grabbed a box of Tastykake Krimpets from the pantry, picked up my bag and shrugged on my coat. "Gotta run, Mom. Love you."

"Love you, kid. Put a hat on," Mom shouted as I shut the door.

My only other client is a guy named Daniel Lakeland. He's a local jeweler, he's super rich and in the middle of an ugly divorce. Tracy, his slutty soon-to-be ex-wife, is the owner of Tracy's Day Spa in town. Daniel hired me to dig up dirt on Tracy's latest side piece so he can look good to the judge.

I tossed my bag in my car, jumped in, and rolled down High Street, the main drag through town. Tracy's Day Spa is on the way to my office. Her building is seven blocks from mine, to be exact. I slowed down, checking for Tracy's car. Her gleaming, white Jaguar F-Type was parked in her reserved space. I hit the gas and headed past the mix of hopeful new businesses and deserted storefronts that make up downtown Pottstown and parked in front of Tito's Tacos. I waved to the owner, Manny, through the window. Manny bought the business from his dad a few years ago, and he's my hot landlord. We also dated briefly when Max and I were in an "off" stretch. I pushed the restaurant door open and warmth, music, and delicious aromas enveloped me. I loved Tito's.

I sat down at the bar. "Hi, Manny. How are you doing?"

"I'm well. Yourself?"

"I'm okay. I stopped by to let you know that I'll have the rent check to you by the end of the week. I'm having some short-term cash flow problems." My cash flow problems were more like medium to long-term, but he didn't need to know that.

"Get it to me when you can. I know you're good for the money." Manny was being kind. The truth is, I'm not always good for the money, like right now.

"Thanks." I waved goodbye and headed out.

I fumbled around in my bag for the keys to the office. Sam and I recently scraped together enough extra money to have our sign made, and Manny attached it to the door for us. It reads *NPI—Normal and Paranormal Investigations. Reasonable Rates*. I found my keys, unlocked the door and ran up the stairs to the second floor.

Our office is one medium-sized room outfitted with desks and chairs purchased at the used office furniture outlet's going out of business sale. Part of the room is used as a reception area, with a second-hand couch and a coffee table Mom and I picked up at a yard sale. Sam painted it to cover the coffee ring stains. We splurged and bought a minifridge from Walmart. We use the bathroom downstairs at Tito's Tacos. The office has great light, the rent is cheap and sometimes we score free burritos.

Sam left me a note that she was out walking Sparkle, her gigantic English mastiff. She adopted him from the SPCA six months ago. Sparkle was a reject and had lived at the shelter for nearly a year. No one wanted him because he's slightly cross-eyed, and his tongue is too long for his mouth. When Sam found him online, she fell in love. She brings Sparkle to the office most days, where he spends his time napping and farting. I sat down at my desk, unwrapped a Krimpet and took a bite. I scrolled through my emails, deleting the spam as I went. My phone rang. I answered it and hit the speaker button.

"Hey, Red. How's it going?"

"Hey, Max." Max is an ex-Borough police officer, and the current owner of O'Conner Investigation Consultants. We met in criminal justice class in college nearly ten years ago. Max is six feet of all night long, lean but muscular, with dark brown hair that isn't going to slide off the back of his head when he hits thirty-five. In addition to my ex-boyfriend, Max is also my ex-employer. And sometimes after a few beers, we forget we aren't a couple anymore, which leads to a night of fantastic sex with minimal regret.

"What do you need, Max? Our breakup is still on, right?"

"It's still on. Just a friendly check-in." Max's firm is my main competition. Right now, he's winning.

"That's sweet. What do you want?"

"Nothing. Tell me about your new client, the one with the junk cars over in West Pottsgrove. What's his name?"

"That's confidential."

"It's Vlad Boyko, isn't it?"

Dammit. "How did you know that, Max?"

"I arrested him a few times. Vlad ran a chop shop when I was in the department, and he dealt with a lot of shady people. He's a criminal."

"Ex-criminal. And now that you know his name, put it in the vault."

"I will, Jess, but he's trouble. His street name is Vlad the Impaler. He did a nickel in the joint for stabbing a guy in the forehead with a screwdriver. He was paroled two years ago. Supposedly, he's gone legit."

"I'm aware of the screwdriver incident."

"Don't piss him off."

"I won't. Besides, I think Vlad likes me. When I first met with him, I told him I'm half Ukrainian and I did a vodka shot with him. We bonded." I could practically see Max shake his head over the phone.

"Let me guess. Vlad's missing some catalytic converters."

"Perhaps."

"Smitty said that Pottstown PD has been investigating catalytic converter thefts for a few months. They're happening all over the Borough and the surrounding townships." Smitty is Detective Joe Smits, Max's ex-partner and good friend.

"Vlad mentioned their investigation. He told me the police spent a few weeks on his case but didn't come up with any suspects."

"Smitty has a few leads, but nothing solid yet. He also mentioned that he talked to a West Pottsgrove officer today who told him a resident called in a complaint last night about shots fired near Vlad Boyko's garage. I don't suppose you were in the vicinity last night?"

"Potentially."

In the background, I could hear Max vigorously tapping a pen on his desk.

"Red, we've talked about you and your risk-taking behaviors." Despite our breakup. Max was protective of me. "You need to be more careful. Don't learn you're not bulletproof the hard way."

"Max, I was totally careful last night. I wasn't shot, and I got a license plate number. It was a good night. I should have this Vlad thing wrapped up in no time. Easy peasy. By the way, can you get Smitty to run the plate for me?"

"Do me a favor. Partner with me on the Boyko case."

"We are partnering, Max. You're conning Smitty into running the plate for me."

The pen tapping became aggressive. "You know what I mean."

"I do, and I'm being careful. It's important to me that I don't rely on you all the time. I don't work for you anymore and I need to handle my cases on my own."

"You're prideful."

"I am not. I'm being independent, and that's different. Will you ask Smitty to run the plate or what?"

Max sighed. "Sure."

I gave him the number, and he put me on hold.

After a few minutes, he came back on the line. "The plate was stolen. It belongs on a Honda with an address in Reading."

"Crap. That lead went nowhere fast."

"Team with me on this one, Jess. Vlad's a bad guy."

"You keep saying that. Did you call just to bug me about him? Don't you have anything else going on?"

"As a matter of fact, I do. I picked up a high-dollar insurance fraud case here in town that I need to get back to. Keep me posted on Vlad."

"You're on a need-to-know basis."

"And Red?"

"Yes?"

"What color panties have you got on?"

"Not helpful." I hung up and shoved the impaler business out of my mind.

A moment later, my phone buzzed with a text from Vlad. It read, *You come now. I don't talk on the phone.*

I texted back, *Be there soon.* I locked up the office, jumped in my car and headed through town to Vlad's garage. Pottstown has the distinction of being wedged between the dump, which thankfully doesn't smell like hot garbage anymore, a nuclear power plant, and a few superfund sites. The town is perched on the banks of the beautiful brown Schuylkill River, a former repository for industrial waste. The river is making a comeback for people who like to float around in kayaks, and once in a while you can see a turtle or two. Pottstown has been described as an authentic urban experience, which means you can get a good cheesesteak here, but park under a streetlight and lock your car first.

I pulled up to Vlad's two-bay garage as James Gang's "Funk #48" blasted through my speakers. The rusty chain-link fence with the newly broken lock encircled the shitshow that was the side lot. The lot was crammed full of engine blocks, doors, windshields, and smashed-up cars in need of a new lease on life. A few shined-up beaters were parked by the street with For Sale signs on them. I locked my car, hiked my bag onto my shoulder, and marched into the office to the sounds of hammering, grinding, and what sounded like Ukrainian cursing came from the half-open garage doors.

I stepped inside the small office. A smartly dressed bleach blond with big blue eyes glanced up from her iPhone and gave me a disapproving up-down look.

"May I help you?" Her accent was the same as Vlad's. Heavy, but nice.

"I'm Jessica Byrne. Vlad asked me to stop by."

She tossed her head to her right. "Through the door. I buzz you in." She hit a button and yelled, "Vlad, the lady detective is here!" Her eyes dropped back to her phone and I entered his office.

Vlad Boyko towered over me at about six feet, four inches. His worn, greased-stained Eagles sweatshirt stretched over two hundred pounds of solid work-type muscles and was paired with worn camouflage pants. A Ukrainian flag hung on the wall behind a battered desk, which held a glass ashtray with a lit cigarette, a bottle of vodka, a shot glass and a black rotary phone. Vlad shut the door, sat down, and put his size twelve combat boots up on the desk. He studied me with brilliant blue eyes that looked like they'd seen some shit, then motioned to two beat-up leather chairs opposite his desk.

"Sit, sit." Vlad's deep voice was as imposing as his stature.

I took off my down coat and perched on the edge the squishy old chair.

"You come over right away. That's good. Most Americans, they're late. Always running around texting but doing nothing."

I didn't disagree with his observation.

"I saw on my security camera you watched my lot last night."

"Yes, my partner Sam and I did."

Vlad ran a giant, calloused hand through his graying hair, took a drag on the cigarette, and blew the smoke out of his nose. "I run a legitimate business here. I pay my taxes. I buy wrecked cars, fix them up, sell them. All my cars have clean titles. I put big lock on the gate, *zlodiyi* break the lock. I buy a watch dog, he run away. Then the police patrol the neighborhood for two weeks, but they catch no one. I see the police parked outside. They do nothing but eat doughnuts, talk on the phone."

I nodded. I thought his assessment of the police was a bit harsh, but I used to date one so I'm biased. And I eat doughnuts and other snack food items when I do surveillance, too. Fortunately, I have my mother's high metabolism.

"So, lady detective, what happened last night?"

"Sam and I saw two men enter your lot, stealing catalytic converters. They took a few shots at us. I managed to get a plate number from their pickup but it didn't pan out."

"Yes. I see on my video camera that *zlodiyi* bring a gun this time," Vlad growled. "But I did not see the shooting."

"So you saw one of them pull a gun?"

"Yes, then he ran out of the camera range."

"They also broke your new lock."

"I see that this morning. They cost me much money." Vlad peered at me through the blue-gray smoke cloud. "You keep watching. When you find out who does this, I'll handle them. I'll take a screwdriver to their *holovy*."

I wasn't sure what body part a *holovy* was, but I had a decent guess. "Vlad, when I figure out who's stealing from you, we're going to let the police handle it."

"Yeah, yeah, the police." He muttered in Ukrainian under his breath.

I was about to impress Vlad with my new plan to catch the thieves when his phone rang. He answered, yelled something about Putin into the phone, and waved me off, which was a good thing because I really didn't have much of a plan yet.

I left Vlad's, cruised back to my office and found a parking space down the street. I power walked up the block, unlocked my door and jogged up the stairs. I stretched out on the couch and took a snooze to make up for the night before. Fifteen minutes later, Sparkle woke me up with a wet nose to the face. I scratched him behind his big, velvety black ears, and he shoved himself under the coffee table. Sam set a takeout bag down, and Sparkle stuck his snout up and sniffed it hopefully.

"I don't thrive in this cold-ass weather," Sam said, taking off her coat and tossing it on to the coatrack. It slipped off, fell on the floor and she left it there. "But Sparkle and I made run to Romeo's Delight, and I picked us up meatballs, garlic knots, and carrot cake. Totally worth the frost bite. Shove over."

I sat up and stretched. Sam plunked down next to me, smoothing out her dress. Sam takes her fashion ideas from Stevie Nicks. Most days Sam wears long, flowing dresses with drapey sleeves, usually black or white, with matching boots and hats. Today her black dress was accompanied by thick black leggings. You can channel Stevie Nicks but still be practical about it.

We dug into lunch. I recently abandoned my New Year's "eat healthier" resolution, and I dunked a garlic knot in the meatball sauce and shoved it in my mouth. Sauce dripped onto the edge of the coffee table. Sparkle's tongue emerged from below and licked it off. After I got a meatball down I said, "Listen, I'm really sorry we got shot at last night."

"Yeah, about that. I wasn't expecting you to take off running. That was not in the plan."

"I know. I needed that plate number, but it's a bust, anyway. The plate's from a stolen vehicle."

"That sucks. Shot at for nothing."

"I have a vehicle description, so it wasn't a totally worthless night."

Sam bit into a meatball, an orgasmic expression spreading across her face. "Damn, I love Romeo's meatballs." She sipped her drink. "So tell me what Vlad's like. I haven't gotten to meet him yet."

"He's a tall Ukrainian guy. In his fifties. A little scary. In addition to Eagles football, he's a fan of vodka and Marlboro Lights. A bit of a loud talker, but he's okay. Supposedly he's been rehabilitated by the state prison system."

"Well, don't get too close to him when he has a sharp tool in his hands. Just saying." Sam selected a garlic knot from the plastic container. "I've got some good news. I have a new client. She called this morning. Her name is Diane Durkle and she has a demon in her attic."

"That's too bad."

"Not for me. She wants me to come over and investigate. The usual, take a look around, and do some EMF readings. Sage the house and shit. Are you in?"

I stuffed a garlic knot in my mouth to hide the smirk. "Sure, I'm in. Set it up."

Three

I left the office at four and headed to the day spa to spy on Tracy. Max and Sam think surveillance is boring, but I like it. I have a natural inquisitiveness that goes back to when I was a little kid, and on occasion it's gotten me into trouble, like last night at Vlad's. When I was in school, knowing the answer to a question wasn't enough for me, I had to know *why*. Every day after school, I was glued to the TV watching old detective shows like *The Rockford Files* and *Magnum, P.I.*, but I didn't relate to the damsels in distress. I was in it for the car chases, explosions and gun fights. I wanted to be like the guys, sneaking around, driving cool cars and solving mysteries.

And now, here I was living the dream. Except I don't live in Malibu or Oahu. It was late winter in southeastern Pennsylvania, and I was slouched down in my bullet-ridden, aging BMW X3, waiting for Daniel Lakeland's wife to leave for the day. I bought the BMW from my Aunt Joanie when she moved into Breezy Creek Active Adult Living Community and started a moonlight bingo league and a singles' club. She gave me a good deal on it, but it came with strings attached. When she needs a ride, I have to oblige her, which means a lot of trips to the salon to get her hair set. The benefits of Aunt Joanie's car are that it has comfortable seats for surveillance and road trips, and it's fast if I need to lose a tail or escape from a crazed gunman, like last night. Despite the good seats, my ass was falling asleep. The dashboard clock read three forty-five and soon, Tracy would emerge from the spa after putting in a hard day of sitting on her ass doing nothing.

In my rearview mirror, I saw Max's giant silver Jeep Grand Wagoneer pull up behind me. I turned down "Whole Lotta Love" and cracked my window three inches. The icy wind blasted right through the crack. January sucks.

Max put his hand on the roof of my car, leaned down, and turned his blue-gray eyes loose on me. "I'm going to need to see your license and registration, miss. And turn Zeppelin back up."

"You couldn't ticket a naked jaywalker. You haven't worn a badge in three years. You're just a lowly PI, same as me, Max."

The truth is, of the two of us, I'm the lowly PI. Max's company specializes in insurance fraud, which sounds really boring, except he caters to corporate and high-net-worth clients. Max's cases involve the gamut of what rich people insure: art, jewelry, luxury cars, yachts, horses, businesses, other rich people, you name it. *My* clients are mainly pissed off spouses in the low-to-medium-net-worth range, with the exception of Daniel Lakeland. Rumor has it, he's worth about twenty million.

"Are you on an important case, Red? I see you pulled out the big guns." Barely concealing the amusement in his eyes, Max motioned to the Tastykake box on my passenger seat.

I grabbed the cellophane Krimpet wrappers and stuffed them in my coat pocket.

He cocked his head toward the day spa. "Is it haunted?"

"You never know. It's an old building. It could be. But for your information, I'm not on one of Sam's cases. And you're not my boss anymore, so I'm not telling you anything else. Bite me."

"I'll bite you anytime you want. Let me know where and when."

"Keep dreaming, Max," I huffed, as I shoved the visual from my mind. "You're blocking my view and blowing my cover. Why don't you board your land yacht and sail back to your bougie office?"

Max has a big, fancy car and a bougie office because three years ago, when Max was a Pottstown police detective, he got shot in the ass by a wealthy personal injury lawyer, Peter Peabody, managing partner of Peabody Lerch and Associates. Peter Peabody got greedy and was caught defrauding his clients. As the investigating detective, Max was a witness for the prosecution. The trial didn't go Peter's way, and he was convicted and given a lengthy prison sentence. The night before he reported to prison, he was partying with a bunch of furries and doing a lot of meth. Peter, high as a kite and dressed in a hamster suit, saw Max and shot him outside the Gas n' Git convenience store. Max was in the hospital for two weeks and had to quit the force. So Max hired his own lawyer and sued Peter for all he was worth. Now Max is loaded. I wish some rich furry would shoot me in my ass, but I don't have that kind of luck.

"Have dinner with me on Saturday night, Jess."

My expression must have appeared noticeably skeptical. "It's not a nookie invite, Red. Only dinner, I promise. We'll catch up."

I pretended to check the calendar on my cell phone. "I can do Friday, not Saturday." My schedule was wide open, as far as dates were concerned, but I wasn't going to let Max know that. On a typical Saturday night, Bruce and I would share a bag of cheese doodles on the couch and be asleep by nine. "Anywhere that serves a good, dry cabernet."

"Carmelo's. Eight."

In my side mirror, I watched him stride back to his SUV. Max's body makes my toes curl and my unit fire up spontaneously. He drove off, and a few moments later Tracy Lakeland flounced out of her building. She fluffed her chemically enhanced blond hair out from underneath the collar of her shearling coat and strutted down the walk to her Jag. Daniel told me Tracy spent too much time on the Home Shopping Channel and needed a hobby besides overspending and sleeping around, so he bought her the day spa a few years ago to try to keep her occupied. It didn't work. Now she also sleeps with her clients.

Tracy held a cell phone to her ear and a cigarette in her free hand. Through my binoculars, I observed her flick the cigarette butt to the ground, squish it out with a spike-heeled boot, and get in the Jag. She backed out, turned right onto High Street and headed west. I set the binoculars on the passenger seat, let a car get in between us and eased my car into the travel lane, following her.

Tracy continued down High Street for a few blocks, then turned right. I followed her at a safe distance as she made a left onto a side street. She stuffed the Jag into an open space on the curb between a Hyundai and a Ford. I cruised on down the street. In my rearview mirror, I watched her cross the street and enter a house. I circled around the block, returned to Earl Street, slipped in behind a sedan, and waited.

Small, historic brick homes in various stages of disrepair made up about three blocks of Earl Street and were in stark contrast to Daniel and Tracy's own house in Rosemont, a neighborhood on the east end of town. Rosemont's streets are lined with fifty-year-old sycamore trees which help to conceal the million-dollar stone and brick homes. Properties are professionally landscaped and backyards contain in-ground swimming pools. Range Rovers, Benzes and Porsches occupy many driveways in Rosemont.

I turned on XM, tuned to Ozzy's Boneyard, and devoured a Krimpet. The box was running low. I sipped my water carefully. Overhydration during surveillance is a rookie mistake.

On a sticky pad, I jotted down the makes, models, and colors of the cars parked on the street near the little brick house. A woman with a white pit bull mix stopped next to the tree by my car as he lifted his leg and took a long leak. I picked up my phone and pretended to have a conversation until he was done and they strolled away. Forty minutes later, well after my back was tight and a crick started in my neck, Tracy left the house, crossed the street, jumped into her Jaguar, and tore off. After a few minutes, I drove past the house she came out of. Just then, a man exited the house and watched me pass. I turned my head, hit the gas, and got out of there.

I took Industrial Parkway to my house in the east end of town. I don't live in Rosemont, like Tracy and Daniel do. I live on the other side of High Street, in a residential neighborhood built for World War II workers who made the steel that helped build the George Washington Bridge and the IRS building. My neighborhood is near the train tracks, the water treatment plant, and Home Depot.

My house is a smallish red brick colonial built in 1941, with an addition on the back and central air. An enormous maple tree takes up most of the tiny front lawn. I pulled into my driveway and climbed the steps to the front door. I found Mom in the kitchen stirring gravy at the stove. I inhaled deeply and dropped my shoulder bag on the floor.

"You made meatloaf?" I knew the answer already. I loved my mom's meatloaf. She doesn't put revolting stuff in it like leftover green beans or carrots or God forbid, peppers. Mom makes dinner most nights, which I love and appreciate, because cooking is not high up in my skillset. I'm more of an eater and cleaner-upper. I'll peel potatoes if I'm available, and I handle all takeout orders. That's our informal arrangement.

"Yes, I made a meatloaf, and there's some nice baby peas, too. I fixed the mashed potatoes with the lactose-free milk, so you can eat them."

Mom is concerned about my new diagnosis of lactose intolerance. I had to reassure her I can lead a fulfilling life. Ice cream is a major food group to her.

I carried everything to the table and we sat down. Right on schedule, Bruce appeared and sat by my left ankle, waiting for his share of the meatloaf. The vet told us Bruce needs to exercise more and eat diet kitty food so he can lose five pounds. He's the snuggliest cat I've ever met. He loves people and he snores.

"How was work today, Jess?" Mom's not a big fan of my new vocation as a PI. When I graduated from college with a degree in Criminal Justice and no hard skills, I got a job as a legal secretary at a sleezy mid-size law firm. When I'd finally had enough of the handsy attorneys and oversized egos, I gave the managing partner the finger, threw my mug and a picture of Bruce in a box, drove the five blocks to Max's new PI firm, and started working for him. At first, I was an administrative assistant. After a year, Max promoted me to an investigator trainee.

"My day wasn't bad for a Monday. My rich client needs to prove his wife is cheating on him so he can save millions in the divorce. He wants results yesterday."

Bruce tapped his paw on my knee and gave me the big green eyes. I slipped him a cat-sized meatloaf chunk. "Just this once, buddy."

"I don't like you following people around and taking photos of them. You're going to get thrown in jail. And I really don't like you chasing ghosts around with Sam. You shouldn't mess around with the paranormal. Your grammy wouldn't approve of that. May God rest her soul."

Mom's fantasy is for me to return to working as a legal secretary in a cushy law office, typing legal briefs, making regular contributions to a 401(k) account, and eventually marrying a lawyer. I happened to briefly date a lawyer when Max and I were broken up, but it didn't take. For Mom, an acceptable alternative would be for me to go back to work for Max. She loves Max. In her eyes, he can do no wrong.

"Mom, what Sam and I do is completely legal. I'm licensed by the county, and Sam is a certified paranormal expert by the powers vested in the internet and the community college's night program. You don't have to worry about me." So what if our office is above a Mexican restaurant, my rent is past due, and our lights are about to be shut off?

"How is Max? Have you two patched things up yet?"

"Nope. We're in the friend zone for the foreseeable future. He asked me to have dinner Friday night, but it's not a date, so don't get all frothy."

Mom's eyes brightened. "Well, it would be nice to see him sometime. You should bring him down to the Otter Club." She forked in some meatloaf and changed the subject. "I read in *The Pottstown Post* today that someone is running around town stealing catalytic converters from people's cars. What is wrong with people?" She shook her head. Mom gets the *Post* delivered daily to the house.

I kept quiet. I wasn't about to tell Mom about Vlad's case. The Otters are responsible for most of the gossip that goes on around town and soon enough, she'd figure out I'd been shot at. That would be no bueno for me.

My phone rang. I stepped into the living room so Mom couldn't eavesdrop.

"Jessica, it's Daniel. What have you got for me? I need to know who's that nympho is screwing ASAP. I'm really done with her this time." Not only is my client super anxious to get rid of his wife, he's not interested in paying her a dollar more in alimony than he's legally required. Daniel owns the Celebration Jewelry chain, and he flips houses on the side to get even richer. He and Tracy have been together since college in the early nineties, and they have two children in Ivy League schools.

"Mr. Lakeland, I understand your need to gather information quickly, but I've only had your case for two weeks. These situations take some time and discretion. I'm making progress, but I don't have solid intel for you yet."

"The sooner I know who he is, the better. Tracy's totally out of hand. I shut down her credit cards last week, so she backed my Mercedes over my golf clubs and dumped hot sauce all over Savannah's upholstery. She knows how I feel about Savannah and those clubs. The new Mercedes is on order. She's lucky the clubs were insured."

I scrunched up my eyes and rubbed my forehead. Savannah the Mercedes and golf clubs so valuable they're insured. I couldn't relate at all.

"I should have more information for you soon, Mr. Lakeland. Please try to stay away from your wife. You know she's an instigator. I'll talk to you tomorrow." Good to know Tracy isn't above major property damage when she's angry. I could only imagine what she'd do to *my* car if she discovered I was shadowing her.

"Sorry, Mom." I slid into the kitchen chair. "That was my new client. He wants out of his marriage, and I need to get him results so he recommends me to all his rich friends with cheating wives. Or husbands."

"If you're going to have clients, they may as well be rich ones." She dumped more mashed potatoes on my plate.

Damn straight.

Four

Mom was still asleep when I left for my office the next morning. I kissed Bruce, gave him some diet kitty crunchies, grabbed my faux-leather bag, and locked up the house. I took High Street and cruised past the day spa. Tracy's Jag was nestled in its reserved space. I hit all the green lights on the way downtown and found a parking space right outside Tito's Tacos. I waved to Manny through the window, and ran up the staircase to my office. The aroma of homemade tortillas followed me upstairs.

Sam swiveled around in her chair when I reached the top of the steps. Her flowing dress spilled to the floor, and her hair cascaded over her shoulders. She crossed her leg and revealed a laced up granny-style boot. A box of sticky buns sat on her desk.

"Hey, Jess. Sparkle has the hiccups this morning."

I dropped my bag at my desk and ruffled Sparkle's head. He did one of those yawn-whines and wagged his tail hello. "What'd he get into this time?"

Sam shrugged. "I'm not sure. He eats so many nonfood items it's tough to keep track. I hope he didn't swallow another one of Jalen's socks. The last one took a while to pass through."

I opened my laptop and checked my emails. One from Daniel read in all caps, *ANY UPDATES? GET PHOTOS OF HER WITH HER SIDE PIECE SOON.* An email from *The Pottstown Post* with the daily headlines included the article about the catalytic converter thefts Mom mentioned.

I scanned the story. "Hey, Sam, did you read this story in the *Post* about the catalytic converter theft ring?"

"Not yet, but I saw a piece about it on *Action News* last night. Apparently, it's big business between Philadelphia and Reading and it's driving the local police nuts."

"This article is about Pottstown PD's investigation. Max said they've been working the case for a few months."

She took a sip of her latte. "How's Max, anyway? Still fine?"

A lot of women think Max is fine, including me. Fortunately, he doesn't have a giant ego about it.

"Yup, he's still fine. We're having dinner on Friday night at Carmelo's. I think he wants to talk me into partnering on cases. But you know how I feel about that."

"Hell yes, I do. We're strong, independent women. We don't need to ride around on Max's coattails. That's an obsolete concept."

"Agreed."

"So what are you going to wear on your date?"

"It's not a date, so I'll probably wear whatever I wear to work that day."

"By that you mean the jeans with the permanent mustard stain you wear three times a week, some tired old gray sweater, and your chunky-heeled, unfeminine boots. In case you're not aware, Friday night is a date night. Tuesday night is business talk night."

I shifted around in my seat. She was probably right. "Fine. I'll compromise and wear nicer boots, but I'm telling you, it's not a date."

Sam rolled her eyes and grabbed a sticky bun from the box. "I tried. When you're sitting in Carmelo's in your mustard jeans you'll be wishing you listened to me."

Sparkle hiccupped and rolled over on his back.

"What's up with the lady with the attic demon?" I asked.

"Diane Durkle? She's been hearing some weird noises in her attic for about a month. She said it sounds like some of her stuff is being moved around and it wakes her up in the middle of the night. She's convinced it's the spirit of her neighbor who died recently. Apparently he was a regular asshole."

"When do you want to go check it out?"

"I called Mrs. Durkle and she said we can come over anytime. She's at the end of her rope."

"How about now?"

Sparkle hiccuped loudly, and a sport sock flew out of his mouth. Blue.

"Mystery solved," Sam said and tossed it in the trash can. Sparkle wagged his tail.

"Let's roll to the demon house."

We left Sparkle to nap, jumped in Sam's immaculate dark-red Mustang and at eleven, we pulled up to Diane Durkle's house on Orange Street. Her two-and-half-story brick colonial, painted white with green shutters, sat on a quarter-acre in the middle of a block of well-maintained homes. Mature landscaping, tall trees and ivy gave the house a stately appearance. Sam killed the engine and gazed up at the attic windows.

"Do you see any creepy-ass faces staring out at us? Any little girl ghosts? Curtains moving around by themselves?"

I glanced up, hoping I would see none of those things. "Nope. All clear."

Sam pulled her digital camera from her purse, grabbed her ghost hunting kit from the back seat, and we got out and stood on the sidewalk. She snapped some photos of the house, and we rang the doorbell. A woman in her late forties or early fifties answered the door. She was tall, blond, and attractive but looked like she hadn't slept well in weeks. A fluffy dog stood mid-calf high beside her.

Sam introduced herself and me to Mrs. Durkle. Sam takes the lead on the paranormal investigations. I'm the self-appointed skeptic.

"Thank God you're here. It's getting worse. The noises upstairs are more frequent and getting louder. Last night I didn't sleep a wink. And Mr. Floof here is a nervous wreck. He's pacing and growling, and that's not like him. He's my sweet little snuggle nugget."

We stepped into the foyer, and Mr. Floof growled and lunged at my ankle. He tried to take a chunk out of it, but my knee boot prevented his little fangs from sinking into my flesh. He left tiny dents in the vegan leather.

Mrs. Durkle picked him up and ushered us into the living room. Sam and I sat down on a loveseat while Mrs. Durkle fixed a pot of tea in the kitchen. She returned moments later carrying a tray with a white flowered teapot, matching teacups, and an assortment of cookies and set it on the coffee table. Mrs. Durkle sat on a couch across from us and Mr. Floof hopped up on her lap and glared at us. She poured us both a cup and motioned to the cookies. "Please have some. I baked them for you. I'm baking quite a bit lately. I'm doing whatever I can to stay occupied through this demon ordeal."

"Thank you, Mrs. Durkle," Sam said. She opened her bag and took a notepad and pen out. "So what makes you believe the noises in the attic are from your deceased neighbor?"

I selected a chocolate chip cookie from the tray and ate it in one bite. Having food in my mouth helps me control the urge to smirk. I finished it off and went in for a peanut butter cookie, and Sam gave me the side-eye.

"Well, I've been in this house for ten years. My former neighbor, George Smeer, never liked me. I don't know why. I'm quiet, respectful, and my house is well maintained. And George *hated* Mr. Floof. Sometimes Mr. Floof would sneak over and poop in his yard when I wasn't keeping an eye on him."

I gave the side-eye back to Sam. Mrs. Durkle continued.

"Anyway, right before George went into hospice care, he left a flaming bag of Mr. Floof's poop on my porch. He tacked to my door that said he was going to come back from the grave and haunt me. So you can understand why I think he's the demon in my attic."

Sam jotted a few notes down. "It makes perfect sense to me, Mrs. Durkle." I did my best to keep a neutral expression on my face. It was a challenge.

I reached for a third cookie. "Do you mind if we go upstairs to the attic now?" I wanted to move this investigation along. We stood up and Mr. Floof snarled at us.

"Go right ahead. I'll show you the way."

The three of us climbed the stairs to the second floor. Mrs. Durkle showed us the door to the attic. "This is as far as

I go. I'm not getting anywhere near that demon. I'll be in the kitchen baking."

"Okay, Mrs. Durkle," Sam said. "We'll let you know what we discover. Please don't use your vacuum cleaner or the blender while we're investigating. It could interfere with our equipment."

I looked the other way so Mrs. Durkle couldn't see my expression. Sam opened the attic door, and I followed her in. I closed the door behind us and we started up the steep, creaky steps to the demon attic.

Sam turned to me. "These are some noisy steps. That's haunted house rule number one. Creaky-ass stairs."

The attic's damp, dusty odor met us when we reached the landing. Cardboard boxes of clothing, books, toys, and Christmas decorations along with miscellaneous pieces of dated furniture were herded into groups throughout the room. Dust danced in the light from two round windows at either end of the attic. I felt no spooky vibes whatsoever. It was a musty, cluttered attic not unlike Aunt Joanie's before she moved to Breezy Creek. Sam pulled the EMF meter out of her bag, switched it on and moved slowly around the room, pointing it at various objects and reporting the readouts to me.

"We got a spike on the meter over here by this stained old rocking chair, Jess. I wonder what the stain is from. Could be blood or ectoplasm."

"That could be from pee or poop." I wrinkled my nose. "And you're standing right next to exposed wires, that's why your meter is spiking."

"That doesn't matter. That old man demon could be sitting in the chair right now." She clicked on her handheld digital recorder. "George, are you with us? You better show yourself. And stop bothering this nice lady and her little dog. I agree with you, the dog's an asshole, but you don't have to worry about him shitting in your yard anymore. You're a demon now, you don't have to clean it up. Go haunt your own attic. Be gone!"

Sam put the recorder in her pocket. She moved around the room, the meter in one hand, her camera in the other, taking readings and snapping photographs. Of what, I wasn't sure. She set the meter down, lit some sage, blew the flame out, and waved the smoke around the room. I stood in the corner with arms crossed, leaning against an antique bureau, taking in the whole scene with my nose tucked inside my sweater. My mind was on Vlad's case, not a crazy lady who believes in ghosts. The bureau began to sway, and we both jumped. Scratching noises came from inside it, a drawer popped open, and the fattest raccoon I'd ever seen squeezed himself out. Growling, it scrambled over to the window, pushed it open, and disappeared.

"Did you see that fat-ass raccoon, Jess?" Sam seemed more afraid of it than of a potential supernatural encounter.

"There's your demon, Sam. George is a fat, possibly rabid raccoon that can open a window latch."

A lightbulb hanging from the ceiling blew out, and we both jumped again. An icy breeze blew past us, and the window rattled and slammed shut. I walked over to the window, made sure it was closed tight and locked it.

"See Sam, it was just a raccoon and a draft. No demon. Case closed."

Sam shoved her equipment into her bag. "Who the hell are we to say there wasn't a raccoon *and* a demon? Let's get the hell out of here. The sage smell makes me ill."

We hightailed it from the attic and met Mrs. Durkle downstairs in the kitchen.

"You won't have any problems with George anymore," Sam said. "He's passed over to the other side. We made sure of that."

"One more thing, Mrs. Durkle," I said. "You may want to have your wiring checked, to be safe."

She pushed a bag of cookies into my hand and thanked us profusely. "I'll send you a check."

"Tell your friends," Sam said, and shut the door behind us.

-At four fifteen, I jumped in my car and rolled down High Street to the day spa to follow Tracy to her love nest. Halfway there, I saw Jimmy the Streaker headed toward the library. Fortunately, Jimmy had clothes on today. He usually streaks on Saturday nights and most federal holidays. In addition to a part-time streaker, Jimmy is a small-time criminal of the herbal variety, and he reluctantly provides me with information for a fee. I yanked my car to the curb, jumped out, and jogged toward him. He saw me, turned and walked in the opposite direction.

I caught up to him and blocked his path. "Hi Jimmy."

"Oh no, Noodle, don't you bother me today. I can't be seen talking to a damn PI. I got a reputation to maintain on the streets."

I grabbed his arm and dragged him into an alley. "I told you to quit calling me Noodle, Jimmy."

"Well, I need to call you something besides your government name. You're white as a sheet and you got them long legs, so Noodle it is."

"Fine, whatever. I'm Noodle."

"You're damn right, you're Noodle. And shouldn't you be hunting down Casper the Friendly Ghost or some shit?"

"*Sam's* the paranormal specialist, not me," I growled.

"Potato, potahto. What the hell do you want, anyway?"

"What can you tell me about the catalytic converter thefts in town, Jimmy?"

He crossed his arms over his chest. "I don't know a damn thing about catalytic converters. I ain't no mechanic. You know I'm in the organic plant business."

I gritted my teeth, fished around in my bag for my wallet, and pulled out a twenty. One of my last twenties to be exact. I held it between two fingers and waved it around in front of him. "I bet you know something now, don't you?" He grabbed for the bill and I yanked it back.

"Okay, Noodle, but you didn't hear it from me. Two guys are running around jacking catties all over town," Jimmy said, eyes focused on the cash. "They're hitting everybody. They hit Squeaky's Garage last night. Man, is Squeaky pissed."

"A name, Jimmy. I need a name."

"For twenty dollars, I don't got a name. Twenty dollars gets you two guys who dress all in black, head to toe. Like some kinda ninjas."

"Yeah, I'm familiar with their work."

"Nobody knows who they are. Rumor is, they're working for...you know...I don't want to say it. It could be culturally insensitive."

"Who, Jimmy?"

"Later, Noodle." Jimmy grabbed the twenty from my hand, ducked around me, and took off down High Street at a full-on sprint. He's really fast, and I didn't have the time or energy to chase after him. Jimmy's speed is probably why he's such a successful streaker.

I stomped back to my car, headed down to the day spa, and parked a half block down. I cranked the seat heater to the highest setting and listened to Tom Petty Radio. His music has an immediate soothing effect on me, which I needed after my altercation with Jimmy.

At four thirty-five, the day spa door flew open and Tracy swooshed out. Today she was decked out in a black coat, probably real cashmere, and tall high-heeled black boots, probably real leather, and matching gloves. I admit I had a touch of wardrobe envy. Most of my closet consisted of Old Navy clearance items.

Tracy steered the Jag west on High Street, and I tailed a half block behind her. As I suspected, she returned to Earl Street. I rounded the corner and pulled to the curb behind an SUV. She continued down the street until she found an open space. She parked, crossed the street, and entered the same two-story brick house.

I settled back into my seat and tried to relax myself as the sunset turned the sky pink and orange. The functioning streetlights blinked on one at a time, and traffic picked up as the work crowd returned home. Around five thirty, Tracy emerged from the house. I sat up. A younger man with short brown hair, in his mid-twenties, stepped out onto the front stoop with her. I raised my phone, zoomed in with the camera, and snapped a few photos. Unfortunately, no kissing or canoodling took place. Nothing that would help Daniel's case. I scrunched down as Tracy trotted across the street, jumped in the Jag, and took off. The man sucked on a vape pen, blew out an enormous smoke cloud, went back inside, and closed the door. I waited a few minutes and drove off, noting the house number as I passed by.

I called Sam. "Are you near your computer?"

"Yeah. What's up?"

"I need you to check an address and tell me who owns the property."

"Hold on a minute." I stopped for a red light, and the sound of Sam clicking away on her laptop filled my car. "Okay, go ahead."

I gave her the address on Earl Street. More clicking.

"Huh," she said. "Well, that's unfortunate."

"What?" I drummed my fingers on the steering wheel.

"The owner's last name is Butz. Jason Butz."

"Butz? That is an unfortunate last name."

"I bet he knows how to fight, though."

Five

Carmelo's is the kind of restaurant where you need to have a reservation, the appetizers are all over twenty bucks, and none are deep fried. I didn't think it was an actual date, but I took Sam's advice and dressed up a bit. I selected a pair of knee boots without Mr. Floof's fang marks, a nice blouse, and put on some sparkly jewelry. I fluffed up my hair, glided through one spritz of perfume, put on my coat, and yelled goodbye to Mom and Harry. They were headed to the Otter Club for dinner. I was meeting Max at the restaurant, which is another reason I downgraded it to a friendly dinner and not a date.

Carmelo's is inside the Moonbeam Ballroom, a historic building that was a former social club with a massive dance hall. Famous big bands performed there back in the forties, and back then it was a hopping joint. Some people claim it's haunted, but Sam hasn't investigated it yet. I pulled in and parked.

Max's Wagoneer was an aisle over from me. I checked my face in the vanity mirror, deemed it acceptable, and entered the restaurant. The greeter pointed to Max, seated at a cozy corner table for two by a window.

Max stood up as I weaved through people and tables to reach him. He helped me take off my coat. Classy move. Max's blue shirt accentuated his eyes. He wore dark jeans, wingtips, and a charcoal-colored blazer. I pretended not to notice anything about him. Max played it cool too.

"Your cabernet is on the way," he said as we sat down. Another classy move.

"Thanks. Nice table."

"Yeah. It's definitely not romantic." The corners of his mouth turned up slightly, and a butterfly flapped around in my stomach.

"So, you wanted to tell me about your new case."

"First, did anything else happen with Vlad?"

"Yes. He saw the robbery on his video cameras when he got into the office the next morning. But not the part when they shot at me and Sam. That part was out of range of both cameras. And the thieves were dressed like ninjas."

"They were wearing actual ninja outfits?"

"No, but they were dressed in all black with their heads and faces covered."

"So Pottstown ninjas," Max said.

"Basically. And I talked to Jimmy the Streaker today. He didn't have any information other than he heard it's two guys dressed in black and Squeaky's Garage was just hit."

"How much did Jimmy cost you?"

"Twenty bucks."

Max shook his head. "Teaming with me on this is still an option, Red."

"I'll let you know if I need help. I've got it covered. Tell me about your new case."

"Right." Max sipped his bourbon. "My new client is a national insurance company with a branch office in the area. It provided a standard, comprehensive policy to a business here in town. The business held the policy for over ten years and was a good client. They paid the premiums on time and never filed a claim in nine years."

The server appeared at our table and placed the cabernet in front of me. It was a hefty pour. She took our orders and returned a few minutes later with warm bread and olive oil. My stomach was totally empty, and I had the growlies. I was in danger of getting buzzed and sloppy in front of Max, so I smooshed a piece of bread around in the oil. Some dripped on the tablecloth.

"Oopsies," I said, and wiped it with my beverage napkin. "Go on."

"Right. Over the past year, the client has filed multiple claims with the insurance company for business-related thefts. The insurance company has reason to believe the items were in fact not stolen. The client is unable to produce adequate receipts for the missing items, claims his employee accidentally shredded the paper receipts and some were lost when they redid their computer system."

"That sounds shady. He could go back to his vendors and get new receipts."

"Right. It sounds shady to me too. The insurance company agrees with my assessment."

I finished off the piece of bread and reached for a second. "So who's the client?"

"I can't tell you that, Red."

"I told you about Vlad."

"That's because you can't say no to me."

He wasn't completely wrong about that. "So, do you want my opinion on how to proceed, or do you need to talk through it?"

"I'm always interested in your thoughts. You have good insight," Max said.

"Did the business you're investigating file police reports on the supposedly stolen items?"

"Yes. Smitty handled one of the calls made by the owner. He thinks it stinks too."

"And you can't get into the business's financials without a court order."

"Right."

"Well, we both know if a person is into an illegal activity like insurance fraud, they're probably into some other criminal activities too. I'd put the insurance fraud to the side for now and try to figure out what else this person is into."

"Yeah. I've been shadowing the owner for a week, but so far, nothing seems irregular."

"Keep at it, something will shake loose."

The server delivered our meals, and we chatted for a while, mostly about college times. Max doesn't talk much about his cop days or when he got shot. He misses life as a police detective more than he lets on.

When we were ready to leave, Max looked past my shoulder at the bar. "Great. Brennan's here."

Brennan is Jamie Brennan, former 82nd Airborne member and now an attorney in town. He's built like a brick shithouse, super smart, with a wicked sense of humor and an equally dirty mind. We dated for about six months when Max and I were broken up. After we ended it, he immediately began schtupping one of his clients, Amanda, and she's now his legal assistant and his baby mama. When Jamie broke it off with Amanda a year after she had his kid, she took his Beretta and shot his pinky toe off. Most of it. There's a little stump. I've seen it.

I glanced over my shoulder. Jamie stood at the bar next to a tall blond. She giggled, and he leaned in and brushed a piece of her hair from her face. A momentary flicker of jealousy flashed over me, and I turned back to Max.

"Let's bail," I said.

Max slipped my coat over my shoulders and put his hand on the small of my back. As we passed the bar, Jamie called out to us.

"Hey, Jessica and Max." He motioned to the blond. "This is Cameron."

Cameron smiled and tossed her hair back, and I said hello.

"How are things going?" Jamie asked.

"Great, busy," I said. Max didn't respond, his eyes narrowed at Jamie.

"How have you been, Max, since the hamster shot you in the ass?" Jamie asked.

Oh shit.

There was moment when I thought Max was going to toss Jamie over the bar. "At least I have all my toes, Brennan," he said, and stomped off.

Cameron scrunched up her face. "What's up with your toes?"

I glared at Jamie. "Not cool, Brennan."

I caught up to Max in the foyer. "Hey, what the hell was that?"

"Jess, you know he's not my favorite guy. For a couple reasons."

"Well, you made that super clear."

"He brought up my ass, so I brought up his toe. I don't see the problem."

Max walked me to my car.

"Well, thanks for dinner. I'm stopping by the Otter Club to meet Mom and Harry." They love it when I stop by. They treat me like I'm a celebrity when I walk in.

"Mind if I join you?"

"You want to go to the Otter Club? On a Friday night?"

"Why not? I haven't seen your mom in a while, and they have good desserts." It was true. The Otters have seriously good desserts. Their chocolate cake with peanut butter frosting is hard to pass up.

"Okay. Whatever makes you happy." Max headed toward his SUV, passing by the back of my car with the fresh bullet hole in it. I hopped inside my car and started the engine.

"Jessica?"

I put my window down. "Yes, Max?"

He stood at my window, looking down at me. "When you came to work for me, what was the first rule I taught you about being a private investigator on day one?"

I scowled at him. "You said, 'First, don't get shot.'"

"Right, that's what I said. So what's with the new hole?"

"Max, *I* wasn't shot. My *car* was shot. It's not the same thing."

He stuffed his hand in his pockets and tapped his shoe on the pavement. "You should have told me about this, Jess. You need to tell me about all the bullets that come near you, not a select few."

"Aw, Max, you still care."

Max bent down, leaned through the driver's window, and attempted to kiss me. I put the window up and he pulled his face out before it got crunched.

"Real nice, Jess."

"We're not back together. You don't have kissing rights."

He stomped over to his land yacht open and drove off. I couldn't tell if he was annoyed with me about the kiss, the bullet hole, or something else. I went with annoyed about the bullet hole. I shoved lusty thoughts out of my head, pulled behind him, and followed him.

I called Mom on my cell phone and told her we had arrived. You don't simply waltz into the Otter Club. It's a process. We stepped inside the vestibule, hit the intercom, and waved to the camera. A moment later we were buzzed in.

We walked beneath the chandelier that hung from the two-story foyer, passing by the portraits of former illustrious rulers and other high-ranking Otter Club officers that have since joined the big otter lodge in the sky. It's been decades since you could whip out your Zippo and light up in the club, but the smell of cigarette smoke clung to the place like the ghosts of dearly departed Otter officers. That and the smell of french fries and beer.

Mom and Harry waved us over from the barroom. Mom lit up when she saw Max, and Harry stood and shook his hand. I love Harry's old-school manners. A few other club members said hello to Max and me as we sat down. A Flyers game played on the TV and conversation filled the room, punctuated with occasional laughter.

"How was dinner, you two?" Mom asked. "Did you have a nice time together?" She was desperate to reunite us.

"Yes. I had the scallops. Max had the New York Strip."

He bent down and gave my mom a quick kiss on the cheek. "I housed it, Mrs. B. Now I need dessert."

We ordered drinks and a piece of chocolate cake with peanut butter icing to share.

"Mom, how's the eighties theme party planning going?"

"Two bands came in to audition this week. A punk band called Acid Reflux and a heavy metal band called Flamethrower. Everyone voted for Flamethrower except for Marjorie Butz. That bitch. She tries to undermine me constantly." Mom hiccuped loudly. "Oh dear. I may have had too much rosé."

The bartender appeared with our drinks, and Harry asked him to bring Mom a cup of coffee.

Max leaned toward me. "Want to go to the eighties dance with me?" I gave him an eyeroll.

"Does Marjorie have any children, Mom?"

"Yes, she has a son named Jason and a daughter named Amy. They're a few years younger than you, and they went to Pottstown School District, anyway. Jason flunked his junior year and was held back."

The bartender returned with coffee for Mom and set the piece of cake and two forks in front of me. I pushed the plate toward Max, and we each shoveled in a bite.

"Are either of you working on any cool cases right now?" Harry asked. "Any serial killers or regular killers? How about pyros? Any pyros?"

"Nothing as interesting as that," Max said. "Mostly divorces, insurance investigations, background checks for employers." He doesn't talk about the missing person cases and cold homicide cases he consults with police departments on. I shook my head no, still working on the cake. There was no way I was telling Mom anything about Vlad's case.

Harry sipped his beer. "Bummer. I was hoping for a good murder story."

Mom looked past Max's shoulder toward the entrance to the barroom. "That bitch Marjorie just walked in." Marjorie made a big production of waving at Mom as she and a man sat down at a high-top table across the room.

"She has some nerve waving at me. And that's her third husband," Mom said.

"Mom, did you stop to consider that maybe Marjorie doesn't like heavy metal music?"

She gave a wave of her hand. "Marjorie mad because she wasn't appointed head of the party planning committee this year. She's a control freak." Mom took the last sip of her wine and yelled across the bar, "Hey, Marjorie! Tomorrow morning I'm gonna hire Flamethrower for the party!"

Marjorie gave my mom the finger across the bar. Mom gave her the double middle fingers back. The bartender shook his head. Mom dumped some sugar in her coffee and took a gulp of it.

"Harry, you should take Mom home before one of them loses an eye." Max choked down some cake.

I scraped the remaining peanut butter icing off the plate with my fork. I tried to pay for the dessert to make the evening seem less like a date, but Max handed his credit card to the bartender before I could stop him. Mom finished half her coffee, and we left the club. Harry said goodbye to us, poured Mom into his car, and they drove off.

Max walked me to my car and drew me close. "Want to come home with me?"

Here's the thing with Max and me. We were good as a couple until we weren't. We had fun in college and talked about marriage someday. After we graduated, we both moved back to Pottstown, got jobs, and dated for another two years. When Max got shot in the ass and had to quit the police department, we struggled to stay together. He needed time to figure his life out, and I tried to be understanding and supportive without getting hurt. That was three years ago and we've been on-again, off-again since. We've both dated other people, but nothing sticks.

Max leaned down and kissed me, and the butterflies started up in my stomach. Things spun around and I stepped back. I beeped the BMW unlocked and fumbled for the door handle behind me.

"I can't. I need to get up early tomorrow." That was a big fat lie. "Thanks for dinner. I'll call you," I said, ungracefully stuffing myself into my car.

"Goodnight, Red," Max said, and shut my door. I watched him walk back to his land yacht. All I wanted to do was go to his beautiful house and spend the night, but after our last breakup, I wasn't sure how I felt about Max. I gave him a wave as he drove away and checked my phone. No messages from Vlad or Daniel Lakeland. One text from Sam said, *How was the date?*

I sent her back wine glass, cake, and kiss emojis, put the car in gear, and headed home.

Six

I woke up at nine on Saturday morning with Bruce wedged up against my side and the house still and quiet. Mom spends most weekends at Harry's. He's got a nice ranch house on a few wooded acres and a pool in Lower Pottsgrove. Harry made his money working as a contractor at the nuclear power plant. The plant's massive cooling towers are a constant reminder to residents that a major catastrophe could happen at any moment. It's Pottstown. You learn to roll with it.

Tracy Lakeland alternated working Saturday mornings at the day spa. She didn't work last Saturday, so I hoped her car would be in the lot this morning. I showered, did my hair and face and dressed in old jeans, boots, and a pullover sweater. Bruce weaved through my ankles, which meant he needed his breakfast right away.

"Okay, Bruce, I'm on it. Let's go get your foodies."

We headed downstairs, and I filled his little ceramic dish with diet kitty crunchies and put fresh water in his countertop fountain. We had a one-way conversation about what he was going to do all day. I peeked in the fridge for to-go breakfast options. Mom had brought home Entenmann's chocolate-covered doughnuts from her last trip to HappyCart. Score. I took two doughnuts and a bottle of water and gave Bruce a smooch goodbye on his orange head.

It was ten thirty when I took the keys to Mom's white Toyota Corolla and left. I try to alternate cars when I do surveillance, and Mom lets me use her car for stakeouts when she doesn't need it, with the standing rule that I'm dead if I trash it. I connected my phone to her car and headed down High Street. I pulled into a space down the block where I could view the parking lot and building entrance. Tracy's F-type sat smugly in its reserved space, silently judging the American cars. I put the seat heater on high, settled back, and started on the first doughnut.

Halfway through the doughnut, a text from Daniel came in. All caps as usual. *OUT OF TOWN FOR THE NEXT FEW DAYS. WHAT'S THE LATEST*? I texted him back, *I'm sitting outside Tracy's building right now.* He texted back, *OK,* and I sent him the photo I'd taken of Tracy and the guy in front the house on Earl Street.

A moment later, he texted back, *THAT'S MY NEPHEW, TONY DIMARIO.*

My phone rang. Before I could say hello, Sam said, "I *told* you it was a date. And you probably wore some ratty-ass sweater and your clunky old boots."

"I did not! I listened to your advice and dressed cute. But not like I was trying too hard. Because I'm not."

"Did you at least show some cleavage?"

"Maybe a hint."

"A hint is better than nothing. Those girls need to be aired out once in a while. And Max needs to be reminded of what he's missing." I was about to make a comment about my girls getting plenty of air, but Tracy burst out of the building.

"Sam, I'll catch up to you later. I'm watching Tracy and she's headed to her car."

"Got it, bye."

I pulled in a few cars behind the Jag. I expected Tracy to head to Jason Butz's house for a tryst, or whatever she was doing over there. Instead, two blocks down, she made a left onto Kramer Street and headed south toward the industrial district and the river. I backed off. She drove underneath the railroad bridge and made a right onto an access road that paralleled the train tracks. I drove straight, pulled behind a building, and watched Tracy follow the access road between an enormous brick warehouse and the tracks. When I lost sight of her car, I pulled out, followed the access road, and scooted behind a dumpster. It's pretty easy to hide a Corolla.

I left the car running, stepped out and peeked around the dumpster. Through my binoculars, I watched as Tracy parked her Jag at the building's far end, nearly one hundred yards away. This side of the warehouse had six gray steel doors spaced along it, with a number spray-painted on each and no windows. Tracy knocked on the last door, someone pushed it open from the inside, and I snapped a photo as she entered.

I jumped in the Corolla, and my phone buzzed with a text from Max. It read, *Why are you hiding behind a dumpster in your mom's car?*

I checked my rearview mirror. His 4Runner was behind the brick office building. Max has two business vehicles, the silver Wagoneer and a dark gray Toyota 4Runner. His personal vehicle is a brand-new black Chevy Camaro. I texted back, *Are you following me? WTH?*

Max replied, *No I'm not. Total coincidence. Let's head over to my office.*

Coincidence my ass, I texted back. Annoyed, I yanked the Corolla around and checked the warehouse in the rearview mirror. No activity. I flew back up the access road from the dumpster hiding spot toward Max's SUV. As I passed his car, I ran my finger across my throat. Who the hell did he think he was, tailing me? Max hit the gas and pulled around me, and I rode his bumper from the industrial park back to High Street. I wanted to call him and yell at him over the phone, but I was going to wait and fix his ass in person.

Max's office is on a tree-lined portion of Charlotte Street in Pottstown's north end, in a restored Victorian home. Max got a deal on the building after a certain lawyer filed bankruptcy and got sent upstate. Max had it repainted and the sign out front read *O'Conner Investigation Consultants*. I pulled in behind him and flung my car door open. He stood next to the 4Runner, looking super-hot in faded jeans, a Flyers sweatshirt, and running shoes. I jumped out, slammed the car door for dramatic effect, and the strap of my shoulder bag got caught. I yanked the door open, pulled out the strap, and slammed the door again. I ignored the smirk on Max's face.

"*Why* in the *hell* were you tailing me?"

"Red, I wasn't following you. Come inside and I'll explain."

Unconvinced, I stomped up the steps and into his building. I wanted to bitch him out, but I really needed to pee. I used the fancy powder room downstairs, then stormed up the curved staircase to his private office on the second floor.

Max was seated behind his executive desk, sunlight pouring through the enormous windows behind him. I faced his desk with my hands on my hips, fuming. He handed me a fun-size Snickers bar from his top desk drawer in an attempt to calm me down. Max keeps a candy stash for me in his desk specifically for these kinds of high-stress situations. I snatched it from him and stuffed it in my mouth.

"What the hell were you doing down at the warehouse, Max?"

"Jess, I wasn't following you. I was down in the industrial park on my own case. Maybe you were following *me*."

"First of all, what you're saying doesn't even make sense. I got there before you did. Second, I was working on my divorce case. What case were you supposedly on?"

"The insurance fraud case I told you about. I followed a person of interest to that location earlier this week. Today, my plan was to surveille to the warehouse and figure out what kind of business is going on down there."

Max opened his drawer and tossed me a fun-size Milky Way bar. I slumped down in a buttery soft leather chair and shrugged my coat off.

"That's a weird coincidence, Max. Did you see anyone go into the building?"

"No, I arrived right before I texted you." Good. Max didn't get a visual on Daniel's wife. He didn't need to stick his nose in my case any further than it already was.

We were silent for a minute. Neither of us was willing to give up any information to each other.

"Well, what about the warehouse? Did you figure out what kind of business is going on there?" I asked.

"Not yet. There's no indication from outside the building what's happening on the inside of it. No signs, the parking and loading areas are incredibly clean, and no machinery or vehicles are parked outside that would give a clue."

"I noticed that." I hadn't noticed that. I was too zeroed in on Tracy. I snarfed down the Milky Way bar.

"You need some vegetables in your life. And some light spanking."

"See? This is why we don't team on cases."

A smile flickered across Max's face. "I checked the property ownership data online, and the building is owned by a company called Nasato Inc. I called the state, and the type of business is listed as general warehouse. They could be doing anything in there." He rummaged around on his desk and pulled a legal pad out from underneath a file folder. "The company's officers are listed as Edward, Joseph, and Vincent Nasato. They own a few industrial-type businesses in Norristown plus the one in Pottstown."

"I don't know that name. And I don't know why my client's wife would be in the industrial park or if it's important, but I'm going to find out. And you better not be around when I do."

Max put his hand up. "I'll stay out of your way, Red." He put his feet up on the desk and laced his fingers behind his head. "So, will you be my date to the eighties dance at the Otter Club?"

"Fine. But only as friends." I tossed the candy wrappers on his desk and left.

I headed back to my house. I avoid my office on weekends if possible, to try to pretend like I have a personal life. When I work from my home office on the weekends, I get to have Bruce as company. He usually naps while I work, but I bounce ideas off him anyway.

Bruce greeted me at the front door. I picked him up, smooched his head, and lugged him upstairs with me. I set him on my desk, and he lay down next to my laptop.

As much as Daniel's divorce case and the warehouse connection bugged the hell out of me, I needed to figure out who was ripping Vlad off, especially since they took shots at Sam and me. Gunfire should probably function as a deterrent to me, but it doesn't. I'd need to stake out Boyko Motors a second time. Vlad had mentioned the thieves were hitting his garage once a week. I called Sam, and she answered on the second ring.

"Hey, Jess. Jalen's over. We're chillin' with a movie."

"Clean or dirty?"

"Dirty."

"Okay, I'll make it quick. I need to stake out Vlad's garage again in case the thieves come back. Are you in?"

"Hell yes, I'm in. Those ninjas were a-holes and they need to be stopped. Besides, I don't think they're real ninjas. Real ninjas don't steal car parts."

"Probably not." I don't actually know what real ninjas do in their spare time.

"I'm borrowing Jalen's gun this time," Sam said. Jalen was a medic in the Army before he went to college.

"No, Sam! No guns! You know my stance on that," I said. I'm not anti-gun. They have their time and place when handled by professionals and those with training and experience. But I'm a klutz. I'm the kind of person who trips walking up the stairs. I shouldn't be trusted with a starter pistol, let alone a real gun that can put holes in people and valuable inanimate objects.

"Jalen's shaking his head no, anyway."

"Good, no guns. I'm going to assume the thieves are morons, and they'll hit Vlad's garage on the same night as last week, so Tuesday, okay?"

"Yup. I'll keep Tuesday night clear."

"Thanks. Kiss Sparkle for me, and tell Jalen I said hi. Make good decisions."

Sam laughed and disconnected. In their relationship, Sam was the one to worry about. Jalen is responsible, an early riser, eats clean, and doesn't swear. It's an opposites attract type of situation, but it works for them.

I refocused on Daniel Lakeland's case. He'd be back in town soon, and I wanted to show him results and get a paycheck. I was curious about the warehouse. Both cases Max and I were working on led us there, and if they were linked, I needed to figure out how. Also, I'm competitive with Max, and I wanted to figure out what was going on at the warehouse before he did.

I'd jotted the names of Nasato Inc.'s officers on a sticky note before I left Max's office. I fished around in my bag, pulled out the sticky note, and removed Bruce's feet from my keyboard. I typed the first name, Edward Nasato, into Google.

After a few minutes of searching and rubbing Bruce's head, I found a news article from 2010. The headline was

Jury Convicts Nasato Brothers on Lesser Charges. Holy shit! I clicked on the link, whipped out my credit card, paid for the lowest subscription rate available for the paper, and opened up the article. Joseph "Fat Joey," Edward "Fat Eddie," and Vincent "Fat Vinnie," brothers in the Nasato gang, were engaged in money laundering, extortion, and illegal casinos in Philadelphia in the nineties and early two thousands. After an undercover sting, the three took plea deals and avoided prosecution on racketeering charges. Each received up to ten years in prison. Great. Gangsters. Just what I needed mixed up in a simple divorce case.

I kept reading. Another article said the three brothers served between five and seven years in prison, and Fat Vinnie was paroled last, in 2017.

Bruce was half asleep, purring and making biscuits on my sleeve.

"What the heck are the Nasato brothers up to in that giant warehouse, and what does Tracy have to do with it?"

Bruce gave me a slow blink. He didn't care.

I'd been counting on Daniel's case to be a straightforward cheating spouse divorce. A few stakeouts, some photographs, and a paycheck. I'd deposit my money, pay the office rent and electric bill, and keep the rest. I could ignore the Nasato warehouse and not tell Daniel about Tracy being there, but that didn't feel right to me. Besides, it might help the divorce case somehow. I needed to return to the warehouse at night so I could get a peek inside the building without being caught by the Fat Brothers or the cops.

My stomach sounded the alarm, and I ran downstairs and checked the fridge for snack options. I found a microwave chicken burrito in the back of the freezer, zapped it, and dumped it on a plate. Eyeing the Entenmann's doughnut box, I contemplated Max's comment about my general lack of vegetable consumption. I shrugged it off, grabbed a doughnut and a glass of iced tea from the fridge and headed back upstairs to my office. I could eat vegetables tomorrow.

I feasted at my desk and shared a piece of chicken with Bruce. He ate it, purring, and curled up on my desk for another nap. My phone rang.

"Hi, Vlad."

"Jessica, you come to my office now. I don't talk on the phone." The usual garage noise and Ukrainian cursing filled the background.

"Now?" I yelled.

"Now!" Vlad the Impaler must think I have no other cases or a personal life. Sadly, that was half right.

"Alright, give me fifteen minutes." I disconnected and told Bruce I'd be back in about an hour. I locked the house and drove to Vlad's garage via Kramer Street, slowing to check for Tracy's Jag at the warehouse. Not there. I hit the gas, headed West Pottsgrove, and pulled to the curb outside Vlad's garage.

In the office, the same blond woman sat at the counter, staring at her iPhone. Her outfit was Chanel and her French manicure was salon quality. My jeans were from Target and my gray sweater had a hole in the armpit.

"Hi, I'm Jessica Byrne. Vlad called me and asked me to stop by."

The woman gave me the same up-down look as last time. "I didn't introduce myself when you were here before. My name is Anastasiya Boyko. Vlad is my husband."

"It's nice to meet you, Anastasiya."

"You do not catch the thieves yet. Are you a lazy lady detective? You rip us off too?"

"No, not at all. I'm here to give Vlad an update."

Anastasiya paused and gave me the once-over one more time and shook her head. "You don't look like a Ukrainian girl. I buzz you in."

Vlad's calloused fingers jabbed at the keyboard as the Flyers game played on the television. He yelled a series of expletives at his laptop, then noticed me standing in the doorway.

He pounded his fist on the desk. "There is my lady detective!" The open bottle of vodka wobbled but remained upright. "Come in. Shut the door."

I closed the office door and sank down into the squishy leather chair. I took a deep breath in an attempt to slow my heart palpitations from the yelling and the fist-pounding.

"You ignore my wife. Anastasiya is moody right now. She acts like a *suka*."

I smiled weakly. I had a decent idea of what *suka* meant.

"What is the plan to catch these bastard thieves?"

"My associate and I are going to stake out your business on Tuesday night. We're hoping the thieves return on the same night as before. My plan is to follow them to wherever they're taking your catalytic converters."

"Yeah. Police staked out my garage for twenty minutes, eat doughnuts and drink coffee, then go home. You will do a better job."

"I'll solve this for you, Vlad, I promise. I'll figure out who the thieves are."

Vlad pounded his fist on the desk again, and I visibly jumped.

"I sharpen my screwdriver for their *holovy*!"

I still didn't know what a *holovy* was, but I got a mental picture of a man with a screwdriver sticking out of his forehead and my stomach turned.

"No need to sharpen your screwdriver, Mr. Boyko."

Vlad poured two shots of Nemiroff and handed one to me.

"*Budmo*," he said, calmly raising his glass. "Cheers."

Seven

I slept off the vodka shot and woke up with a jolt at nine thirty. Bruce let me know he needed a nighttime snack. I inhaled a bowl of knock off Apple Jacks, changed into my own version of the ninja outfit, and yanked my backpack from the coat closet. I dumped out the contents on the floor and put in my flashlight, lock kit, multitool, pepper spray, and cell phone along with a bag of M&M's and a fruit punch juice box. Sneaking around and possibly breaking into a mob-owned warehouse was probably stupid and definitely illegal, but it had to be done. Daniel would be back in town soon, and I had to give him something to work with for his divorce.

Mom and Bruce were asleep when I left. I threw the backpack into my car and headed over to Kramer Street. I left my car on a residential street two blocks away and walked down Kramer, passed beneath the railroad bridge and into the deserted industrial park.

I stopped behind the dumpster where I'd hidden the Corolla in the morning and assessed the situation. One car was parked at the other end of the warehouse, where Tracy had entered earlier. It wasn't the Jag. I didn't want to risk being spotted sneaking down the access road, so I took the long way around the building. From the dumpster, I power walked to the warehouse's east side, which consisted of a loading dock with ten bays. A single tractor trailer was backed up to the loading dock with the engine off. Hearing nothing but the traffic out on Route 422, I followed along the wall and peeked around the corner. Dead as a doornail and horror movie dark. I took a deep breath to calm my banging heartbeat. So far, no gangsters in sight.

I kept moving, feeling my way along the cold brick wall. A car passed by on Kramer Street, and I plastered myself to the building until it was out of sight. Other than being discovered by a mobster, or the cops, my other major fear was being bitten by a giant, rabid industrial park rat.

My foot hit something solid and I fell face-first onto the asphalt. The thing said, "*Oomph*," grabbed me, and flipped me over on my back. I tried to smack the shit out of whoever it was with my flashlight, but they snatched it from me. A hand covered my mouth, someone straddled my stomach with their knees, pinning my arms to my sides. They stuck the flashlight in my face, blinding me. I kicked and tried to bite the hand on my mouth.

"Ow! Jessica!" Max growled, rubbing his hand. "What hell are you doing out here?" He clicked the flashlight off.

"Get off me!" I hissed. "I was about to figure out what's going on inside this warehouse until I tripped over your dumb ass."

Max stood up, hauled me up off the ground, and I snatched my flashlight back from him. He pressed against me in the darkness, his lips mushed into the side of my head.

"Shhh. You know this building is owned by criminals, right?" I could feel his breath in my ear. It was nice.

"I know it's owned by gangsters," I whispered. "I figured that out this afternoon, no thanks to you. You could've told me."

"Red, we're not working together. You don't want that. And you shouldn't be here."

"Why in the hell not?"

"It's not safe for you. I'm an armed ex-cop and you have a tiny flashlight and a pink backpack."

"For your information, I brought my black backpack tonight and have some M&M's in it." I had to bring something to the table.

"Do you see what I mean?"

"Well, I'm not leaving. I'm on a job. Same as you."

"Fine. Stay behind me."

"No problem. The mutant rats can bite you first."

We moved toward the corner of the building. A row of small windows spanned the last third of the warehouse, about ten feet off the ground.

I touched Max's arm and pointed to the windows. "Boost me up."

"Red, that's not a good idea. Someone could still be inside. You saw the car, right?"

"They could have left by now."

"Let's keep going around the building and check for the car. If it's gone, we'll come back here and I'll boost you up."

"Fine."

We turned the corner to the warehouse's far side. A single floodlight shone down revealing bricked-in windows. In silence, we followed a narrow driveway and peered around the corner. The same car was outside, about twenty feet from us. After a minute or two, the door banged open and two men exited the warehouse. The shorter guy carried a briefcase. He clicked the car's trunk open, dropped the box in, and slammed it closed. The taller guy locked the warehouse door and walked to the car.

"Did you hear that?" the short guy said.

Max pushed me against the wall, threw his arm across me, and pulled out his Glock. I clamped my hand over my mouth. Shit shit shit.

I waited for them to discover us and shoot us dead. The taller guy said, "I don't hear anything. You always think you hear something. You're a big scaredy cat." They jumped in the car and sped off.

I blew out a breath, unclenched my ass cheeks, and the butterflies in my stomach landed somewhere. Max stuffed the Glock back in his pants, and we retraced our steps back to the windows.

"So how are we going to do this, Red?"

"Squat down and I'll sit on your shoulders." Max chuckled and stooped down on one knee, facing the wall. I scooted onto his shoulders. He stood up slowly and wrapped his arms around my legs. If I craned my neck, I could barely see in the windows.

"Max, can you stand on your tippy-toes?"

"My tippy-toes? You're kidding me, right? You need to back off the candy and muffins."

"Oh, real nice." He wasn't wrong about me cutting back on snacks though. I wobbled on his shoulders as I felt him try to stand on his toes.

"Not gonna happen, Red. I'll blow out a calf muscle. Do your best. And hurry up."

I rubbed the grimy glass pane with my glove. I flicked on my flashlight and shined it down and around the room, revealing an open area with long work benches.

"Tell me what you see, Jess." Max swayed to the left.

"Keep still! Let's see, there's tables with beakers on them, and things that look like camping stoves, and jugs of chemicals all over the place."

"Drug lab. Put your hand down to me." I felt Max grope around for my hand, and he shoved his phone into it. "Get some photos."

I took off my glove and held it in my teeth. The phone was locked.

"What's your code?"

He hesitated. "It's your birthday. I never changed it."

"Aww."

I entered the code, clicked a bunch of photos of the lab, and passed his phone back down to him.

"Okay, you can put me down now." Max slowly crouched down until my feet hit the ground and I stood up.

Max jumped up and stretched his neck. "Let's get out of here, Red. Where's your car?"

"Up the street. Where are you?"

"Same." We retraced our route around the warehouse and were nearly to the railroad bridge when police sirens sounded in the distance. We picked up our pace.

"They're getting closer, Max" I started jogging.

"Crap. We may have tripped a silent alarm."

The sirens were blaring.

"Hide!" Max yelled, and vaulted over the side of a dumpster. He stuck his hand out, dragged me up, and I tumbled ass over tea kettles into the stinky void. Go to your happy place, I told myself, but the threat of being arrested for trespassing and what might lurk at the bottom of the dumpster prevented that. I squeezed Max's hand as the sirens screamed past us, continued up Kramer Street, and faded into the distance.

"False alarm, Red."

"I cannot believe I'm sitting in a dumpster right now."

Max clicked on his flashlight. "First time?"

"Max, you're an ex-cop. If the police had stopped, couldn't you have talked your way out of the trespassing?" I stood up, stepped in something squishy, and flinched. I balanced on some crammed-full garbage bags, swung my leg over the side of the dumpster, and scrambled out.

"I choose my battles wisely." Max flicked something wet out of my hair, and we dusted ourselves off. Something gross was stuck to my boot and I really didn't want to know what it was.

We strolled up Kramer Street, sharing my M&M's and the juice box. We reached my car, and I beeped it open and got in.

"I'm sorry I tripped over you and called you a dumbass earlier," I said.

"And I'm sorry I said you need to back off the sweets. I love your body."

"Too bad you can't have it." I put the car in gear and zoomed off.

Eight

Once a month, I meet Mom and Harry at the Otter Club for Sunday brunch. The Otters have a sprawling buffet of eggs to order, pancakes, regular French toast, stuffed French toast, Belgian waffles, bacon, sausage, quiche, three kinds of potatoes, oatmeal, cereal, yogurt, fruit, doughnuts, and pastries. Mimosas are extra. I usually go alone, but Max and I had things to discuss since our mutual discovery at the industrial park the previous evening. I rolled over to the nightstand and checked my phone. Nine thirty. Mom and Harry would arrive by ten. I texted Max, *Otter Club at 10?* and jumped in the shower, fluffed up my hair, and did cursory makeup. Max texted back, *Pick you up*. I threw on some dark jeans, stepped into knee boots, and yanked a nonratty sweater over my head. I shook some diet food into Bruce's bowl and gave him some pets while I waited for my ride.

Max rolled up to my house in the Camaro at five minutes before ten. I shrugged on one of my mom's nice coats as he rang the doorbell. I said goodbye to Bruce and locked up the house.

"Good morning, Red," Max said, as he opened the car door for me. I got in, he shut the door and jumped into the driver's seat. I love the Camaro and Max knows it. He looks so good driving it, it's hard not to stare at him. But right now, I was trying to figure things out in my head about us, so I kept my eyes forward and my thoughts not perverted.

Max glanced over at me. "You look hot." He put the Camaro in gear and pulled away from the curb.

"Thanks. I didn't wash my hair today." My attempt to deflect the compliment.

"I love it when you're a little dirty." Fail.

"So, there's a drug lab in the giant warehouse."

"Could be, Red. It's a decent guess."

"Do we need to tell Smitty or someone at Pottstown PD?"

"Well, since we aren't one hundred percent certain of what we saw and we came upon the information somewhat illegally, we don't need to tell Smitty yet."

"Will you send me the photos I took while I was on your shoulders last night?"

From the corner of my eye, I saw Max suppress a grin. "Sure, Red. I'm looking forward to the next time I'm in between your legs."

Dear Lord.

We found a parking space on the street near the Otter Club, got buzzed in, and hung up our coats. Mom and Harry had a table for four near the front windows overlooking the public plaza across the street. We said hello, I gave her and Harry a smooch, and Max and I took our place at the end of the buffet line. As we stood talking, I could feel my mom's friends giving Max and me the hairy eyeball, which I interpreted as *when are those two going to make up and get married already?* I tried to ignore the glances and focused on food selection. We piled our plates and headed back to the table. A mimosa was waiting for me, and Max poured coffee from the carafe on the table.

"Jessica, don't forget to take your Lactaid," Mom said, handing me a tablet from her purse. "You don't need another bout of the scoots. Remember New Year's?"

"Thanks, *Mom*." I glared at her and swallowed the pill. Max did his best to not choke on his coffee.

"How's the eighties party planning going? It's this Saturday night, right?" Max asked, changing the subject from my overly sensitive digestive tract.

"It's going fine. Tomorrow I'm giving the deposit to Flamethrower. We have to tell them no pyrotechnics though. They're not going to like it, but it's against the fire code. Their band is known for elaborate pyrotechnic shows, and their fans are called Flamers. We're lucky to get them at the last minute. They're very popular."

I couldn't confirm or deny that. I had never witnessed a Flamethrower show.

"They play the VFW once a month and bring in a big crowd. We sell the most chicken wings that night," Harry said.

"I love wings. The hotter, the better," Max offered, shoveling a link sausage into his mouth.

Marjorie Butz barged up to our table and stood between my seat and Max's. "Hello, everyone. Enjoying the brunch?" She made a sweeping gesture with her right hand toward the buffet and nearly smacked a passing busboy in the face. He scurried off, and she made a point of resting her left hand on the table.

"Wow, Marjorie, that's quite a rock," Harry said. "Where'd you get that?" We all looked down at her hand. Marjorie wore an obnoxiously large oval-shaped sapphire cocktail ring with diamond baguettes on a thick band. Her long, fake nails were painted blue to match the stone.

"Thank you, Harry." Marjorie flapped her hand around. "My son, Jason, gave it to me for my birthday. And the band is made of platinum. Only the best for his mother." Marjorie pointed at my mom's hand. "When are you going to upgrade that tiny thing?" She was referring to the not-small, over-one-carat diamond ring Harry gave her twenty years ago. Oh Jesus, not good.

Mom picked up a pancake from her plate and flung it frisbee-style at Marjorie. It slapped Marjorie in the forehead, and butter and syrup dripped down her face. Marjorie was about to throw her mimosa in Mom's face when a hand reached out and caught her arm. It was the Otter Club's illustrious ruler, Jack McFarland. He was recently voted in when the last Illustrious Ruler renounced his membership, moved to Arizona, and joined the Loyal Order of the Prairie Dogs.

"Val and Marjorie. Your behavior is unbecoming of an Otter Club member, and it won't be tolerated. If it continues you'll both be fined and suspended. No eighties party." He muttered something about women members under his breath as he walked away. Mom and Marjorie gave each other the finger, and Marjorie stomped off.

"Probably a lab-created sapphire. And that Jason is a bum," Mom said.

"What's Jason's story, anyway, Mrs. B.?"

"Oh, that one. He refuses to hold a job. Marjorie gave him the house to live in rent-free. I heard he wakes and bakes, but she thinks he shits vanilla ice cream."

I bit the inside of my lip to keep from laughing and shoved hashbrowns into my mouth. Max stared intently at his Belgian waffle.

"That's your last drink, Val," Harry said gently.

Mom threw back the last of her mimosa and set the glass down. She picked up a danish, dunked it in Harry's coffee, took a bite, and said, "That bitch. Now she's on my shit list."

Harry put his arm around my mom and kissed her head. "No shit list, Valentina. You heard Jack. He'll revoke your party privileges." A couple of Mom and Harry's friends stopped by the table to chat about the upcoming party and to congratulate Mom on the pancake incident. Max and I finished up, said our goodbyes, and left the club.

"Never a dull moment with those two," Max said, as we walked to the car.

"Mom told me Marjorie had a major crush on Harry back in high school. He wasn't into her, and she never got over it. Plus she's an asshole."

"Wasn't that forty years ago?"

"At least."

We got in the Camaro and Max started the engine. "Where to, Jess?"

"I don't want to be in an office on a Sunday, but we need to discuss the drug lab situation."

"My place?"

I gave him the eyeball.

"I'll behave. I definitely won't put the moves on you."

"You have no moves." This was a blatant lie. Max has all the moves and uses them to perfection.

He put the Camaro in gear, gave it some gas and headed toward the Hanover Street bridge and the Chester County side of the river.

After Max received the settlement from being shot in the ass by the hamster, he bought ten acres with a stone farmhouse in North Coventry Township. The house was built in the late 1800s and is absolutely gorgeous. Every room has a fireplace, except the johns. Max renovated the house with central air, a new kitchen, and a garage next to the barn. French doors from the kitchen open to a flagstone patio with a view of the rear of property. The acreage is a mix of woods and meadow, with one enormous old sycamore tree beside a stream-fed pond. Beyond the pond is a stone barn Max uses for storage. I told him he should get some sheep or chickens, or maybe a pony. Or a pool. Right now, that's a hard no.

Max steered down the winding, tree-lined driveway and put the Camaro in the garage. Inside, I sat down at the island, and he opened the refrigerator and peered inside. He grabbed two bottles of water from the fridge and booted the door closed with his foot.

We sat in the living room, which held whiskey-colored leather couches and off-white fabric chairs, probably picked out by his sister Emma. The room had a masculine ambiance but wasn't in your face about it. Max carried a few logs in from the stack on the patio and started a fire. I sank into a couch, and Max sat down in a club chair.

"So my client's divorce case and your fraud investigation now include a drug ring somehow," I said.

"It seems so. If you came back to work for me, we could talk about our cases more openly. We'd know who each other was investigating and why."

"I know, Max. But I like having my own business. It's important to me, and Sam and I work great together."

"I'd bring her in too. No paranormal stuff though. She would have to do that on her own time."

The idea was tempting, I'll admit. No more overhead costs to worry about, Sam and I would get steady paychecks, and I'd have access to his resources and staff. And of course, I'd get to work with Max.

"It's a generous offer, but I have to do this my own way, okay?"

"I understand. Think about it though."

"I will. I promise." I took off my boots, curled up on the couch, and stared at the fire. "I have to tell Daniel his wife may be involved with a drug dealer. Or may be a drug dealer."

"Looks that way. And he'll want hard evidence so he can bury her at the settlement table and reduce his payout to her. Maybe even help put her in jail."

"Crap. I'm going to have to stake out the warehouse again."

"Me too. But we're doing it together. No way you're going to the warehouse by yourself with a can of hair spray and a juice box."

"Mace and a big flashlight."

"You know what I mean, Red."

• • • •

I WOKE UP AN HOUR LATER on Max's couch with an afghan thrown over me. Max had left a note on the coffee table that said he was out for a run on the Schuylkill River Trail and would be back by two. I put some music on and puttered around the house. Brunch was wearing off, and I checked for snack options in Max's cupboards. Max eats healthy about 95 percent of the time. I didn't find much by way of treats and settled on a cup of tea. I gazed out the French doors at the pond and the woods, sipping my tea and rolling my two cases around in my mind. When I was halfway through my mug, Max returned from his run, his face flushed from the cold. He was sweaty but not in a repulsive way.

"Hey, Jess. You conked out while we were talking, so I covered you up and hit the trail. I needed to burn off the Belgian waffle. That sucker was substantial."

"Thanks for the blanket." It was an excellent nap, fueled by French toast and a mimosa. "How far did you run?"

"I made it about three miles before I started to feel the ass injury. The last mile wasn't pretty. You should come with me next time. I saw ducks in the river. You like ducks."

"I do like ducks. But right now I should get back to the house. I have a few things to do."

"I'll take you home right after I get a shower." He gave me the eyeball. "Want to join me? I mean, your shoes are already off."

That was a dumb question. Of course I wanted to join Max in the shower. But considering the state of our relationship, which was undetermined, I politely declined and stayed downstairs.

While I waited, a text came in from Daniel. *WHAT'S THE LATEST?* I texted back, *She may be into something illegal, not sure yet.* He answered, *CALL YOU FIRST THING TOMORROW.* I wasn't sure what he meant by first thing, but I assumed it was earlier than I'm usually awake. I replied, *OK, talk soon.*

Fifteen minutes later, Max drove me back to my house. When he pulled up, Bruce was feet up in the picture window, catching some low-angle winter sunshine. Max walked me to the front door. Bruce rolled over and meowed at me silently through the glass.

"Jess, I understand if you don't want to come back to work for me, but how about teaming with me on Vlad's case?"

"I appreciate your concern, Max, but you don't have to worry about me. I'll be fine." I eyed my boots. He wanted to protect me, and I wasn't letting him.

Max pushed a piece of my hair back, tilted my chin up, and gave me a kiss on the lips. "You're tough. And prideful." He turned and left.

I needed to walk off the brunch and mull things over. Max had me confused with the kiss, and my cases were bugging the hell out of me. I changed into workout gear, laced up my sneakers and took a power walk down to Ash Street Park. In the summertime, the park is teaming with groundhogs and little kids running around, but now it was deserted. A few brave squirrels scrounged for nuts in the crunchy, frozen grass. Walking helps my brain crank on my cases. I planned out the next few workdays in my head.

I pulled my phone out and called Jamie.

"Hey, Jessica."

"Hey, Jamie." The usual two-second span of awkward silence followed where we both envisioned the last time we had sex, which was years ago. I shoved the thought out of my mind. "Do you have time for a quick meeting tomorrow?"

"I'm actually in the office today. I have a brief due tomorrow at four and I'm in court half the day. I can give you about ten minutes."

"I'll be right over." I power walked back to my car, jumped inside, and ten minutes later, scaled the steps to Jamie's office. It was on the third floor of a circa-1970s office building that held an orthodontist office, accountants, and a reiki healer. I stepped inside, and Amanda pretended to be thrilled to see me. I suppressed a glare. I didn't know she was there, too.

"Hey, girl, hey!" she said, and tossed her blond hair over her shoulder. "How have you been?" She couldn't care less how I've been. She'd be ecstatic if I got hit by a SEPTA bus. She must have had a mommy makeover since the last time I visited Jamie. Her boobs were up to her chin, her butt was super perky, and her face didn't move that much when she talked.

"I'm fine. How's Jamie Junior?"

"JJ's wonderful. We're so proud of him. His nursery school teacher says he's highly gifted. But I already knew that."

Amanda has a room temperature IQ, so whatever smarts JJ had, they were from his daddy.

She furrowed her brow as best she could. "Jessica, I don't see you in Jamie's calendar."

"I'm not. I called him and he said to come right over." That pissed her off, which pleased me.

"I'll tell him you're here." She and her boobs bounced into Jamie's office, and I heard a muffled argument. Stupid Amanda.

She reappeared a moment later and gave me a withering look. "You can go in now, but he's very busy today. And you're not a paying client."

"Didn't you use to pay him with your crotch, Amanda?" I said, waltzed into Jamie's office, and slammed the door in her face.

"Hi, Jessica." Jamie came around his desk and gave me a hug. Instead of letting it linger a second too long, I pulled away. "Have a seat. What did you want to talk about?"

"What can you tell me about the Nasato brothers?" I asked. I threw my coat on the chair next to me and tried to avoid direct eye contact with him.

"I'll tell you what I know if you assure me you're not mixed up with them."

"I wouldn't call it mixed up, exactly."

"I don't like the sound of that, Jess. The Nasato brothers are semiorganized crime. Fingers in a lot of sleezy pies. They want people to think they're Mafia. In reality, the Nasato brothers are ex-cons and mob wannabes, which in my opinion makes them even more dangerous than the actual mob. The Nasato brothers have something to prove."

"They may be directly involved with the wife of one of my clients."

"Jess, I'll give you some free legal advice. If you want to remain above ground, stay away from them. Far away."

"That's the plan."

"It better be." He gave me a long look. "What was with you and Max at Carmelo's the other night? Are you two back together?"

"Nope. We're just friends." Max's kiss last night rushed back to me and my face heated up. I changed the subject.

"What's up with Amanda? She was pretty territorial today."

"The only good thing that came out of me and Amanda was JJ. Amanda was a momentary lapse of reason after you and I broke up. And Cameron's a client."

"So was Amanda."

"I learned my lesson the hard way. Never again."

Amanda buzzed in on the intercom. "Jamie, we're on a deadline."

I stood up. "Thanks, Jamie."

"Let me know if you need me." There were a few different ways I needed Jamie, but I kept that to myself.

When I got back to my house, Mom was in the kitchen peeling potatoes. She comes home from Harry's in time to have dinner with me on Sunday evenings.

"Hi, Jess. Pork chops sound okay?"

"Hi, Mom." I gave her a kiss. "Sounds awesome. How was your weekend?"

"Good. Harry and I made a stop at Party Bazaar and got all the decorations for the eighties party this Saturday night. You're coming, right?"

Shit. I hadn't given it much thought. The Otters do have good food though, and I'm a fan of heavy metal music, and rock music in general.

"Yeah, Mom, I'll stop by the party. I'm curious to hear Flamethrower."

"They said they're going to melt our faces."

"They set a high bar."

Mashed potatoes are a staple on Mom's dinner menu. I have no complaints about this. We dove into the potatoes, pork chops with gravy, and sweet corn. For dessert, Mom put an Entenmann's chocolate fudge cake on the table between us, and we got two forks and dug in. After all that food I fought the urge to nap and cleaned up the dishes. When I finished, I grabbed my jacket, yelled goodbye to Mom, and backed the car out, headed to Jason Butz's house. I didn't expect much activity on a Sunday night, but I had some time to kill, and I was curious. I followed the Parkway along the Schuylkill River to Hanover Street and made the left onto Earl Street. Tracy's Jag wasn't there. On a hunch, I turned the car around and headed back toward Rosemont.

Historically, doctors and lawyers lived in Rosemont. The neighborhood is right next to St. Agnes Hospital. Homes in Rosemont are large, the architecture is distinctive and varied, and vinyl siding is nonexistent. Today, Rosemont is a mix of old money, new money, and up-and-comers who got a deal on the rare Rosemont home that wasn't well maintained over the decades. The Lakelands' corner property was on a tree-lined street in the neighborhood's north side. When Daniel and Tracy separated, Daniel temporarily moved out, although he returned regularly to check on the house, get clothes, and pick up mail.

The Lakelands' five-thousand-square-foot residence was stone with black shutters. An open wrought iron gate framed the driveway, and landscape lights lit the driveway's edge. I approached the house from the side street, where the driveway and the carriage house–style garage were. I pulled over about a half block away, killed the lights, and left the engine running. I fumbled around in my bag for my binoculars. A tan pickup truck sat in the driveway, and I assumed Tracy's Jaguar was in the garage. Lights blazed in the downstairs windows.

I texted Sam. *Outside Tracy's house. Pickup truck in driveway.*

Sparkle says she's a cheatin' ho, she texted back.

Just need to prove it.

In this type of neighborhood, strange cars on the street are noticed and picked up by security cameras, so I wouldn't stay in my location for very long. Not that I was doing anything illegal, but I didn't need nervous rich people putting a video of my car on some online neighborhood busybody group. After a few minutes, a man walked out of Tracy's garage, threw an object into the back of the pickup, lit a cigarette, and got in his truck.

He backed out, and as he drove away, I snapped a photo of his tailgate, which had a dent on the left side. I counted sixty seconds and headed back home.

Nine

I tossed and turned all night, and at six a.m., I gave up on sleep, took a shower, and got to the office at seven on Monday morning. It was way too early for Tracy to be at the day spa. I cruised Jason Butz's house, but her car wasn't there either. I parked outside of Tito's Tacos, charged up the steps, unlocked the office, and cranked up the heat. I read the headlines and checked my emails for a half hour. No texts or emails from Daniel. At quarter after eight, I made a pot of coffee for Sam and a microwaved a mug of hot chocolate for myself. A few minutes later, Sam and Sparkle bounded up the steps. Sparkle burst through the door and flung himself at me. I braced for impact and tried to divert the sloppy kisses to my cheek as I gave him some pets. He found one of his office bones, lay down on the rug, and started gnawing on it.

Sam brought a half dozen jelly doughnuts with her from Dingle's Doughnuts down the street from our office. She sat down at her desk with her coffee, and I told her about the stakeout at the warehouse, tripping over Max, the Nasato brothers, the drug lab, the dumpster, and the meeting with Jamie.

"So you're telling me there's a Fat Eddie, a Fat Joey, and a Fat Vinnie?" Sam asked, biting into a Boston cream. "Those aren't very original nicknames. I would expect more from the Nasato crime family. They have an image to uphold in the community. People expect good gangster nicknames nowadays."

I dunked a jelly doughnut in my hot chocolate. A blob of jelly plopped out onto my boot, and Sparkle licked it off. Sam pretended not to notice.

"Maybe the mob is trying to keep a lower profile, so the nicknames aren't as flashy as they used to be. Or they were trying to keep it simple."

"Could be. So, the Fat Brothers are cooking up drugs in the industrial district. And somehow Tracy is in on it. Maybe she's a drug mule and we can follow her to LA or Miami. Get some paid beach time and do the star map thing. We could go see where the Kardashians live."

I didn't care about the Kardashians at all, but a beach trip sounded good to me. January was getting on my nerves.

"I'm not sure how Tracy's involved yet. Max and I are going to go back to the warehouse for another stakeout."

"I thought we were strong independent women," Sam said.

I stuffed the other half of the doughnut in my mouth and sipped my hot chocolate. "We are." I paused while I got the doughnut down. "Why? What do you have in mind?"

"I say we stake out the warehouse ourselves. Max is hot and smart and all, but we can do our own investigations. I mean, he got in your way once already, right? See what I'm saying?"

Sam had a point. It was too easy for me to lean on Max every time things got a little scary. I didn't want to make it a habit. If I was going to rely on Max all the time, I may as well go back to work for him. Which I didn't want to do.

"Okay, Sam. Are you free tonight?"

"Hell yes, I'm free."

"Let's meet at my house at ten."

"It's on." The office phone rang and Sam answered. "NPI, Normal and Paranormal Investigations." After a series of mm-hmms, uh-huhs, and no kiddings, Sam hung up.

"A man says his grammy's cat is haunting her. He asked if we could come over in the next couple days to investigate."

I did a mental eye roll. I didn't really have the time to deal with a ghost cat, but I'd squeeze it in somehow, especially since Sam was helping me. "Okay, let's see how it goes tonight and we'll set up a time with him tomorrow.

"Sounds like a plan."

• • • •

THAT NIGHT, MOM PACKED it in early and so did Bruce, who was a lump of sleeping cat under the blankets on my bed. For the stakeout at the warehouse, I dressed in the usual all black, with a heavy sweatshirt, jacket, cargo pants, and running shoes. I added gloves and a black beanie so my ears wouldn't freeze. Frozen ears are also a rookie mistake. I threw some snacks, my lock kit, mace, and a flashlight in my backpack and shoved my phone into my pants pocket. Sam knocked on my front door at five minutes to ten.

"It's cold as a bastard out tonight," she said, barging inside. "Makes me have to pee." She ran upstairs to the bathroom and slammed the door. When she was finished, I grabbed my pack and locked up the house. We piled into my car and headed over to the industrial district. I left the car on the same side street as Saturday night, and we power walked down Kramer Street into the industrial park.

We stopped behind the dumpster, and I shivered at the thought of its contents. I pointed into the darkness. "The drug lab is way down there. We think it only takes up a portion of the building."

"That's a good location for a drug lab. Nice and secluded. Those mob wannabes must have a good real estate agent." Sam didn't catch the look I shot her. She's so earnest sometimes, I can't always tell when she's joking.

A light at the end of the warehouse shined down on two parked cars. We took the same route around the building as Max and I had on Saturday night so we could approach the drug lab entrance from the northwest corner. My stomach growled as we made our way through the darkness. Snack time. I set my backpack down, crouched and fumbled around inside it until I came up with a Tastykake Krimpet. I zipped up the pack and stood. Sam was way ahead of me and had nearly disappeared into the night. Yelling while trespassing at a gangster warehouse was not an option.

Something cold and hard dug into my back and a hand covered my mouth. I dropped my Tastykake and backpack. Someone spun me around, and headlights flicked on and blinded me. The only thing I could make out was the grill of a brand-new Cadillac.

A burly man with what I assumed was a gun between my shoulder blades said, "Move or I'll put a hole in you." Yeah, probably a gun. Shit.

He pushed me over to the car, stuffed me into the back seat, and said, "Shove over."

I scooched across the seat and yanked vainly on the locked door handle. The man heaved himself into the back seat next to me, shut the door, and stuck the gun in my side. Two more burly guys wearing velour tracksuits sat in the front seats. The driver hit the gas, peeled out, and headed toward Industrial Parkway.

The man in the driver's seat said, "How do you like my new Cadillac? It's electric. Nobody can hear it under five miles per hour. It takes kidnapping people to a whole 'nother level."

"Who are you and where are you taking me?" I asked, trying to use my defiant voice.

"Who am *I*? I'm Eddie freakin' Nasato, your worst nightmare. Next to me is my brother Joey, and the one with the gun in your side is Vinnie." Double shit. I just got kidnapped by mob wannabes. Jamie was going to be pissed. So was Max.

"Say hi to our new friend, guys," Eddie said.

"Hello," the brothers mumbled.

"We're gonna take you for a little ride and have a nice chat." Fat Eddie eased the car onto Route 422 and headed east.

Fat Joey turned around in his seat. "Yeah, we got some items to discuss." He looked like he should have "Duh" tattooed on his forehead.

Fat Vinnie stuck the gun deeper into my side and said, "Yeah, we need to talk." The Fat Brothers spoke with heavy Philly accents and each appeared to be in the three-hundred-pound range, all with slicked-back hair.

"First off, who in the hell are you?" Fat Eddie asked.

That surprised me. I thought since he kidnapped me, he had that information already. Fat Joey said, "Yeah, what's your name?"

I wasn't sure whether to lie or not, so I stalled. "I'm no one. I was out for a walk to get some exercise. My doctor says I have abnormally high cholesterol for a person my age." I pointed to my running shoes as proof of my exercise.

"Don't freakin' lie to me," Fat Eddie said. Fat Vinnie poked the gun farther into my ribs and said, "Don't be untruthful." Fat Joey turned in his seat toward me. "Yeah, don't be a fibber."

Before I could give them a false name, my stomach growled surprisingly loudly.

"Pardon," I said. "I'm hungry. I was about to eat a Tastykake when you abducted me."

"Hey, Eddie." Fat Vinnie leaned toward the front seat. "Whatshername here needs a snack. And I didn't have no dinner yet either."

Fat Joey said, "I could eat."

Fat Eddie stared in the rearview mirror at us. "So what do you want me to do? You want me to go through a freakin' drive-through in the middle of a kidnapping?"

Fat Vinnie dug the gun into my side again, which was starting to annoy me. "Whatshername ain't gonna try nothin', right?"

"Nope," I said. I did need a snack. I get agitated if my blood sugar drops too low, plus I figured it was another good stall tactic. It would give me more time to come up with an escape plan.

"There's a freakin' Wendy's off the next exit," Fat Eddie said. "That's where we're going." I hadn't pegged mobster-types as fans of fast food. He glared at me in the rearview mirror. "You try anything, they're going to find your body floating in the Schuylkill River in the springtime."

Dick.

Even though Fat Vinnie had the gun in my side, I suspected Fat Eddie was the mean one of the three, and Fat Vinnie might be the softie. I might be able to get somewhere with him. I met eyes with Fat Eddie in the rearview mirror. "I'm not going to try anything."

We traveled down the highway in silence. Fat Eddie pulled the Cadillac into the right lane and took the Oaks exit to Egypt Road. We crossed through the intersection and pulled up to the Wendy's drive-through. We were the only car in line. Fat Eddie stopped the car, and he and Fat Joey gazed at the menu. After about ten seconds, a bored-sounding woman came on the intercom.

"Welcome to Wendy's. Home of the Baconator. May I take your order?"

Fat Eddie said, "We're gonna need a few seconds, honey." I resisted the urge to scream, climb over Fat Eddie, and crawl through the driver's window. I really didn't want to get shot. Fat Vinnie's huge gun was currently stuck in my hip underneath my jacket.

Fat Joey leaned toward Fat Eddie and said to the microphone, "Uh, yeah, I'll try one of them pretzel Baconators, hold the onions, and I'll take a large fries and a large peppermint Frosty."

Fat Vinnie ordered next, leaning forward and putting more pressure on the gun. "I want a loaded nacho double cheeseburger, extra pickles, a large fries, and a large strawberry lemonade."

"Do you want the combo?" the woman asked.

"Yeah...yeah, I want the combo." He didn't sound sure about it.

Fat Eddie ordered next. "I want two ten-piece crispy chicken nuggets, a large fry, and a large chocolate Frosty."

"Okay, that's the number eight combo. Do you want any dipping sauce?"

"No sauce. And add in another large fries."

"Will that be all?"

The Fat Brothers all turned and eyeballed me. Fat Eddie asked, "What do you want, Whatshername?"

I didn't think I'd be able to swallow solid food right now with the huge lump of fear in my throat. "I'll have a small chocolate Frosty," I croaked out.

"Give her a large chocolate Frosty, and a small fries," Fat Eddie said to the microphone.

"That'll be thirty-six seventy-five. Please pull around."

Fat Eddie pulled the Cadillac up to the window. I wanted to make eyeballs at the woman from the backseat, but Fat Joey was turned around in his seat, glaring at me.

"Thirty-six seventy-five," the woman said when we reached the window.

Fat Eddie took a thick roll of cash from his pocket, pulled off a bill, and handed it to her.

She gave him the change. "Here's your order. Thank you for choosing Wendy's." She handed a drink carrier and two bags of food to Fat Eddie and slammed the window shut. My heart sank. My window of opportunity had literally closed in Fat Eddie's face. He handed the bags and drinks off to Fat Joey and drove away, making a left onto Egypt Road and heading toward Norristown.

Fat Joey pawed through the bags and handed a fat sandwich to Fat Vinnie. Vinnie opened the wrapper with one hand and pulled up the bun as he held the gun to my side. "Joey, you gave me your freakin' Baconator. You have my nacho double cheeseburger." They switched sandwiches, and Fat Joey handed me my Frosty, a spoon, and my french fries.

Fat Eddie stuffed some chicken nuggets in his mouth. "Don't get any ketchup or any of that Frosty crap on my freakin' new upholstery."

I looked at my Frosty. I realized I didn't have a Lactaid tablet, so I couldn't eat the Frosty unless I wanted to get stomach cramps and diarrhea while in the middle of being kidnapped. Now the Fat Brothers would be pissed at me for snooping around their warehouse and wasting their money.

Fat Vinnie turned to me. "Whatsamatter with your Frosty? Did someone spit it in?"

"No, it's fine. But I, uh, I need a Lactaid tablet."

Fat Eddie looked in the rearview mirror. "What'd Whatshername say? Did she say someone spit in her Frosty?"

"No. Whatshername says she needs a Lactaid," Fat Vinnie said.

Everyone got quiet for a moment as they considered the implications. Fat Eddie said, "My wife has that freakin' lactose interference. Joey, look around in the glove box for a Lactaid. She puts those damn pills everywhere."

Fat Joey emptied out the glove box contents into his lap, which consisted of a Glock, two boxes of ammo, handcuffs, a taser, brass knuckles, and a pink makeup bag. Gingerly, he zipped opened up the makeup bag, fished around in it, and pulled out a Lactaid tablet. He handed it to me.

"Thanks." Hands shaking, I removed it from its little pouch, put it in my mouth, and scooped in a spoonful of Frosty. The Frosty slid down my dried-out throat, made it over the lump, and hit my stomach. I dipped a fry in my Frosty and swallowed hard to get it down. I hadn't devised an escape plan from this mess. I guessed the Fat Brothers were taking me to Norristown to do God knows what to me.

I forced myself to eat the Frosty as we continued along Egypt Road. Fat Eddie turned right onto West Main Street and headed into Norristown. After a few blocks, he turned south on a side street. We were near the river, which did not make me feel great.

Fat Eddie pulled up beside a one-story brick building and killed the engine. The structure looked like it had been a machine shop or factory decades ago. It was much smaller than the Nasato's brick warehouse in Pottstown.

"Gimme my freakin' gun, Joey," Fat Eddie said.

Fat Joey handed him the Glock from the glovebox. Fat Eddie yanked my door open and dragged me from the backseat. Fat Joey came around the car and snatched my food from me. Eddie stuck his gun in my back and marched me into the building. Fat Joey and Fat Vinnie followed behind me, carrying the fast food.

We entered a big empty room. A faint chemical odor hung in the air. A row of blacked-out windows were too small to squeeze through. The room had another exit on the opposite wall. Three plastic chairs sat near a folding table, and another metal chair sat apart from the others on a sheet of plastic. The table held a sledgehammer, pliers, a knife, and zip ties, and a stained area rug lay on the floor. My knees buckled when I realized what the plastic was for. Fat Eddie dragged me to the metal chair and pushed me down, and he and Fat Joey zip-tied me to it with my arms behind me. Fat Joey sat down and pointed his gun at me and Joey stuck a straw in my Frosty and gave me a sip.

"Would you quit it with that, Joe," Fat Eddie said, and set a chair down opposite me, his gun casually pointed in my direction.

"It's unfortunate that it has to come to this because you seem like a nice-type person, but business is business. It's not personal. It's just that we don't like loose ends, and to us, you're a loose end. You understand, right?"

I nodded slowly, even though I understood nothing. My eyes darted around the room, searching for anything to help me escape the building. Other than the torture devices on the table, there was nothing. I was tied up alone with three psychos and totally screwed.

Fat Eddie continued. "On our security cameras, we saw you snooping around in the dark at the Pottstown warehouse the other night. We can't have you interfering with our operations. It's been very freakin' lucrative, and we can't have you messing it up. Now who the hell are you?" He picked up the hammer and swung it leisurely in the air like he was hitting a baseball.

Shit. I hadn't noticed the cameras when I snooped at the warehouse.

I really wanted to tell him to eat a big bag of dicks, but since he was the one holding the hammer and I was the idiot strapped to the chair, I didn't. "I told you already. I lost my cat, and I was looking for him and getting some exercise."

"Bullshit. We saw you looking through the window with your boyfriend. Now talk or I'll break both your kneecaps before we throw you in the river."

I had nothing to lose at this point, so I figured I'd stall for time with another bullshit story. "Okay, okay, I'll tell you the truth this time, but you won't believe me."

"I'm all ears," Eddie said.

"The truth is, I'm a paranormal researcher, and we heard a rumor that your warehouse is haunted. I was down there conducting research." It wasn't a *total* lie.

Fat Vinnie and Fat Joey exchanged glances. "We do hear weird noises in there, Ed, especially at night."

"Is it a scratching sound?" I asked.

They looked at each other, then back at me. They shook their heads no.

"Is it a moaning sound?"

"Yeah...yeah," Vinnie said. "A moaning sound. Creeps us out."

I nodded vigorously. "Yup. Just what I thought. You've got a ghost in there. Could be a poltergeist. Very mischievous." Poltergeist, my ass.

"Would you three shut up?" Eddie yelled, rubbing his hand with his forehead.

A massive explosion outside rocked the shop building. The door I'd been marched through blew off, windows burst and shattered glass flew everywhere, cutting my forehead. The Fat Brothers hit the floor, yelling and cursing. When the dust settled, they jumped up and ran outside.

Still zip-tied to the chair, I attempted to stand up. My plan was to smash the chair against the wall and free myself like heroes do in action movies. Unfortunately, I wasn't an action hero. I lost my balance and tipped over on my back like a helpless turtle. Pissed, I rocked my way onto my side and watched as fire consumed the Cadillac and threatened to catch the building on fire. Turtle situation or not, this was my chance to escape the Fat Brothers. There was no way I was dying in an inferno in this stinky old building. Still on my side, I used my feet to wriggle and lurch inch by inch toward the opposite door. Within a minute, sparks ignited the rug and seconds later, flames raced up the wall. I shoved myself another foot closer to the door as smoke scorched my lungs. Tears poured from my eyes and I struggled to breathe. Mom and Bruce and Max rushed through my brain, and I let out a scream of frustration.

The door burst open. Instead of a fireman, there stood Max, gun in hand, dressed for combat and looking like a hot superhero. Max put his finger up to his lips in a "shhh" motion. He hauled me and the chair upright, grabbed the pliers from the table, and snipped the zip ties off of my wrists and ankles.

Max grabbed me by the hand. "No crying right now. Let's go!"

We burst out the door as the flames closed in on us. The Cadillac's front bumper had blown completely over the building and lay mangled on the sidewalk in front of us. I hurdled it, and we hauled ass down the street through the billowing smoke toward Max's 4Runner. We jumped in and Max floored it. As we raced past the shop building, we saw Fat Eddie's mangled Cadillac burning out of control.

Ten

I picked glass out of my hair and flicked it out the window as Max flew up the street and out of Norristown. Blood ran down my forehead, and I dabbed it with Wawa napkins from the glove box. Max kept checking his rearview mirror for a tail.

He gave me a sideways glance. "Are you hurt? Did they touch you?"

"No. They wanted to, but they didn't get the chance. How did you find me?"

"Nope. Uh-uh, Jessica. You don't have questions right now, *I* have questions right now." Shit. I was nearly killed, and Max was pissed at me.

"What in the actual hell were you and Sam doing at the warehouse in Pottstown? A *mob* warehouse. We were going to stake it out together, remember?"

"Mob *wannabes*," I said quietly. "They're mob adjacent. It's different."

"Don't get technical with me right now."

"Fine. Sam and I were talking, and she said we were strong independent women and we should do the stakeout by ourselves."

Max shifted around violently in the driver's seat. His hands gripped the wheel tighter. "Sam should stick to ghost hunting and bigfoot and whatever else she's into."

"I'm trying to handle my cases on my own." I gave him the eyes and tried to squish a tear out, which wasn't exactly difficult to do at the moment. I rubbed his arm.

"Do you want to stop and get a Frosty from Wendy's?" The Frosty that the mob wannabes bought me had made me feel slightly better when I was stressed during the kidnapping.

"No, Jessica. I do not want a Frosty from Wendy's. I want to know exactly what happened tonight. Start talking." He took a deep breath and tried to calm himself.

"So, Sam and I were making our way around the back of the warehouse, like you and I did the other night. I stopped to get a snack out of my backpack, but Sam kept going and we got separated. I guess she couldn't see me in the dark."

"Wait a minute. You stopped for a snack? In the middle of doing surveillance on dangerous criminals. Let me guess, Jessica. Was it M&Ms? Ding Dongs? *HoHos?*"

I didn't grasp why Max was so upset. He's aware that I'm a habitual snacker. "*No.* I was getting a *Tastykake* out of my backpack because my stomach started growling. My blood sugar drops when I'm hungry. Then I can't function. You know that. *Anyway*, the next thing I knew, someone stuck a gun in my back. The Nasato brothers snuck up on me in an electric Cadillac. You can't hear those things at all when they go really slow."

Max tried to suppress a smirk. "Well, Sam watched what happened from the shadows. She called me right away and said you got shoved into a car and kidnapped. She's extremely upset."

Shit! Sam! I texted Sam that I was safe. I turned to Max. "Okay, but how did you locate me? How did you figure out where those guys took me?"

Max cleared his throat and put some music on the radio. "Did you say you wanted to stop for that Frosty?" he asked gently, picking a piece of glass out of my hair.

"No, I had one tonight with the Nasato brothers."

Max's annoyance switched to confusion. "Wait. The Fat Brothers stopped for fast food? While they were in the middle of a kidnapping?"

"It surprised me too, but they aren't called the Fat Brothers for nothing."

"So the nicknames aren't ironic? Like calling a tall guy Shorty?"

"Nope, they're definitely not ironic. They're large men. I could have outrun them at a fast walk, but they had guns on me the entire time."

"Maybe the brothers started out skinny," Max said. "Pasta will put weight on you quick."

"Max, quit stalling. Tell me right now how you found me in Norristown."

Max drew in a breath and blew it out. "Back when you worked for me, I put a tracking app on your phone to keep you safe when you were out on cases. I didn't remove it when you left my company. I'm sorry."

Now I was pissed. "You did what now? You've been tracking me this whole time?"

Max gave me the eyes. It's surprising how well they work on me. "I was concerned for your safety," he said. "I worry about you. Were you hurt?"

I tried to remind myself Max had just saved me from being kneecapped, shot and thrown in the Schuylkill River.

And I couldn't say he didn't have to worry about me because obviously that wasn't true.

"No. Like I said, you blew up the car before they got to the pain part," I said.

Max gave me a weird look. "The car? I didn't blow it up. I wasn't sure how I was going to burst in and get you, but I didn't blow that car up."

We were both silent for a moment. "I don't get it," I said. "Who blew up the Cadillac? A rival gang?"

"We may never know the answer to that, Red. But I'm glad someone did. It was the ultimate distraction."

The adrenaline rush of my first car explosion was wearing off, and I closed my eyes while Max drove us home. My eyes snapped open when he pulled up to the curb. He walked me to the front door.

"We're talking about this more tomorrow, Red. Get some sleep." Max pulled me close, and I smooshed into his chest for a moment.

"Thank you for saving me, even if it was paranoid and invasive."

Max planted a kiss on my lips and returned to his car. He waited until I was inside the house, then drove off.

I face-planted on my bed and awoke at seven the next morning to the smell of eggs and bacon cooking. Bruce was taking a bath on one of my pillows. I added some pajama pants to my tee shirt, stuffed my feet into my slippers, and shuffled downstairs to the kitchen. Mom stood at the stove manning the frying pans.

"Want some eggs, Jess? And how about some nice bacon?"

I gave my mom a side hug and smooch. "Sounds awesome. I'll throw the toast in."

"You got in late last night," she said. "I saw Max's car."

Mom can be a light sleeper. And nosy. "Yes. We spent some time together last night." I tried to keep my explanations vague to avoid the third degree.

"That's nice. I like Max."

"I do too."

Mom smiled. "You could bring him to the Otter Club's eighties party on Saturday night."

"We're going as friends." I could think of about ten other things I'd rather do with Max, and none involved wearing clothes.

"You two make everything so complicated." She slid two dippy eggs and some bacon onto my plate. I buttered the toast, put them on our plates, and poured some orange juice for both of us. I stabbed an egg and sopped its guts up with the toast. Fat Eddie's stupid face flashed into my mind, and I shoved it out.

"Harry's going to come to the party dressed as Eddie Van Halen, and I'm going to dress up as Lita Ford."

"That's cool, Mom. I love it." Now I had a reason to go to the party and observe that spectacle. "Do I have to come in a costume?" Please God, let there be no costume requirement.

"Costumes are optional, but we're giving away prizes for most radical and most bitchin'."

"I'm not promising I'll show up in a costume, Mom, but I'll be there."

I finished breakfast and cleaned up the dishes. Bruce and I headed upstairs and showered and fluffed up my hair. I pulled on jeans and boots and dropped a sweater over my head. I shrugged on a jacket, yelled goodbye to Mom, and jumped in my car. Headed downtown, I passed by the day spa. Tracy's car wasn't there, and I drove over to check Jason Butz's house. Her car wasn't there either. I parked at my office, stopped in at Tito's Tacos and chatted with Manny for a few minutes, then ran upstairs to my office.

Sparkle shimmied over to me and flopped on his side by way of a greeting, his thick tail slapping the aging hardwood. I gave him some belly rubs and a kiss. Sam swiveled around in her chair.

"You better tell me what the hell happened last night. I almost died of heart failure when I saw you get shoved into that car by those fat guys. I picked up your backpack. It's by your desk."

"Thanks, Sam." I sat down, rummaged through the backpack, and pulled out the Tastykake Junior I had intended to eat when I got kidnapped. I snarfed it down in a couple bites. I turned my laptop on and caught Sam up on what happened after I got stuffed into the Cadillac, including the fast-food stop, the machine shop in Norristown, the zip ties, the explosion and fire, and Max saving my ass.

"Could be the mob wannabes' Cadillac spontaneously combusted," Sam said after I finished telling the story. "That's a real phenomenon. It happens to people all the time. You sit down to watch *Real Wives* and the next thing you know, you're dead on the couch. The only thing that's left of you is one of your feet."

"Gross. You need to stop watching *The UnXplained with William Shatner*," I said.

"The hell I don't. William Shatner is a national treasure. His show provides valuable information to the public on topics not covered by mainstream media. How else would we get the latest updates about Nessie, Bigfoot, the Bermuda Triangle, and unidentified submerged objects?"

I'm a fan of *The UnXplained* too, but I wasn't going to admit it to Sam.

"Anyway, I'm glad you're okay," she said. "But we need to set a time to meet with the guy who said his grammy's recently deceased cat is haunting her. Are you up for it?"

"Yes. What's his name?"

"Steve Sneevley. He and his grammy live over on Tulip Street. The cat's name was Big John. I tried to communicate with Big John on the Ouija board last night, but the only words it spelled out was 'moo shu pork.' Which is weird, because I had a craving for moo shu yesterday."

"No kidding."

My cell phone buzzed with a text from Vlad. It read, *You please come here now. I don't talk on the phone.* I texted back, *See you in a few minutes.*

"Tell Steve we'll be at his house in about an hour. Text me his address and I'll meet you there. I have to leave. Vlad the Yeller is beckoning."

"Do you want to take Sparkle with you?" We both eyed Sparkle, asleep on his back, feet in the air with his tongue hanging from the side of his mouth, drying up.

"Forget it," we both said.

I pulled to the curb outside Vlad's garage as the mechanics checked me out, nodding and no doubt saying something about redheads in Ukrainian. I hurried from the cold into the office, where Anastasiya sat at the front desk, engrossed in her iPhone. Vlad was yelling behind his office door. It wasn't his normal yelling. Today he sounded angry.

She glanced up at me, unconcerned about the yelling. "Have a seat. I buzz you in soon."

I sat down in the reception area that consisted of a single flowery couch that sagged in the middle. Anastasiya eyes dropped to her phone. A few minutes later the yelling stopped, and Anastasiya picked up the desk phone and spoke in Ukrainian. She set the receiver down.

"My husband will see you now," she said, as she buzzed me in. She gave me the usual up-down look as I trudged into the office.

I was not excited to deal with Vlad's bad mood, but he brightened when he saw me.

"How is my lady detective today?" he asked, leaning back in his aging executive chair. He looked pleased with himself. "All in one piece?"

That was a weird thing to say. "Yup, I'm all here." I sat down in the squishy leather chair.

"Yeah, *dobre*, good." He sat forward, leaned across the desk, and in a low voice said conspiratorially, "I bomb those lazy mob bastards." He slammed his fist on his desk. "That Cadillac blew fifty feet in the air!"

I was dumbstruck. After a two-second delay, I managed to get out, "That was *you*?"

"You work for me, yes? I make sure you don't waste my money. Last week, I put a tracking device on your car. I see you go to that big warehouse in Pottstown. Second time you go there, I follow you. I see a fat guy stuff you in a Cadillac and drive away. I follow the fat guy."

"You followed us through the Wendy's drive-through?" I need to start putting tracking devices on people's phones and cars. Apparently it's the in thing to do nowadays.

"No. I park at the Wawa next door and watch those fat guys order greasy food. Lazy American phony mobsters." Vlad relaxed back into his seat and laced his fingers behind his head. "When I was young, I train as an explosives expert in the Ukrainian Army. I can blow up anything. I always carry a dynamite stick with me."

"Why didn't you come inside to get me? I was zip-tied to a chair."

"After I blow up the Cadillac, I see a man dressed like an army guy holding a gun running toward the building. A minute later, the same man runs back up the street with you. You seem okay, so I leave. Blowing stuff up is a parole violation. I'm not going back to prison."

"Well, thank you for following the Cadillac and blowing it up, Vlad. The explosion gave Max a chance to kick the door in and free me. Max is my ex-boyfriend. I used to work for him, but we broke up and I quit." I stopped babbling and took a breath. "Tonight, I'm doing a stakeout here. But you have to let me do this alone. No following me."

"I promise. I take tonight off. I stay home and sharpen my screwdriver for the *zlodiyi*." Vlad poured two shots of Nemiroff and handed one to me.

"Those fat bastards don't mess with my lady detective. I make that Cadillac go boom." He raised his glass with a smile. "*Budmo.*"

• • • •

TULIP STREET IS LOCATED in the west end of Pottstown. Brick Cape Cod style houses on tidy, third-of-an-acre lots lined the street. I found the Sneevley's address, pulled in behind Sam's car, approached the front door, and rang the bell.

A man way over six feet tall in his mid-thirties answered the door. Beside him stood a little old woman who was barely up to his chest.

"Come in, dear," she said, gesturing to the dining room area. "I'm Ruth Sneevley, and this is my grandson Stevie."

Sam was sitting at the table with her notepad out. She turned to me and said, "Hi, Jess."

Sam, Mrs. Sneevley, and I sat down at the table. A teapot and a loaf of banana bread sat in front of Mrs. Sneevley. She sliced off pieces of bread for me and Sam and another for Steve.

"So, Mrs. Sneevley, your grandson here said your cat recently passed away. I'm so sorry," Sam said. "Jessica and I are both animal lovers."

"Thank you, dear. Big John was over twenty pounds and all black. I had Big John from the time he was a kitten. He was such a good, friendly cat. He kept me company. I love black cats," she said, pouring us tea.

"We're not usually superstitious people," Steve offered.

"Anyway, Big John escaped a few weeks ago. He'd been hit by a car right out in front of our house. At least it happened fast for him," Mrs. Sneevley said. "Stevie here buried him in the backyard for me. We had a nice service for him. The neighbors attended and brought us a tuna casserole."

"Now Grammy says she sees him and hears him meowing," Steve said, shaking his head. "I don't know what to think."

"I *do* see him and I *do* hear him and I'm *not* senile. He's come back from the dead, and I need you two girls to send his spirit back to cat heaven or wherever it is that dead cats go. He needs peace, and his meowing is driving me nuts."

I shoved a bite of banana bread into my mouth and smoothed the lace tablecloth in front of me. A ghost cat. This was a new one for Sam.

"Can we have a look at Big John's grave?" Sam asked, chugging the rest of her tea. "That would be the best place to start our investigation."

"It's out back under the evergreen tree. We'll leave you to it," Steve said.

Sam and I trudged out the back door into the cold and headed toward a tall spruce tree in the corner of the yard. A wooden cross with "Big John" painted on it marked the grave. A bouquet of artificial flowers had been placed across the mounded earth. Sam and I stood somberly at the foot of the grave, paying our respects to the departed cat.

"Poor kitty," I said. "He didn't deserve to go out like that."

Sam examined around the gravesite. "Well, the grave's not disturbed, so we don't have a zombie cat situation. Probably a straightforward cat haunting," she said. "Should be simple enough to deal with."

"Good to know," I said, shifting my weight back and forth, trying to stay warm.

Sam stood next to me and closed her eyes. "Big John, you have to move on now. You can't be bothering your grammy anymore. Go on to kitty heaven in peace."

Sam continued encouraging the spirit of Big John to move on. She told him it was time to cross the Rainbow Bridge. A tear welled up in my eye, and I reached into my bag for a tissue. I didn't have any, so I dashed the tear with my glove and snorted a little snot back up my nose. I stared down at my feet, hoping it would be over soon. That's when a hefty black cat sat down next to my right leg, a blue collar around his neck. His tail curled around his toes as he looked at the grave.

I bent down. The little round tag read *Hello, my name is Big John.* The Sneevley's home phone number was printed underneath.

"Uh, Sam."

"Don't interrupt me, Jess, his spirit is almost free. I can feel it."

"Sam, we have a situation here."

Her eyes snapped open, and she turned and looked at me. I pointed down to the fat cat sitting placidly next to me. "Big John isn't dead."

The expression on her face was priceless. "Are you telling me that's Big John right there?"

"Yup. Says so right on his collar."

"Well, who in the hell is in the grave then?"

"Search me. Some other dead cat, I guess." It was sad knowing someone lost their pet, but I couldn't help being relieved that it wasn't Big John. I already felt like I knew him. I reached down, hauled him up, and we headed back inside the Sneevley's house.

Grammy Sneevley burst into tears when I put Big John in her lap. "What on earth..." she said. He purred loudly, and she buried her face in his thick black fur.

Steve scratched his head. We had clearly blown his mind. "Grammy, what in the hell did I bury out back?"

"Someone else's dead cat," she said. She started to laugh, mopping her eyes with a pink handkerchief.

"I was sure I buried Big John. Or maybe I buried a raccoon. One's been nosing around the trash cans for the past few weeks. He didn't look right." He walked us to the front door. "Well, it's good to know Grammy's not crazy and we're not being haunted by a ghost cat. We'll send you a check. Thank you." He shut the door behind us.

"Well, that case ended on a real positive note," Sam said. "Big John has a few miles left on him. And I set some other kitty spirit free."

Or a rabid raccoon. I wasn't going to pick at that scab.

If Sam could make money from people's raccoon problems, who was I to judge?

"See you tonight?" I asked.

"Damn straight. I'm starting to enjoy ninja hunting."

Eleven

It was right after eleven when Sam and I rolled to a stop around the corner from Vlad's garage. It wasn't safe to park at Doogal's Lawn and Tree Service, since I'd blown our cover last week when we got shot at by the catalytic converter thieves. From our new hiding spot on the street beside a vacant lot, we could observe Vlad's business safely. Tonight, I was determined to tail the thieves without being detected. There could be no gunfire tonight. Mom let me borrow the Corolla, and returning it to her with holes in it was not an option. And I definitely didn't want holes in Sam or me. If the thieves showed up tonight, they'd be on high alert. Sitting in the car on the street felt too exposed.

"Let's get out and hide in the weeds, Sam. I don't want the ninjas to spot us in Mom's car, and there's not much room in here for us to duck down and hide."

"I'm okay with that. It's too hot in here. I've been waiting for an occasion to wear my pink designer thermal underwear, and tonight is the night. I'm prepared for this stakeout. Warm and fashionable."

I was bundled up in all black and overheating, too. Sam picked up her camera, I grabbed my binoculars and a Maryanne's Moist Muffins box filled with banana nut muffins, and we scrunched down in the tall weeds.

"I better not come across any vermin in these weeds. I'm not in the mood for vermin. Or vermin poop," Sam said.

I thought we had a fifty-fifty chance of a run-in with an angry vacant-lot rat, especially since we had snacks with us.

"Sam, vermin is the least of our worries. I'm more worried about the ninjas taking another shot at us."

As we hunkered down in our hiding spot, an occasional car traveled by, continued down Rice Street and passed by Vlad's garage. The freight train rumbled by in the distance.

Sam gazed up at the stars in the clear night sky. "It's an excellent night for UFO spotting. Nice and clear. This weedy vacant lot is exactly the type of place an alien spacecraft would land too, according to *Ancient Aliens*. That show provides a lot of valuable information for up-and-coming ufologists such as myself."

"It is a nice night. Cold as a mother, but a good night for ninja spotting. Let's hope they show up."

"You keep a lookout for the ninjas, I'll watch for the grays."

Forty-five minutes later, after my core body temperature had dropped to the danger zone, a loud pickup truck approached us. We flattened ourselves down to the ground as the truck passed by, rounded the corner, and stopped in front of Vlad's garage. Crouched, Sam focused her camera and started snapping photos. Two men jumped out and grabbed their tools from the truck bed. One cut right through the heavy chain that Vlad had padlocked around the gate last week. In a matter of minutes, they stole five catalytic converters in the motion-triggered light. The thieves loaded them into the bed of the truck, covered them with a tarp and jumped into the front of the pickup.

"Come on, Sam. We have to go now," I whispered, scanning around for her. She was squatted in the weeds a few yards away, pants down.

"You know the cold makes me have to pee," she hissed at me.

"Sam, they're leaving and we're going to lose them." I sprinted to the Corolla and cranked the engine. I was leaving with or without her. With the muffin box clamped in her teeth, Sam hobbled to the car as she hiked her pants up along the way. She jumped in and we took off. The thieves headed to High Street and made a left. I stomped the gas in pursuit, leaving about a half block between us. Their asses were mine tonight.

"I hope the ninjas stop at the Gas n' Git. I could use a slushie. These designer long johns are making my ass sweat," Sam said.

"Thanks for the update."

The thieves rounded the curve, drove under the railroad bridge, and continued toward Hanover Street. My guess was that the pickup truck would turn right at the light and get on the highway and head east to Norristown or Philadelphia. My heart raced and I gripped the wheel. The light changed, and they drove straight through the intersection onto Industrial Parkway. The car in front of me turned right and I had no cover between the Corolla and the pickup. That's when I noticed the dent in the pickup's tailgate.

"Sam, that's the truck I saw at Tracy's house the other night. It has the same dent."

"Are you sure? There's a lot of dented pickup trucks in Pottstown. It's the unofficial vehicle of Pottstown."

"I'm sure of it." I handed her my phone. "Check my photos for a picture of a license plate. I bet you it's the same."

Sam swiped through the photos until she found it. "I'll be damned. It's the same pickup."

"I knew it!" I shadowed the truck down the parkway, keeping my distance. It hurtled through the S-curve, bounced over the train tracks, and continued down the street beside the Schuylkill River.

"Where are those stupid ninjas going, anyway? Sam asked.

"I think I know."

The truck turned left onto Kramer Street, traveled north, and turned onto an access driveway between the warehouse and the tracks. I slowed long enough to see the pickup stop at the end of the warehouse and the men jump out. Sam snapped some photos and I hit the gas, tearing off down the street, headed back home.

"Sam, they aren't cooking drugs in the warehouse," I said. "They're processing the precious metals out of Vlad's stolen catalytic converters. That's what all the chemicals and beakers and crap were for that I saw the night I was sitting on Max's shoulders, spying."

"Those are some nontraditional ninjas," Sam said. "And since when does the fake mob partner with ninjas, anyway?"

She had a valid question. I turned onto Andrews Street and pulled into my driveway. Sam jumped in her car and took off for home. Inside, I hung up my coat and dragged myself upstairs. I kicked off my running shoes, crawled under my comforter, and fell asleep face down, with Bruce snuggled next to me, snoring.

• • • •

MAX RANG MY CELL PHONE at eight. I grabbed it off the bedside table, knocked the lamp over, and said, "You are not going to believe what I have to tell you."

"You're naked, and you want me to come over right away."

"As a matter of fact, I am still in bed. But I fell asleep in a sweatshirt and running tights."

"Need me to come over and remove them, Red?" Crap. I considered that scenario briefly, then moved on.

"Sam and I were watching Vlad's business last night, and we followed the thieves back to their hidey-hole."

"Oh yeah, and where is their hole located?"

"How bad do you want to know?" I enjoyed having information that Max didn't. It didn't happen to me all that often.

"I want to know really, really bad," he said in his bedroom voice. Dammit. Now I did want him to come over.

"It's the big warehouse off Kramer Street, where I got kidnapped. Max, they aren't cooking meth in there. It's where the catalytic converters are being processed for the platinum. And the ninja-mobile is the same pickup I saw at Tracy's house a few nights ago."

Max was silent. I may have blown his mind.

"My client is going to love this turn of events," he said eventually. "And I never should have let you quit working for me. Nice work."

"You couldn't have stopped me, Max. And I know something else you don't." This was going to be the best day ever.

"Don't tell me yet. How about you stay in bed, I'll make a stop for sticky buns and come to your place, and you can tell me then. I'll get the extra-sticky sticky buns. We'll make a morning of it."

"I know who blew up Fat Eddie's Cadillac."

Another moment of silence.

"Jessica, I need you to tell me now." Max was desperate for the information and using his sexy voice on me.

"I'll tell you, but you have to promise to keep it in the vault."

"It's in the vault. Now who did it?"

"Vlad did it."

"How in the hell...?"

I explained about Vlad putting a tracking device on my car to make sure I wasn't wasting his money. "Either way, right after Vlad blew up the Cadillac, he saw you run toward the shop building. He stayed long enough to watch us run back up the street. Vlad figured I was safe, so he left. Please don't report him to the police. They'll send him back to the clink. He helped save my life."

"Well, since no one got hurt from the explosion, and it was Fat Eddie's car and building, I don't feel an ethical obligation to make a report to Smitty."

"Thank you."

"I never thought I'd say this sentence in my lifetime, but tell Vlad the Impaler I said thank you for blowing up the Cadillac."

"I will. Can you get Smitty to run another license plate for me?" I texted him the photo of the dented tailgate.

"Sure thing, Red."

"I owe you one."

"Yeah, you do. And I can't wait to call that favor in." Max was relentless this morning.

We disconnected, and I headed for the shower. I let the water pound my right side, which was bruised and sore where Fat Vinnie had the gun stuck on me in the Cadillac. When I was done, I called Sam. I had a plan.

"Are you in the mood for a mani-pedi on the company, Sam?"

"Hell yes. I could use a color refresh. What's up?"

"We're going to do some recon at Tracy's Day Spa. We have an appointment at ten thirty."

"This is going to be an adventure. I've never been to Tracy's Day Spa. I always go to Dames and Dudes. You can count on me. I excel at listening in on other people's conversations. I'm real casual about it."

"Can you pick me up? I don't want Tracy to see my car."

"No problem."

It was risky going into the day spa, but I needed to figure out what Tracy was up to before Daniel returned. People talk too much in salons. Must be all the chemicals in the air.

A note from Mom on the kitchen counter read, *Harry and I went to the Sunrise Café for breakfast. You were snoring, didn't want to wake you up. Love you.* I decided on a healthy breakfast this morning, strawberry coconut-milk yogurt. I let Bruce lick the yogurt cup when I finished, then he climbed to the top of his kitty tree and washed his face.

Sam's pristine dark red Mustang pulled up at twenty after ten. I said goodbye to Bruce, locked up, and jumped in her car. Despite our tendency to snack, her car remains immaculate, with never a crumb or a piece of lint to be found inside, and it always has a slight scent of vanilla. She may get it washed more than once a week.

We rolled down High Street and pulled into the day spa lot. Tracy's Jag waited in its reserved space. Before we went inside, I said, "Our objective today is to gather information. Don't be obvious. If Tracy asks you stuff about yourself, keep it ambiguous."

"Got it. Eavesdrop, don't get busted, and lie my ass off."

"Exactly."

A woman in her early twenties greeted us when we entered the building. We gave her our names and sat down in the reception area, which looked like it had been designed by an interior decorator in whites, silver, and creams. It would have been a relaxing atmosphere if I weren't on a job. I grabbed an aging *Us Weekly* and pretended to read it while scanning the room. So far, no sign of Tracy.

After a few minutes, we were led to a back room where the manicures and pedicures were done. We picked out our toenail polish colors, ditched our shoes and socks, and each took a seat in the massaging pedicure chairs. I cranked my chair onto the highest setting, sat back, and tried to calm myself. The truth is, I struggle with getting pedicures. My feet are extremely ticklish, so my pedicures are spent fighting the urge to kick the woman in the face. Sam didn't appear to have that problem. I tried to focus on the generic new age music playing in the background. I squirmed around in my seat, and the pedicure lady told me to hold still.

Tracy swooshed into the room, as perfect as ever. "Are you ladies enjoying yourselves? Can I get you anything?"

I was busy biting my lip and white-knuckling the chair but managed to get out, "I'm fine, thanks."

Sam asked for a glass of water, and Tracy swooshed away. Sam started discussing her bunions with her pedicure lady. I wasn't going to make it. I needed to kick something. I sunk my fingers into the chair arms and gritted my teeth.

Tracy returned with two bottles of water and handed them to Sam and me. She narrowed her eyes and gave me the once-over. "You look very familiar. I must know you from somewhere. Are you a member of Creekview Country Club?"

"Nope."

"Have you been in the spa before?"

"Nope, first time here." I stared down at my toes and hoped she'd walk away. The scrubbing and moisturizing of my feet was finally over with, and my pedicurist painted my toenails. Thank God. Painting it much less ticklish than scrubbing. Sam's lady started painting a daisy on her big toenail.

Tracy eyed the woman working on me. "Sheree, doesn't she look familiar?"

Sheree glanced up at me for a moment. "Hmm...she looks like Ashley. Not Ashley M., Ashley T."

"That's it. She looks like Ashley T. with all that red hair."

Satisfied, Tracy left the room, and I relaxed. Sam had a smirk on her face. Tracy was clueless.

After our pedicures were complete, Sam and I were ushered to another room for our manicures. We selected our polish colors and sat next to each other. I chose a pink and white gel manicure for my stubby nails. Sam selected a dark purple polish with glitter on her long, perfect nails.

Sheree gazed at my hands. "Are you a nail biter?"

"No. Kind of. They break constantly."

Rita, the woman doing Sam's nails, looked over at me. "Take biotin," she offered with a smile. Sheree nodded in agreement.

I leaned back in my seat and watched Tracy on the phone in the reception area. She raised her voice. Through the doorway, I watched her pace as she yapped on her cell phone to someone named Tony. The conversation got heated, and her volume varied from loud to hushed to shrill. Sheree and Rita glanced at each other, and Rita rolled her eyes and shook her head. Tracy mentioned a package a few times. The last thing she said before she stormed out of building was, "Make it happen, Tony!"

Twelve

After our nails were done cooking under the UV lights, I used my low-credit-limit company card and paid for the mani-pedis. We said goodbye to Sheree and Rita and left. It was noon, and Tracy's Jaguar was gone from the lot. Sam stuck her hands out and admired her nails when we were back in the Mustang.

"Dames and Dudes may have lost a client. I really like that Rita. She understands nails on a spiritual level."

"I like my nails too." I stuck my hands out for Sam to admire.

"Look at that. Sheree turned nothing into something."

"I know. And I'm going to start taking biotin too."

"I'm starving, Jess. Being pampered took it out of me. I'm in the mood for Jerry's Gyros. Are you in?"

"Definitely." I'm a big Jerry's Gyros fan.

She put the Mustang in gear and we headed across town. Sam put on the premium sound system and put it on an R&B station.

"So what do you suppose Tracy was yelling about on the phone?" I asked.

"Who knows. I feel sorry for that Tony guy she was talking to. Tracy sounds like a classic narcissist." Sam thinks every other person she meets is a narcissist, but she may be right about Tracy.

"She definitely seems demanding."

"And what did she mean by 'get it done'?"

"I'm not sure," I said. "Daniel told me her nephew-in-law Tony DiMario does work for them at their house, like repairs and remodeling. She could have been yelling at him about a project he hasn't finished. Or maybe he's involved with the catalytic converter ring and that's what she was upset about."

"Both are good guesses."

"I'll have to tell Daniel about Tracy's possible involvement in the catalytic converter ring when he gets back in town, which should be sometime today. He's probably going to want to meet with me in person to discuss it."

We rolled up to Jerry's Gyros, parked and ambled up to the counter. We ordered chicken gyros and tzatziki dip with pita bread to share. We got drinks at the self-serve fountain, paid, and hauled it all back to the Mustang.

"We need to solve the dessert issue," Sam said. The only dessert Jerry's Gyros had on the menu was baklava. Not a fan.

"You know where I want to go for dessert," I said. "It's right around the corner. But I'm not going to say it."

"Maryanne's Moist Muffins *again*?"

"Yes, dammit. And I hate that name." I hate the word moist. It reminds me of a moldy basement or a sweaty crotch.

"It's an unfortunate name, but her muffins really are moist," Sam said. "No other word accurately describes those muffins besides moist."

"Stop saying it, Sam! Get me a double chocolate chip muffin. I'll wait in the car."

A few moments later Sam returned to the car with the white bakery bag. We picked up Sparkle at Sam's condo, headed to the office, set up in the reception area, and feasted. Sparkle got a plain piece of pita bread. He wagged his tail and lay down on the area rug to work on it. I scooped some dip with a pita and took a bite. The dip plopped onto the rug, and Sparkle took care of it. You could always count on Sparkle for emergency cleanups. And the muffins did not disappoint. Moist as ever.

After we finished eating Sam said, "We accomplished a lot so far today. We combined self-care with undercover work, and we had delicious Greek food to nourish our bodies. It was nice to have finally some me time."

We reconvened at our desks and Sam played the office messages on speakerphone. The first message was from a potential new client. The next was the unmistakable voice of Fat Eddie.

"Hello, Jessica, this is Eddie Nasato. Remember, your worst freakin' nightmare? I'm disappointed we didn't get to finish our talk the other night. Next time we meet, I'm gonna bring all the tools in my collection. You're going to pay for destroying my brand-new electric Cadillac *and* burning my building down. I'll see you real soon, Jessica."

Shit. My mind raced. "Sam, I never gave the Fat Brothers my name. After they got their food from Wendy's they were busy stuffing their faces and didn't talk that much. I guess they figured they'd get my name out of me sometime that night, but the Cadillac blew up and Max kicked the door in before they could hurt me."

Sam's eyes bugged out. "Don't tell me these mob wannabe guys are after you. *You* didn't blow up their stupid

Cadillac. They don't even have their facts straight. See, this is why you need a damn gun. For these kinds of situations."

I was more worried about Mom's and Sam's safety than my own. I wouldn't put anything past the Fat Brothers.

"Sam, I need you to stay at Jalen's for a few days to be on the safe side. Don't come into the office for the rest of the week. Forward the office phone to your cell phone."

"You'll get no argument from me. No way in hell I'm staying at my place with the Fat Brothers mad at you. It's not going to take them very long to figure out who I am too."

"Okay. I need to call Harry and tell him what's up."

I dialed Harry and told him the situation with the Nasato brothers, including the kidnapping, the explosion, and the fire. I swore Harry to secrecy and asked him if he could convince Mom to stay at his place for a few days. I can tell Harry the truth and he doesn't freak out like Mom does. Harry was in Desert Storm, and he's always strapped.

"Jess, how about I take her to Amish Country. She loves Amish Country. She can't say no to it."

"That sounds like a good plan, Harry. How soon can you pick her up at my place?"

"I'm leaving now. I'll go get her and bring her back to my house. I'll pack, get more ammo from the basement, and we'll leave."

"That works. I'll see you when you get here." We disconnected.

"Sam, when does Jalen get off work today?"

"Three. He's on the seven to three shift this week."

"Okay. Let's go to my house. Jalen can pick you up, go to your place together to get your stuff, then head to his place to be safe." Sam texted Jalen the plan and forwarded the office phone to her cell phone.

We locked up the office, stuffed Sparkle in the back seat of the Mustang, and flew across town to my house. Harry hadn't arrived yet and the front door was unlocked. Panicked, I ran in the house, yelling "Mom" at the top of my lungs, with Sam and Sparkle right behind me.

Mom was sitting at her sewing machine in the family room, making a new potholder with bunnies on it.

"Hi, Mom!" I tried to change the sound of my voice from frantic to sunny and carefree.

"Hi, Mrs. B.," Sam said, trying to match my tone.

"Hi, girls. Why aren't you at work?" Sparkle stuck his snout in Mom's lap. She ruffled Sparkle's fur and told him what a good boy he was.

"Uh, we were in the neighborhood and we haven't eaten yet, so we're having a late lunch," I said, giving Sam the hairy eyeball.

"Oh yeah, I'm famished," Sam said.

I dragged Sam into the kitchen, and we grabbed peanut butter and jelly from the fridge and made two sandwiches we did not need or want.

Someone knocked on the front door and I jumped about a foot. I peeked through the curtains on the picture window in the living room. Harry stood on the front step, facing the street, surveying the neighborhood. I let him inside.

"Be cool, or she'll figure out something's up," I said.

"Got it. We're on a top secret mission."

We headed back to the family room.

"Hi, doll," Harry said, kissing my mom. "That's a nice potholder you're working on."

"Thanks, honey," Mom said. "Well, this is a nice surprise, everyone here at the same time."

I shoved a bite of PBJ into my mouth despite being stuffed full of Jerry's Gyros takeout and a Moist Muffin.

"Say, Val, I found a coupon for the Amish Feast Smorgasbord in the glove box, and it's going to expire tonight," Harry said. "What say you and I make a getaway out of it and stay for a few days? We can hit that quilt shop you like before it closes tonight."

Harry was a genius. In addition to not being able to say no to Amish Country, Mom couldn't resist the allure of an about-to-expire coupon. She pressed the foot pedal down on the sewing machine, finished the potholder, and cut the thread.

"That sounds fun, Harry, but we need to be back on Saturday in time for the eighties party. We have to decorate Saturday afternoon. And Flamethrower is showing up early to warm up. The party starts at six."

Shit. I'd forgotten about the damn eighties party at the Otter Club.

"Sure, Val, we'll drive back on Saturday morning." Harry shot me a look that said *I did my best.*

I ran down to the basement and dragged Mom's suitcase up the steps. My phone rang. It was Max. "Did you hear the news yet?" he asked.

"Hold on a minute." I handed the suitcase to Harry. Sam, Sparkle, and I ran upstairs to my office. Bruce was taking a bath on my office chair, so we all sat on the floor.

"What news? I'm dealing with a situation right now." I stuffed the remaining PBJ in my mouth. I'm a stress eater in addition to being a sweets-o-holic. I sucked down some of my diet fruit punch from Jerry's Gyros.

Max continued. "I talked to Smitty today about another case I'm working on, and he told me Daniel Lakeland was stabbed. So I told him I'm investigating Daniel for insurance fraud."

My eyes bugged out of my head, my stomach turned over, and I nearly spilled the fruit punch all over the carpet. "Max, Daniel's my client."

"Not anymore, Jess, he's dead. They found him in his car in a back alley early this morning, half frozen with a screwdriver in his forehead."

I felt the immediate urge to hork up the PBJ, gyro, and muffin. I took a deep breath and swallowed it back down. I stared at Sam while Max was talking, and she gave me a *what the hell is wrong* look.

"Daniel's dead, stabbed with a screwdriver," I said to her. I set the phone down and paced the room. "You're on speaker, Max, Sam is here."

"Hey, Sam. Jessica, the screwdriver is Vlad's MO. The medical examiner said Daniel's time of death was a few days before, Sunday night or early Monday morning."

"I can't believe this is happening! Why would Vlad kill Daniel? I need to talk to Vlad right now," I said, staring down at the phone.

"Absolutely not. If you call him and talk to him about it, and you don't go to the police with what he tells you, you could be charged as an accessory after the fact. You don't need that kind of heat right now."

"Dammit. This cannot be happening." My mind was racing on full throttle. "Vlad must have returned to the Pottstown warehouse after he blew up the Cadillac in Norristown. Vlad could have seen Daniel at the warehouse, put it together, and killed him. Oh my God."

"It's possible, Jess. It doesn't look good for Vlad."

"Why were you investigating Daniel, Max?" Sam asked.

"Daniel made a suspicious amount of insurance claims for stolen merchandise out of his jewelry shops. The insurance company asked me to determine if they were legitimate claims or fraud."

"I remember reading an article about the jewelry thefts in *The Pottstown Post*, but Daniel never mentioned it to me. He only wanted me to get the goods on Tracy for the divorce."

"Can you come to my office to discuss this?"

"No. I need you to come to me. I'm at my house. I'll explain what's going on when you get here."

"Okay, I'll be right over." Max disconnected.

Ten minutes later, Max pulled up to the house in his Wagoneer. I let him in, he said hello to Mom and Harry, and the two of us headed upstairs to my office. The doorbell rang.

"It's Jalen," Sam said, checking the street from the window. "I'm out of here."

"You two stick together," I said to her. "Please don't go out anywhere by yourself for the next couple of days. And it wouldn't hurt if Jalen was strapped."

Max looked at me. "What's going on?"

"Mob wannabes," Sam and I said. She leashed up Sparkle, and they left.

"Jess, tell me what happened."

"I got a creepy message from Fat Eddie today on the office phone. He was the one who owned the Cadillac that exploded and the one who was about to kneecap me when you kicked the door down in Norristown."

"What did he say?"

"He said he knew my name, and I was going to pay for blowing up his Cadillac and setting his building on fire, even though I didn't do those things, and that he was bringing more tools the next time he abducts me. So Sam's going to stay with Jalen to be safe. I told Harry the situation and he's taking Mom to Amish Country for a few days. Mom doesn't know any of this, so act normal around her. Dammit, I can't believe I'm jammed up with gangsters. Even if they aren't real mob guys."

Max looked pissed. "Well, you can't stay here by yourself with the Nasato brothers searching for you. You're staying with me for a while."

I blew out a breath. Max was right. I wouldn't be safe here alone. I couldn't fight off mob wannabes who had something to prove with my out-of-date pepper spray and Mom's pickleball paddle.

"Fine. I'll stay with you, but I need to bring Bruce along. We're a package deal."

"Bruce is always welcome at my house. Now let's get moving."

Harry yelled up the stairs, "We're leaving, kids!"

Max and I walked downstairs to say goodbye.

"Okay, you two have fun!" I said, all light and cheery. "See you in a few days." I hugged them both and mouthed, *Thank you* to Harry. After Mom stepped onto the porch, he turned and patted his side, which was his gentleman's way of saying *I'm locked and loaded.*

I shut the door behind them and watched as they pulled away. I plopped onto the couch.

"Daniel was frozen?" I asked.

"Yes. Smitty said Daniel was in the trunk of his car for at least twenty-four hours, maybe more. They couldn't get the screwdriver out of his forehead until he thawed out."

My stomach turned over, and I put my head down until the sick feeling passed.

"Come on, Red. Let's get you and Bruce out of here."

I rummaged around in the basement and found Bruce's travel carrier and other supplies and shoved them in a bag. I ran back upstairs to my bedroom. Bruce was snoring on my office chair, and I stuffed him into the carrier. He didn't wake up until I got him locked in. I jammed some clothes in an overnight bag, grabbed my travel bag of bathroom stuff, and shoved that in the bag. We scanned the street for unfamiliar cars. The coast was clear. Max grabbed Bruce's carrier, and we locked up and left.

Thirteen

The drive to Max's house was silent as we checked for tails and processed what had happened. Max steered the SUV down the curving driveway and pulled the Wagoneer into the garage next to the Camaro. I grabbed the bags, Max took Bruce, and we entered his house through a back door. Max set the security system, threw some logs in the fireplace, and started a fire. I let Bruce out of his carrier in the living room, and he scooted under the couch with his tail sticking out.

"Bruce needs a half an hour to adjust. He'll come out when he's hungry," I said, and slouched into a suede couch. "I feel responsible for Daniel's death. Vlad kept talking about sharpening his screwdriver for the *zlodiyi*, which is the Ukrainian word for thieves. I didn't think he was going to actually *do* anything."

"Even after he admitted to you that he blew up the Cadillac?"

I bit my lip and stared down at my boots, willing myself not to tear up. You can't be a PI and cry all the time.

"Listen," Max said, his voice softening, "we're not sure Vlad killed Daniel. Let's not jump to conclusions. And you're not responsible for his actions, even if he did it."

All of that was true, but it didn't make me feel any better.

Max disappeared into the kitchen and returned with a cup of coffee for himself, hot chocolate for me, and a bag of chocolate chip cookies in his teeth. He handed me the mug, set the bag on the coffee table, and said, "We need to talk."

This is one of the worst sentences anyone can hear, in my opinion. Nothing good ever comes after someone says those words to you. Max and I had been broken up for years, so I wasn't sure what he was going to lay on me now. I dumped a few cookies out onto the table, dunked one in the hot chocolate, took a bite, and braced myself.

"Sure, what do want to talk about?" It's going to be alright, I told myself. Everything is going to be fine. Your client is dead and crazy gangster types are after you, but you're fine.

"Jess, hear me out before you give me your answer," Max said. "You've just lost your client, and it could be a long time until you get paid for your work on his case, if you ever do. And if Vlad goes to jail, you probably won't get paid on that account either."

Shit. I hadn't considered that. Without the money from those cases, I couldn't make my office rent and my mortgage would be a struggle. And I hated asking Mom to float me a loan. I'd get the obligatory fiscal responsibility lecture and how I don't need so many pairs of shoes. This lecture was closely followed by the settle-down-and-get-married speech.

"If you come work for me on this case, I'll pay you what you're already owed from Vlad and Daniel, including Sam's time. We need to be a team on this, Red. We can settle up later when Daniel's estate pays you. I don't care about the money. You can't go back to your house or office until the Nasato brothers situation is sorted out, anyway." He turned the blue-gray eyes loose on me. I gazed into them a moment too long.

I sipped the hot chocolate and considered Max's offer. I was beginning to feel as though I had failed as a PI. Being kidnapped by gangsters, learning your client was murdered and your other client is a potential murder suspect is a lot to process in forty-eight hours, even for me.

"Fine," I said. "I need the money to make my office rent, and I need to figure out who killed Daniel and why. I owe that to him. And if Vlad ends up in jail, he'll still want me to figure out who's stealing from him, I know it."

"So we're partners on Daniel's case?"

"Yes. But just this one time, Max."

"Fine. If we assume Daniel was at the warehouse, he was probably involved with the Nasato brothers on some level, which can negatively impact the duration of your life. The problem is, we have no proof of his involvement."

It was true, we didn't.

I grabbed another cookie. "What about Vlad? Did he have mob connections when you dealt with him on the force?"

"We could never connect Vlad to organized crime. He was his own boss, as far as we could tell."

"Did Vlad ever kill anyone before?" I realized that I should probably know the answer to that question, but I didn't.

"In the US, no. But let's not forget he put a hole in a man's forehead with a screwdriver. The guy lived, but he was in the hospital for a month. And I don't know Vlad's criminal history in Ukraine."

"Neither do I. I only knew he had been an explosives specialist in the army."

"I was leaning toward the jewelry thefts being an inside job by one of Daniel's shop employees, but since the murder, I'm not so sure."

"Maybe Daniel got in over his head with the Nasato brothers or stole from them. Could he have been that stupid?"

"Anything's possible at this point," Max said.

"Sam and I did some undercover work today at Tracy's Day Spa. We went in for mani-pedis and to eavesdrop."

"Risky, Red. I like it. What did you find out?"

"We overheard Tracy having a heated phone conversation with her nephew-in-law Tony. At least I think she was talking to her nephew. She ended the conversation by yelling, '*Make it happen!*' In retrospect, it could mean doing a murder. Isn't the spouse always guilty, anyway?"

"Usually, but these people are into a lot of stuff. We have three strong suspects right now that we need to run down. The Nasato brothers, Vlad Boyko, and Tracy Lakeland."

"Does your client want you to continue to work the insurance fraud case with Daniel being dead?" I crunched my cookie but couldn't get it past the new lump in my throat. I sucked down some hot chocolate that was now warm chocolate, and the cookie slowly worked its way down my throat and dropped into the pit of my stomach.

"Yes. I called them as soon as Smitty told me about Daniel's murder. The company is out a lot of money on the stolen jewelry claims, and if they were made fraudulently, they'll want to be made whole by Daniel's estate."

"We need more information on Daniel's business dealings. Since I'm his PI, maybe I could get into his Pottstown store tomorrow and look around."

"Red, you *were* his PI. And by tomorrow morning, his jewelry stores will be full of police looking for clues to his murder, if they haven't been through them already."

I didn't want to suggest what I was about to, but we were out of moves. "Are you up for a B and E?" Personally, I'm not a fan of breaking and entering. If I was caught, it would mean the end of my PI license and the possibility of some jail time. Not to mention public humiliation and endless lectures from my mom.

Max hesitated. He's not a fan of illegal entry either, being an ex-cop and all. "If it will help get the Nasato brothers off of you, I'm in."

We left Max's house in the 4Runner at midnight dressed like old-timey cat burglars. Our objective was to break into Celebration Jewelry without getting busted. Daniel owned three jewelry stores with Tracy. The original store was in Lower Pottsgrove Township, in a strip mall off High Street, and the others were in Collegeville and Boyertown. We drove to the Lower Pottsgrove store to search for financial records. Max pulled the 4Runner behind the strip mall and cut the lights. A skinny row of evergreen trees buffered the paved area behind the strip mall from the bank next door. Traffic was light, and no cops were in sight.

"How in the hell are we going to break into a jewelry shop, Max? Aren't they heavily secured? And what about the cameras inside?" I wanted to stay in the 4Runner, where it was warm and legal to be.

"I can bypass the security systems, Red, and the less you know about how I do it, the better. We learned a lot of criminals' techniques on the force. Now I try to use my skills to benefit the greater good." Max handed me a pair of latex gloves. I slid them on, and we sneaked to the back door of the shop.

Max got us into the building and disabled the cameras in less than two minutes. His skills were scary and impressive at the same time. He flicked on a Maglite, and we tiptoed through the store and found a door to an office. He picked that lock and we entered.

"So it's going to be a situation where he's got two sets of books, right? One for the IRS and one for his real money? Isn't that what TV criminals do?" I whispered.

"It's possible. Check for ledgers, notebooks, and receipts, and I'll try to get into his computer. My skills end at safecracking, so we're going to have to leave that alone."

A three-drawered file cabinet stood in the corner behind Daniel's desk. I made my way to it and tripped over a briefcase, kicking it across the room. I face-planted hard onto the low-pile office carpet.

"Ow! What the hell!" I yelled, rubbing my knee. It definitely had a brush burn on it. I could tell.

"Shhh!" Max hissed.

"You shhh." We froze, kept shushing each other, and listened for a sign that we were busted. It was deadly quiet, except for my heartbeat slamming in my ears.

Max knelt beside me. "Are you alright?" He put his hand down to me and hauled me up off the floor.

"Yes. I didn't see his stupid black briefcase."

The briefcase's contents had scattered across the floor, and Max rifled through the papers.

"Some bank statements and a copy of your PI contract," he said.

He handed the contract to me, and I folded it and stuffed it in my pocket. Max pulled out his phone and took photos of the statements. He closed the briefcase and put it back where it had been before I stumbled over it.

I yanked a drawer on the file cabinet, hoping I'd get lucky, but it was locked. My heart pounding, I stuck my penlight in my teeth and fiddled with the lock with my multitool until it opened. I flipped through the files, scanning each one. Copies of utility bills were mixed in with receipts for the purchase of diamonds and other gems. In the bottom drawer, stuffed in the back, I found a file with the words "Fat Boys" scrawled on it. I grabbed the file, sat down on the floor, and opened it. It held old-style receipts torn from a pad with the name "Diamond Goods Inc." stamped on the top. On the top receipt in barely legible print was written, *4.8 oz pt, 1.0 oz rd., rec'd 11/10/23, DRS.* The remaining receipts were similar to the first but with different numbers and dates, going back four years. I didn't know what any of it meant, but I pulled out my phone and took a few photographs. Anything could be a clue at this point.

"Red, we need to leave soon."

"Okay. I found some funky receipts in a folder marked 'Fat Boys.'"

"I'm not having any luck with his computer. I'm going to take his trash." Max dumped the wastebasket into his backpack.

"Isn't that stealing evidence and obstruction of justice or something?"

"We're ass deep in this break in now, Jess. And it's only stealing evidence if it's actually evidence of a crime. And right now, I feel it's a gray area."

On our way out, Max put Daniel's office phone on speaker and played his messages. The first two messages were from store customers. The third message was the unmistakable voice of Fat Eddie. His nasally voice was burned into my brain forever. He said, "A little bird told me what you're up to, Danny Boy, and I'm disappointed. Very disappointed. Call me. Don't make me come looking for you."

"Not good," I said. "Let's get out of here."

We slipped back out into the cold, Max reset the security system and we took off. When we arrived back at Max's house, both of us were too amped up from the break-in to sleep. We sat by the fire and examined the photos we'd taken of the receipts and statements.

"I'm assuming the folder called Fat Boys is a reference to the Nasato brothers. So the folder has to do with the catalytic converter thefts," I said.

"Seems that way. And the writing on the Diamond Goods Inc. receipts you took photos of could be quantities of materials. One precious metal found in catalytic converters is platinum. I forget what the others are."

I pulled out my phone and looked it up. "The other precious metals are rhodium and palladium. I don't remember them from chemistry class."

"Me either. So on the receipts, 'pt' is platinum, 'rd' is rhodium, and 'pd' is palladium." Max read from his phone. "Google says the value of an ounce of platinum is roughly a thousand dollars right now. About the same for palladium."

I checked *rhodium* on my phone. "Rhodium is even more valuable. Right now, it's worth forty-five hundred dollars per ounce, and it been as much as twenty thousand per ounce. That's nuts."

"That is nuts. I'd guess it would probably take several catalytic converters to get an ounce of platinum. It might vary on the type of car or the way it's processed."

"So Daniel bought precious metals from the Nasato brothers' theft ring at a cheaper price to make jewelry for his stores. And after Vlad followed me over to the warehouse the other night, he somehow figured it out. Maybe he saw Daniel at the warehouse, figured he'd make an easy target, and he killed him."

Max sat back in his club chair and yawned. "Red, I'm exhausted. It's after two and I need to be up by seven. Do you want to go through the bank statements and the backpack trash tomorrow?"

"Sounds like a plan. Where am I sleeping?"

"You're welcome to sleep wherever you like, including with me."

As incredibly tempting as that sounded, I didn't want it to get weird between us, especially since we were working this case together and he was my protection from the Nasato brothers.

I smiled. "I'll take the guest room, but thanks for the offer." I grabbed my bag and headed upstairs. Max followed.

"Extra blankets are in the closet. Feel free to sleep naked," he said, and shut the door.

I dumped my bag, sat down on the edge of the bed, and checked my texts. One was from Harry earlier in the evening telling me he and Mom were safe at the Amish Mule Bed and Breakfast. It was late, but I texted back, *Glad you're ok, I'm safe too. Stay in touch.* Sam's text said she and Jalen were chillin' with Netflix. I texted back, *I'm with Max, kiss Sparkle for me.* I washed my face and brushed my teeth in the hall bath, got changed into a tee shirt and collapsed in bed. Bruce jumped up and lay down at my feet. The high thread count sheets felt like silk. I pulled the puffy comforter up around me as my head sank back into the plush pillows. Max's mother or his sister, Emma, must have picked all this stuff out for him.

It felt odd to be sleeping down the hall from Max, but it would have felt odd to sleep next to him, too. We were in different spaces right now.

Max knocked lightly on the door. "Goodnight, Red."

"Night, Max."

Fourteen

Max showering in the ensuite bathroom down the hall woke me up. He was singing "Takin' Care of Business" by BTO. I was tempted to join him—or at least take a peek. Max in the shower is a sight to behold. The extra time and close quarters with him were making me weak, and I was afraid I'd cave into my pent-up sexual frustration. I pulled my hair up into a ponytail, put on a sweatshirt and pajama pants, and headed downstairs to the kitchen to channel the frustration into food.

I figured since Max put me up for the night, I'd make us breakfast. I found pancake mix in the cupboard and went to it. Max came downstairs a few minutes later with damp hair, in faded jeans and a Shippensburg University sweatshirt. I tried not to stare. I was a mess, but the pancake operation was in full swing. He poured himself coffee, made me a hot chocolate, and sat down at the island.

"There's something about a woman who's cooking for me without a bra that's a turn-on," he said.

"Is it the thought of maple syrup being this close to my boobs?" I said, laughing.

Max launched himself at me, pushed me up against the refrigerator, and kissed me deeply. I didn't fight it. I leaned in.

"I didn't sleep much last night with you down the hall," Max said when the kiss came to a natural breaking point. I ducked under his arm to save a pancake before it ignited. I

140

piled our plates, and we sat down to eat. The kiss had me super flustered.

"It's been hard for me too, Max. But we haven't been a couple in ages."

His eyes softened. He brushed a piece of my hair away from my face. "Jess, when I had to quit the force after I got shot, I was screwed up for a long time. I completely lost my identity, and I took it out on our relationship. I acted like a giant ass."

I swirled some pancake around in a syrup puddle on my plate and stuffed it into my mouth. "I'm sorry you got shot in the ass by the furry and you had to quit the force. I know you went through a terrible time. But you *did* act like a giant ass."

"I'm apologizing to you for that. I never meant to take it out on you. My head is on straight now. Let me make it up to you, Red. Be my girl."

He turned the eyes on me. Shit, nowhere to hide. I stuffed more pancake into my mouth as a stall tactic.

Max's phone rang. He kept the look trained on me as he answered it.

"Hey, Smitty, what's up?" His expression changed, and he put the phone on speaker and set it on the counter. "Jess is here with me. She should hear this."

"Hi, Jess," Smitty said. "Last night, we arrested Vlad Boyko for the murder of Daniel Lakeland. He'll probably be arraigned tomorrow. Right now, he's in County."

Max and I stared at each other.

"Smitty, Daniel was my client," I said. "He hired me to help him with his divorce."

"Sorry, Jess. I understand there was a lot of money in their marriage. Vlad looks good for this, but Daniel's wife may too. And you're going to have to come in for an interview."

"Smitty, I'm working this case for the insurance company," Max said. "They want me to continue the investigation. Jess and I are working on Daniel's case together and we're going need to meet with you soon."

"Okay. Before the end of my shift today? Four p.m.?"

"That works."

We disconnected with Smitty. My stomach rumbled. The pancakes weren't sitting right, probably due to all the stress. Max handed me a Sprite from the fridge. I took a few sips, had a fairly large burp, and felt better.

"Nice one," he said. Max was used to it.

"Should we spill the beans to Smitty?" I asked.

"We have to at this point."

"Even the B and E? And the trash stealing?"

"I may leave that part out."

I dumped my plate in the dishwasher. "Do you want to go through the bank statements and the backpack trash after I get a shower?"

"Want to shower together?"

"You literally had one twenty minutes ago."

"What's your point, Jess? And you didn't give me an answer about the other thing."

"What other thing?" Play dumb. Another one of my stall tactics.

"The girlfriend thing."

"Oh, that thing. Max, I need to take it slow. I was pretty wrecked when we ended it, but I knew you were going through a bad time that I couldn't fix. I tried to be what you needed me to be. But I got hurt in the process, and now I need to protect myself, you know? I don't want to go through that again. Ever."

A tear tried to exit my eye and sat on the edge of my lid, waiting for me to say another word so it could be free. Max saw the tear and wiped it away. He drew me into his shoulder.

"We can go as slow as you want, Red."

"Fine. But we're on a trial basis. Don't mess up."

My steamy shower wasn't relaxing. My mind was spinning and I couldn't focus. Daniel, Vlad, Max, my mom and Sam's safety, the B and E, and the Fat Brothers all flashed through my brain. I wrapped up in one of Max's fluffy, oversized towels and stared at myself in the mirror. Working at the asshole law firm would be so much simpler for me. It would only require that I ignore the dead-end job part of it and the constant sexual harassment. I got dressed and called Sam.

"Hey, Sam, did I wake you up?"

"No, Sparkle needed to tinkle so I woke up around seven. Jalen's at work."

"Okay. Please lie low today. Be careful."

"I can stay busy inside. I have my laptop with me. I'm going to do some more online coursework on ufology and Jalen's stun gun is next to me. He won't let me have his real gun. The office phone is forwarded to my cell phone, and I'll let you know if stupid Fat Eddie calls."

"Good. Let all the calls go to voicemail."

"Fine by me. But I wouldn't mind doing some krav maga shit on Fat Eddie. He sounds like he needs an ass kicking."

I'd like to watch Sam take that clown to the mat.

"So Max made me a deal last night."

"What'd that sexy fox have in mind?"

"If we work with him on Daniel's case, he'll pay us what we're owed from Vlad and Daniel. He'll cover our nut."

"He's hot, rich, and generous, which is a rare combination, like a unicorn combined with Mothman. You better hold on to him."

"Interesting comparison. Oh, and he and I are sort of back together too. Only on a trial basis."

"You better lock that man all the way down."

"Maybe someday." We disconnected, and I made one more phone call. This one was to Jamie.

"Jessica."

"Jamie, I have a favor to ask you."

"Shoot."

"I have a client who may need legal representation. He's up against some serious charges." I told him everything, and he listened patiently until I was finished.

"I warned you about the Nasato brothers, didn't I?"

"You did. I didn't realize how quiet electric Cadillacs are."

"Listen. I'll determine if Vlad has retained counsel, and if not, I'll get in touch with him at the jail."

"Thanks, Jamie."

"And Jessica, whatever trouble Vlad's gotten himself into, it's not your job to fix it."

"Right."

I headed downstairs. Max yelled to me from his office off the dining room. "Jess, in here."

Max's home office held a desk, meeting table with four chairs, big screen TV, bookcases, wingback chair, and couch. None of his furniture was purchased at yard sales and secondhand stores like mine.

Max swiveled around and looked at me. "How much does Vlad owe you?"

I did some quick math in my head. "About a thousand dollars."

"And Daniel?"

"About the same. Rough numbers."

He turned back to the desk and a moment later handed me a check. "Have Sam add up her time. If it's more than that, tell me."

"Thanks, Max."

"Just stay safe and work this case with me. That's all I want."

I pulled out my phone and deposited the signed check into my business account. I sent Sam a text telling her she could pay Manny the office rent, the electric bill, and herself. I instantly felt better knowing I owed fewer people money.

Max grabbed his backpack from the couch and dumped Daniel's trash out onto the table. He handed me a pair of latex gloves, and we sat down and started picking through it. Mixed in with the candy bar wrappers were a few crumpled sticky notes with phone numbers scrawled on them. I flattened them out, photographed them, and put them in a stack. Max found a piece of legal pad paper with notations about platinum rings and another piece of paper about rings plated with rhodium. He took pictures of them and sat back, running his hand through his hair. He opened the bank statement photos on his laptop and we scooted closer together to examine them.

"Good. The bank statements are for Celebration Jewelry, not his personal accounts," he said. He scrolled through them slowly and we searched for clues.

"Each statement shows a lot of payments to Diamond Goods Inc., mostly under ten thousand dollars," I said.

"Yeah, right under the IRS's radar." Max kept scrolling.

I pointed to the screen. "Are those other large deposits from Barkley Insurance the payouts from your client to Celebration Jewelry for the stolen jewelry?"

"Looks like it. We need to figure out who owns Diamond Goods Inc.," Max said. He ran the business name through a few of his databases that I can't afford. After a few minutes, he pointed to the screen, "I got it. Diamond Goods is incorporated in the British Virgin Islands."

"Is it a shell company?"

"Could be."

"Who's the owner?"

Max put the database on the screen and scrolled down. "Some guy named Ronald Dalton. Probably no one close to the people forming the shell corp. They pay some rando who needs cash to sign the papers and make it seem legitimate."

"No trace back. Nothing for the IRS to track down, which is what criminals want," I said.

"Exactly."

"So how do you think Daniel got roped in with the brothers in the first place?"

"It's hard to say. He could have been approached by Fat Eddie or another brother with an offer he couldn't refuse type of situation."

"Fat Eddie is a complete psycho," I said. "He was getting off on scaring me and looking forward to hurting me right before you kicked the door in, which was hot, by the way. Eddie's so crazy he made the brother with the gun in my side seem nice."

"Fat Eddie's lucky his Cadillac blew up. I would have killed him if he laid a hand on you."

I had never heard Max speak that way, and the look in his eyes wasn't one I wanted to see again anytime soon.

"Well, Vlad bailed us out and now he's in the clink for murder," I said. "I feel like it's my fault because I was snooping at the warehouse and he followed me there."

"It's not your fault. And the clink might be the best place for Vlad right now if he's mixed up with the Nasato brothers. Although they can always arrange to have someone get to him in jail."

Sam called my phone. I put it on speaker and set it down on the table. "Hey, Sam. I'm here with Max."

"Hey, guys. Jess, I think I might be able to help you with your investigation."

"How's that?" I asked.

"Well, since Daniel Lakeland is in the spirit world now, I figured I could try to make contact with him. My Ouija board is over here at Jalen's. He doesn't like me to use the Ouija board when he's home, but Jalen's gone until three."

Max and I exchanged glances. I knew she was trying to be helpful.

"Sure, Sam, give it a shot." I looked at Max and shrugged. He shook his head.

"Oh, and another thing," Sam said. "Stupid Fat Eddie called with another creepy-ass message for you, Jess."

"Sam, you should have led with that. Can you play it for us?" Max asked.

"Yeah, hold on." After a few seconds the message began. "Hello, Jessica. Do you miss me? I miss you and your beautiful red hair. My tools are sharpened and ready for you. It's unfortunate what happened to Daniel, and if you don't want a hole in *your* forehead, you'd better call me by midnight tonight. If not, I'll get to you, Jessica, and your mother. It's your choice."

Okay, now I was pissed. That asshat was going down.

"I know he didn't threaten your mom," Sam said. "That guy has deep-seated issues. He needs a team of experienced anger management specialists. He's a classic narcissist."

Max's eyes narrowed. "I don't like this, Jess. He enjoys tormenting you. And we already know he's sadistic."

"I'm not afraid of that fat bastard," I said. Actually, I was terrified of Fat Eddie, but sometimes acting brave helps me feel brave. Sometimes.

"Me neither," Sam said. "All Fat Eddie needs is an attitude adjustment. He may have some unresolved mother issues or an inferiority complex."

"He's no one to mess with," Max said. "Fat Eddie's been linked to at least three murders in Philly over the last few years, but he's never been convicted for involvement with any of them. He slithers out of it with the help of his high-priced lawyers."

"Like Teflon Don," Sam said. "He's Nonstick Fat Eddie."

"Let's call him," I said. "Let's get Eddie talking. Maybe he'll talk about the catalytic converter ring, kidnapping me, or his deal with Daniel."

"Or he could say something freaky," Sam said.

"What's the endgame, Red?"

"We hope he incriminates himself. We'll record the conversation. I'm way past caring whether it's legal or not."

"Since he threatened you and your mom, that's probably not an issue now," Max said.

"So we're calling him," I said.

Max blew out a breath and shook his head as if to say *I can't believe I'm agreeing to this.* "Fine."

"He shouldn't have brought my mom into it. Don't mess with my mom."

Fifteen

Max and I met with Detective Joe Smits and his partner, Detective Tamika Johnson, at four fifteen at the police department downtown. They didn't make us sit in an interrogation room like two criminals. Instead, the four of us sat in a small conference room on the second floor. A bowl of Hershey's Kisses sat on the table, and I ate one to calm my nerves. From the taste of it, the bowl had probably been sitting there since at least Halloween.

"What's going on with Vlad?" I asked.

"The judge denied bond," Smitty said. "Given Vlad's prior conviction for assault and his dual citizenship in Ukraine, the judge determined him to be a flight risk."

That made me feel worse about the whole situation, even though I wasn't sure if Vlad killed Daniel.

"We have evidence linking Vlad to the murder," Tamika said.

I shot Max a look. "What evidence?" we asked.

"Vlad's fingerprint is on the screwdriver used to kill Daniel," Smitty said.

It took a minute for that to sink in. "Why would he leave the murder weapon behind? That makes no sense," I said.

"Criminals do dumb stuff all the time," Tamika said. "That's why they're criminals."

"The chief wants the case solved quickly," Smitty said. "This is a high-profile case for Pottstown. As you know, Lakeland was worth millions."

"The other night Jess and I were doing surveillance on a warehouse in town, and we made a discovery that in retrospect may be related to Daniel's murder. We wanted to share it with you in exchange for something." Max shifted around in his seat.

Smitty crossed his arms over his chest. "Go on."

"Our surveillance initially led us to believe part of the warehouse was being used as a drug lab," I said. "But later I determined that actually, it's where the Nasato gang breaks down stolen catalytic converters to get the precious metals. Sam and I followed the ninjas to the warehouse from Vlad's garage."

"You followed who now?" Tamika asked.

"The ninjas. The Pottstown ninjas. The ones stealing all the catalytic converters."

"They're not called *ninjas*. People who steal catalytic converters are called *cutters*," Tamika said.

"Well, these guys dress like ninjas," I said. "All in black, head to toe."

"I won't ask about the nature of your surveillance because I honestly don't want to know," Smitty said. "I've had officers working that case for two months. We have a joint task force with the surrounding townships. We haven't been able to pinpoint the base of operations. Where is it?"

"It's in part the big brick warehouse off of Kramer Street. At the end of the driveway," Max said.

"Vlad's garage was obviously one of the businesses targeted," I said.

"The Nasato brothers are running the operation," Max said. "Fat Eddie, Fat Joey, and Fat Vinnie."

"Yes, we know about the Nasato gang," Tamika said. "They used to conduct most of their activities in south Philly, but they've been expanding into the suburbs in the last few years."

"You haven't told us what you want in exchange for the information," Smitty said.

"Protection," Max said. "The Fat Brothers are aware that Jessica knows about their operation, and they're threatening her and her mother." Max was playing it close to the vest. He left out my kidnapping and the car explosion.

"I sent Mom out of town with her boyfriend, Harry. To be safe, Sam's staying with her boyfriend, Jalen Marks. I'm staying with Max for now." I saw a nearly imperceptible smile flicker over Smitty's face.

"I'll increase patrols in your neighborhood, Jess, and I'll call North Coventry PD about covering your place, Max."

I gave Jalen's address to Smitty and asked if he could keep an eye on Sam too. I glanced down at the table. A pile of six Hershey's Kisses foil wrappers sat in front of me. I had no memory of eating five Kisses.

Max looked at the pile. "Are you alright, Jess?"

I rolled the wrappers into a ball. "Yup, perfect."

"Thanks for the intel, guys. I'm going to have officers sit on the warehouse twenty-four seven until I get some evidence, then I'm going to shut it down. Arresting the Nasato brothers would be a big win for the department."

"Watch out for Fat Eddie. He's demented," I said.

Max shot me a look, and we stood up to leave.

"Let's get a beer soon and catch up, Smitty," Max said. They shook hands, and we left.

We piled into the Wagoneer and headed toward Max's place.

"I need to talk to Vlad. Let's go visit him in jail." I said.

"What's that going to get you, Jessica?"

"If Vlad looks me in the eye and says he didn't kill Daniel, I think I'll be able tell if he's being truthful or not."

"You're going to want to believe he's telling the truth no matter what Vlad says to you, because you want him to be innocent. The best thing you can do for him right now is keep investigating. If Vlad didn't do the murder, the evidence will bear it out."

Max was probably right. I wanted to visit Vlad for my own reasons.

"I hope he's doing alright in jail," I said.

"I wouldn't worry too much about him. He's probably already running D block." Max looked at me. "Do you want to risk a trip to the grocery store? You need vegetables in your life. More than I currently have in my refrigerator."

"Sure. I could go for some veggies, I guess. And cupcakes or something."

Max drove down South Hanover Street toward the HappyCart shopping center and I checked for tails in the side mirror.

Few people were in the store, and we cruised through the produce section, picking up stuff to make salads. I gazed longingly at a box of Entenmann's chocolate chip cookies at the end of an aisle, and Max tossed a box in the cart. We grabbed another bag of diet kitty crunchies and a few toys for Bruce.

We paid, loaded everything into the Wagoneer, and got in the front seat. A piece of paper under the windshield wiper flapped in the icy breeze. Max opened the door, yanked it off the windshield, and read it.

"Jessica, get out of the car. Now."

Max doesn't call me by my full name unless there's a problem. I leaped out from Wagoneer and backed up a few paces. "What's going on? What's happening?"

He walked over and handed the note to me. "It's from your secret admirer."

It read, *Jessica, What did you tell the cops? Tick tock, tick tock. Yours, Eddie.*

We both turned, scanning the parking lot for Fat Eddie's Cadillac in the sea of SUVs, minivans, and shopping carts. Max walked around the Wagoneer, examining it, then crawled underneath it to check for explosives. He scooted back out and said, "I'm pretty sure it's clean, but I'm calling the police to have them bring over a sniffer dog."

Within minutes, the HappyCart parking lot turned into a war zone as squad cars, ambulances, and fire trucks descended upon us, sirens blaring and air horns blasting. Within minute, a news helicopter hovered overhead adding to the chaos. Police, EMTs, and fire personnel milled around and shouted at each other. A group of gawkers and people live streaming the commotion formed outside the police tape.

Twenty minutes later the sniffer dog, a black Labrador retriever named Slayer, showed up with his handler. Slayer circled around the SUV a few times, sniffed the inside, lay down on the ground, and pronounced the Wagoneer free of any bombs. He got a tennis ball.

Max used the remote start on the Wagoneer. The crowd gasped as the engine started, and when it didn't blow up, someone yelled, "That sucked."

The police, fire, and ambulance vehicles cleared out, the crowd of disappointed gawkers dispersed, and the helicopter flew off to the next potential headline.

Max and I jumped back in the Wagoneer and left. We were both on high alert for the Fat Brothers. The butterflies in my stomach had multiplied, and I felt ill, either from the police department's stale Hershey's Kisses, Fat Eddie's note, or the possibility of being blown to bits in the HappyCart parking lot. Max took a winding route back to his house. When we arrived, he pulled the Glock from his hip and cleared the house before we carried in the groceries.

"I figured everything was okay when I saw Bruce asleep on the island," he said, as we put the groceries away. "He'd have been hiding if a stranger was in the house."

"For sure. He was giving you the all clear." I ruffled Bruce's fur and kissed his head. I tossed him the new catnip fish toy, and he batted it into the living room and attacked it.

"Looks like you picked a winner, Jess." Max said. He carried a stack of wood in from the patio, set the security alarm, and started a fire.

"Do you want a glass of wine?" he asked.

"Red wine helps settle your stomach. That's science, right?"

"I've definitely heard that." Max took a beer from the fridge for himself and poured a glass of cabernet for me.

He tucked the Entenmann's box under his arm and carried everything over to the coffee table and set it down. He sat next to me on the couch and put his arm around me.

"I know the Nasato brothers want to kill you and all, but I'm glad we agreed to give us a another try. I really want to kiss you and do other things."

I bit into a cookie, washed it down with a sip of wine, and attempted to relax into the couch. "I'd like to kiss you and do other things too, Max, but we're on a trial basis right now."

Undeterred, he leaned in for a kiss, and my phone buzzed with a text from Mom. She sent a photo of herself in an Amish bonnet with the message, *Fun in Amish Country! I got us matching quilts and a dozen whoopie pies!* Another text came through from Harry. *We're doing fine. I've got plenty of ammo.*

I woke up two hours later on Max's shoulder. The Eagles game was on and my wine was empty.

"Did I accidentally fall asleep?"

"Yes. You drank half of your wine, ate a couple more cookies, snuggled in, and you were out cold. I finished the wine for you."

"Did I snore?"

"Nope. You drooled some. My shirt is damp right here."

"Oops." I dabbed at the spot with a napkin. "What time is it?"

"Almost time to call Fat Eddie, if you're still up for it."

"Yes, I'm up for it. That assclown doesn't scare me."

"He should scare you. He's dangerous."

We headed back to Max's office and sat down at the table. "Fat Eddie will want to meet in person. He's going to want another chance to grab you."

"If he thinks I already told the cops what I know about the catalytic converter ring, what's the point of kidnapping me for a second time?"

"First, never underestimate a criminal's capacity for revenge. He's a sadistic psycho who gets off on hurting people. He's skated on three murders so far, so he probably feels invincible. Second, if he kills you, you can't testify against him."

That hadn't occurred to me. "I don't get why he didn't shoot me when he had the chance, right when he kidnapped me in Pottstown."

"For someone like Eddie, it's more about the chase, and unfortunately the torture, than it is murder."

"Are you going to talk to him too?"

"It's better if it's only you who talks to him. If he hears a male voice, it could throw off the whole dynamic, and we want to keep him on the phone as long as possible. The more Eddie talks, the more likely he'll incriminate himself."

"Fine."

"Are you ready?"

"Yes. Let's get this over with."

Max pulled a burner phone out of his desk drawer, powered it up, dialed Fat Eddie's number, and put it on speaker. I set my phone on the table and put it on record. Fat Eddie picked up on the third ring.

"Is this my beautiful redhead?" Fat Eddie practically sounded aroused. Gross.

"This is Jessica. You wanted to talk to me?"

"I have so much to tell you," Fat Eddie said, "and more things to show you."

I almost gagged up a cookie. "Really? What would you like to talk about first, Mr. Nasato?"

"Please, Jessica, call me Eddie. We should be on a first name basis by now."

"Fine. What do you want to talk about, *Eddie*."

"I want to talk about what I'm going to do to you, but we need to talk about business. First, my Cadillac. Who blew it up for you? My brothers and I saw you run away with a guy that night. The same guy as at HappyCart today. It won't be long until I figure out who he is. Then he's dead too."

Max stood with arms crossed over his chest, his jaw set, glaring at the phone.

"I have no idea who blew up your Cadillac, Eddie. Are you sure it wasn't a battery malfunction? You should call the manufacturer and complain. It's probably still under warranty."

"I know the sound of a freakin' bomb when I hear one. That's okay, Jessica. I'll get the truth out of you soon enough. And I already got my replacement Cadillac. Exactly the same, but it's black."

"I hope that one doesn't blow up too. That would unfortunate." I enjoyed screwing with him, and it kept him talking.

"That's not going to happen, Jessica. Now, I'd like to talk to you about what you saw the night you and your boyfriend were trespassing at my freakin' warehouse."

Max slid me a note that said, *Say drug lab. We don't want to show our hand yet.*

"Well, Eddie, like I told you when you kidnapped me, my friend and I were ghost hunting at your warehouse. When I looked in the window, I saw scales, cookers, and lots of jugs of chemicals. Like I imagine a drug lab would look."

In the background I heard Fat Vinnie say, "Hey Eddie, do you want olives on it?"

Eddie tried to muffle the phone with his hand. "Can't you see I'm talking here? Yes, olives. Dumbass. Pardon the interruption, Jessica, that was my moron brother. So you think I run a drug lab? I don't deal in that crap. My current project is much more profitable than coke or meth."

"What could possibly make more money than your own drug lab?"

"Nice try. You're trying to get me to incriminate myself on the freakin' phone. I know your boyfriend is with you and you're probably recording me."

"Nope. It's just me, myself, and I," I said, watching Max's eyes.

"Yeah, right. I almost forgot to mention the most important thing," Fat Eddie said. "Since you blew up my Cadillac, I took your car. Vinnie boosted it from your house this morning. It's pretty nice, but not as nice as my new Caddy."

Dammit, why did I leave my car at my house? Rookie mistake. Max paced the room, staring at the loaded Glock on his desk.

"Eddie, did you just admit to car theft?" I asked.

He ignored me. "If you want your car back, you meet me. We'll have some fun. If you bring cops, we're gonna have a real problem."

"I'll consider your offer and get back to you." I hit End Call on the burner phone. I couldn't listen to Fat Eddie's stupid voice any longer.

"Sorry Max. I couldn't talk to him anymore. He's an ass. I hoped he'd mention the catalytic converters and the jewelry scam, but you heard him, he wasn't going to go into that."

"Red, you did great. But we have to pull the police in on this. If you're going to meet Eddie, you'll need more protection than I can provide. I'm not letting anything happen to you."

"Fine by me."

"The only issue with pulling Smitty and Tamika in is we're going to have to tell them the whole story."

"Well, cops or no cops, Fat Eddie is coming for me, so we may as well tell Smitty and Tamika everything."

"We'll talk to them tomorrow."

Max and I headed upstairs to bed. I slept next to Max. Max slept next to his gun.

Sixteen

Max was already downstairs making breakfast when my eyes opened. I hit the shower, dressed for combat, lost in thought as I sat on the edge of the bed and laced up my hiking boots. I had no idea what today would bring, but I wanted to be ready to kick Eddie in the balls if I needed to.

Max stood at the stove making eggs with green stuff in it. He reached out, pulled me to him, and gave me a kiss that made me dizzy.

"You look hot in those boots, Red. Have a seat, we're ready to eat." The toast popped up, and he picked it up with two fingers and sat down next to me. The green stuff in the eggs turned out to be spinach, which I deemed acceptable in the omelet format.

"I'll call Smitty and set up a meeting for later today," Max said.

"Okay. Tell them to be on the lookout for Fat Eddie's car when we come in."

"Fat Eddie really is stupid enough to follow us to Pottstown PD," Max said, shoveling in some eggs.

"Stupid, brazen, or a combination of both," I said. My phone rang and a number I didn't recognize appeared on the screen. "Hello?"

"Jessica? This is Anastasiya Boyko, Vlad's wife."

"Yes, Anastasiya. How are you doing?"

"Not so good. Vlad always says to me, don't talk on the phone. Will you meet me? I must talk to you about Vlad. Please." She sounded frightened and upset.

"When?"

"In one hour. Dingle's Donuts."

"Okay. See you then."

"Thank you," she said, and hung up.

Max looked skeptical. "Who are you meeting?"

"Vlad's wife, Anastasiya. She wants to talk, and she won't do it over the phone. I'm meeting her at Dingle's in an hour."

"I'm going with you," Max said firmly.

"No arguments from me," I said.

We rolled up to the curb outside Dingle's Donuts at ten in the morning. Mr. and Mrs. Dingle were about a hundred years old. Their shop is an institution in Pottstown, and everyone loves them.

Max was in full ex-cop mode. His Glock sat next to him in the center console. "I'll check the bathrooms and make sure no one's in there hiding. I'll give you a sign if it's all clear. Then I'll be posted right out here by the entrance."

"Got it." I tucked my hair up under a baseball cap and adjusted my dark shades.

"Wait here."

Max holstered his gun, pulled his jacket over it, and entered the doughnut shop. I watched as he headed to the back of the shop and out of sight. He returned a moment later, gave me a nod, and stood outside by the entrance, pretending to read his phone.

Another minute passed. Anastasiya rounded the corner and walked briskly toward Dingle's. She looked as chic as ever, with sunglasses on her head, and wearing a long coat and spike-heeled boots. She entered the shop and approached the counter. I hopped out of the 4Runner and the bells on the door jingled cheerily as I entered. I stood in line behind her and lightly touched her arm.

"Hey." I took off my sunglasses.

Tears welled up in her eyes. Anastasiya and I placed our orders, paid, and took our drinks and doughnuts to a table. I took a seat facing the window, with a clear view of Max and the street.

"You must help my husband," Anastasiya said. Her quiet voice trembled. "He did not do what the police say he did."

I gingerly tested my hot chocolate for temperature. "The police have some good evidence against Vlad. His fingerprint left on a screwdriver. Did Vlad talk to Jamie Brennan?"

"Yes, we retain him. He's a smart man. Thank you."

"Tell me why Vlad didn't do this." I took a bite of my jelly doughnut, and a jelly blob squirted out the bottom and oozed onto the table.

Anastasiya handed me a napkin, and I sopped up the jelly as best I could.

"Jamie told us about the screwdriver the police found. I know Vlad did not kill this man for one reason. But you won't believe me when I tell you."

"Try me."

"He's cheap." Her voice steadied a bit. "Vlad is a cheap man. He would never leave a good tool behind. Never. When he stabbed that man a few years ago, he took his screwdriver with him. Besides, Vlad is a changed man now. We start a family. I'm pregnant." Tears welled up in her eyes and threatened to spill down her cheeks. "You must help him. We will make it right with you when Vlad is out of jail. We will pay you double, triple your fee."

I pointed to Max. "The man standing outside is Max O'Conner. He's an ex-cop, and he's a private investigator like me. We're working together on Vlad's case. If Vlad is innocent like you say he is, we'll do everything we can to prove it." I hoped to God Vlad was innocent.

A tear rolled down Anastasiya's cheek, and she dashed it with a napkin. The bells chimed, and a mom and two kids came in the shop and stood staring at the doughnut trays, trying to decide.

"Will you visit him in jail? He says he must talk to you. I beg you." Another tear slid down her cheek.

"If you put Max and me on the visitors list, we'll go talk to him."

"Okay, I'll call the jail and schedule your visit for Monday."

Anastasiya wiped more tears away and stood up. "Thank you. I'll tell Vlad you will help him."

We left the shop together, and I introduced her to Max. Anastasiya said goodbye to us, retraced her steps back down the street, around the corner and out of sight.

"You know, I could use a coffee," Max said. "And we can soften Smitty and Tamika up with a dozen doughnuts."

We returned to the shop and ordered a dozen chocolate frosted and jelly doughnuts.

"I promised her we'd visit Vlad in jail," I said while we waited for our order.

"I figured that was going to come up," Max said. "It may take a few days to get on the visitors list, but I'll try to pull a few strings."

Mr. Dingle handed us our order, we thanked him and left.

"Anastasiya wants us to visit Vlad on Monday," I said, as we piled into the 4Runner.

"Okay. I have meetings in the morning. Let's see if we can make it in the afternoon." His phone buzzed with a text. "Smitty says we can come over to meet with him and Tamika now."

"Let's get this over with."

Max drove around the block and over to the police department. No Cadillacs in sight. He pulled into a visitor spot at the back of Borough Hall, I grabbed the doughnuts, and we headed inside. We waited at the front desk for a few minutes before Tamika appeared and led us to the meeting room upstairs. The three of us sat down, and I pushed the bowl of Hershey's Kisses away from me and opened the box of doughnuts. Smitty came in a few minutes later and tossed a legal pad on the table and took a seat next to Tamika.

Tamika took a doughnut from the box. "Did something new happen since our meeting yesterday?"

Max cleared his throat. "Yesterday we didn't discuss with you how the Fat Brothers came to know about Jessica," he said.

"Right," Smitty said. "Care to let us in on how that happened?"

I took a breath. "I was doing surveillance on the Kramer Street warehouse with Sam earlier this week, and I sort of got abducted by the Fat Brothers. I may have been, uh, looking around on their property."

"So you were trespassing, then you got kidnapped. By gangsters," Tamika said. Max shifted around in his seat.

"Yes. The three of them stuffed me into a Cadillac and took me through the drive-through at Wendy's. After that, they drove me to an old building in Norristown. Close to the river."

"Hold up," Tamika said. "The Fat Brothers took you through the *drive-through*?"

"Yes. And I couldn't scream for help because Fat Vinnie had a gun stuck in my side. I was afraid the drive-through lady or I would get shot. But they did buy me some fries and a Frosty."

"What flavor?" Tamika asked. Smitty gave her a look.

"Chocolate."

"Mm-hmm." She made a note on her tablet.

"Did you happen to hear about the recent car explosion in Norristown?" Max asked.

"We heard about it. Was that you guys?" Smitty asked.

"Yes. No. I mean, the Fat Brothers took me to Norristown, marched me at gunpoint into the building, and zip-tied me to a chair. And Fat Eddie was getting ready to break my leg with a sledgehammer. Max rescued me right after someone blew up Fat Eddie's Cadillac, parked outside."

Smitty frowned. "Max, I have to ask. Did you blow up the Cadillac?"

"No, I definitely did not blow it up. That was not me."

"Right," Tamika said. "And you expect us to believe that?"

"I know it's hard to believe, but I had nothing to do with that car exploding. Come on, Smitty, you know I'm not a bomb guy."

"If it wasn't you, who blew up the Cadillac?" Smitty asked. "The timing is a little too perfect."

He looked from Max to me and back to Max. Tamika stared a hole through me. I took a bite of my jelly doughnut as a delay tactic. Just like in the doughnut shop, a jelly blob dropped out onto the conference table. Tamika shook her head, handed me a napkin, and I mopped up the jelly and handed the napkin back to her.

"I don't want your damn jelly napkin. Throw it in the trash. Now who blew up the Cadillac?"

I handed the balled up napkin to Max, and he tossed it in the trashcan across the room. I took my sweet time chewing my doughnut. I'd never make it as a criminal. My heart pounded in my ears and my pits were working overtime. I had to think fast.

I swallowed. "Listen, I'll make you a deal. Don't ask us who blew up the Cadillac right now, and you can use me to get to Fat Eddie. He wants to meet. You can get him for the catalytic converter ring and kidnapping me."

"Big deal. We were going to make you do that anyway," Tamika said.

"We're giving you a lot, and I'm taking all the risk," I said.

"Fat Eddie stole Jess's car this morning, and he's using it to get her to meet with him," Max said. "For the record, I'm not a fan of this idea. The guy is sick. He's threatened to kill her more than once."

"I don't like it much either, but I'll agree to it. We're running the op, and you'll do what you're told," Smitty said, eyeballing both of us.

"You got it," Max said.

"Did Fat Eddie say when this meeting is supposed to take place?" Tamika asked.

I shook my head. "No."

I played last night's conversation for them from my phone. When it finished, Tamika said, "Are you sure you want to do this, Jessica?"

"He threatened my mom, and he needs to go down."

"When do you want to meet him?" Smitty asked.

"Tomorrow morning. I have the eighties party at the Otter Club tomorrow night."

Max turned to me. "You're still going to that, Jess? It's not safe. Even if we get Fat Eddie, there will be two other Fat Brothers still at large."

"I have to go to the party. Mom's in charge of it, and I have to be there to help her. And protect her." I teared up. Dammit. I willed myself not to bawl in front of the cops.

"Then I'm going with you. Strapped," Max said.

"I'll talk to Jack McFarland at the Otter Club," Smitty said. "We'll put some plainclothes officers at the party and unmarked cars outside."

"I want you and Tamika inside with us," I said.

"Don't worry. No one's going to mess up your momma's eighties party," Tamika said.

"She's dressing up as Lita Ford," I said quietly. I caught Max suppressing a smirk. Smitty stared at the table, and Tamika shuffled some papers around.

"Jess, when you call Fat Eddie about the meeting, get him to agree to a public place," Smitty said. "How about the parking lot at Riverview Park? The one by the pavilion."

"I'll try to get him to agree to it. I'll let you know what he says." I took a chocolate frosted doughnut from the box and ate it in three bites. All this stress was not good for my BMI.

"Has Tracy Lakeland come in to make a statement about Daniel's murder yet?" I asked.

"Yes," Smitty said. "She came in without a lawyer the day after we found his body. She met with Tamika and me. Tracy said she and Daniel have been living separately for several months and she doesn't have any idea who would have had a motive to kill him. She appeared to be genuinely upset."

"What's your impression?" Max asked.

"I think she has millions of reasons to murder her husband," Tamika said.

"About twenty million," I said.

"So we're good for the meet?" Max said.

"I have to clear it with the chief," Smitty said. "Call Fat Eddie soon. We're going to need time to coordinate this."

"One more thing," Max said. He opened his backpack and took out the small trash bag he had liberated from Daniel's jewelry shop. "Jess and I were surveilling Daniel's shop in Lower Pottsgrove last night to see who might show up, and I found this by the dumpster out back. Some trash from the jewelry shop." He handed the bag to Smitty.

"Oh, that itty-bitty bag was sitting all alone by the dumpster?" Tamika asked with a smirk.

"Yeah. Sitting on the ground. Someone was too lazy to throw it in, I guess."

"Mm-hmm." Tamika locked eyes with Max, and I started to pit out again.

"Well, thanks, guys," Max said, jumping up. "We'll be in touch."

I said goodbye, and we beat it out of there.

"I don't like lying to Smitty and Tamika," I said, when we were back in the 4Runner.

"I don't either, Red. That's why I don't like B and Es. They tend to get messy. But we gave them what we took. We're square with them."

"Let's stop at my house before we head back to your place," I said, as we pulled onto Hanover Street.

"You got it, Red."

Max and I rolled to my neighborhood with no Cadillacs in sight. Mom's car was parked in the driveway, but my car was gone.

"Crap," I said. "I was holding out hope that Fat Eddie was bluffing."

"No such luck. Do you need to grab any stuff while we're here?"

"I could use some more underwear."

"Red, you need less underwear," Max said.

"Not helpful."

I brought in the mail and Mom's newspapers and unlocked the front door. Max pulled his Glock and made me wait downstairs in the foyer while he cleared the house.

"We're good!" he yelled, barreling down the steps.

I checked Mom's bedroom and the family room to see if anything had been stolen. All appeared to be in order, and nothing had been taken from her jewelry armoire or the hollowed-out dictionary she kept a stash of money in.

We ran up to my bedroom. I don't have much expensive jewelry, but what I did have was in my jewelry box, and my laptop was in my office. I don't have a secret money stash.

"I guess the Fat Brothers didn't bother breaking in, Max. It's bad enough Fat Eddie stole my car. If they'd robbed my house, I'd blow up Fat Eddie's new Cadillac myself."

Max posted himself by the bedroom window and kept an eye on the street. I grabbed an overnight bag from the closet and opened my underwear drawer.

"Max, your wish came true," I said, my skin crawling. "I have no underwear."

He turned form the window and winked at me. "How's that a problem?"

"No, you don't understand. My underwear are *gone*. Fat Eddie stole all my underwear." I sank down onto the bed, completely skeeved out. "What is his deal? It's so gross that he was in my bedroom. And why does he need *all* my underwear? He couldn't leave me one pair?"

Max left the window and stared into the empty drawer. "Let's go to my place. I'll call a locksmith for you. And you're getting a security system. I'll pay for it." He slammed the drawer shut.

I didn't argue. I tried to shake off the skeevy feeling as we cruised back to Max's place. The thought of what Eddie might do with my underwear made me want to hurl.

Back at Max's house, I dumped my bags in the foyer. We used the burner phone to call Eddie. He picked up right away.

"Hello, my beautiful Jessica. Say you'll meet me and make me a happy man."

Gross. Max paced around the office.

"Why the hell did you steal my underwear? That was totally uncalled for, Eddie."

"They're my souvenir. Something to remember you by when you're gone."

Max looked like his head might explode.

"Whatever, Eddie. I need my car back. Can we meet tomorrow morning?"

"That's fine with me, Jessica. Let's meet at my warehouse on Kramer Street."

"Nope," I said firmly. "Let's meet in a public place. How about Riverview Park? That's not too far from your warehouse."

"And two blocks from the freakin' cops. How convenient for you."

"Come on, Eddie. You're a gangster. You're not afraid of the police."

"That's true, I'm not. But you have to come alone. If I even smell a cop, you can kiss your car goodbye forever. It'll be flattened by nighttime."

"Fine, Eddie, no cops. What time?"

"Ten o'clock," Eddie said. "And dress pretty for me."

I ignored that comment. "Okay, ten o'clock tomorrow morning, in Riverview Park by the pavilion."

"I can't wait."

I ended the call.

"I really want to kick his ass," Max said.

"Me too. I hate his face."

Seventeen

The next morning, Max and I awoke early. After the conversation with Fat Eddie the night before, we called Smitty and made plans for the Riverview Park meeting. At eight, Max and I headed to Pottstown PD. Smitty and Tamika were going over the plan with two undercover officers. Max, Smitty, and Officer José Martinez were dressed in exercise clothes and would pose as runners in the park. Two more officers would pose as park maintenance workers. They'd have visuals on me while I met with Eddie.

At eight thirty, Max, Smitty, José and the two other officers left to take their positions in the park. Some technician guy put a GPS tracker in my hiking boot. Tamika took me into her office, drew the blinds, and attached a wire to my bra. Then the tech came back in, tested it, and gave me the thumbs up.

Things were moving fast. I paced while chain-eating stale Hershey's Kisses in the conference room until Tamika popped her head in and said it was time to go. I shrugged on my jacket. In a pocket I'd stashed a can of pepper spray and a paring knife I borrowed from Max's utensil drawer. I told myself I was ready to kick some ass. Fat Eddie had had his fun with me, and now I was going to take him down.

At nine, I left the police department on foot and headed east on High Street. When I rounded the corner, Tamika followed about thirty paces behind me to ensure I wasn't grabbed before I made it to the park. She pretended to talk on her phone but had an earpiece so she could communicate with Smitty and the officers. Weak-kneed but determined, I tromped down the street, trying not to hyperventilate in the freezing winter air. I crossed the railroad tracks and made a right onto the footpath that led into the park. The two undercover cops were there, one running a leaf blower, and the other pruning shrubs near the pavilion. Next to him was a wheelbarrow. Both wore neon yellow public works sweatshirts, and a public works truck was parked nearby. All in all, it looked pretty convincing. I glanced over my shoulder to catch Tamika's eye but she had disappeared. My car was parked at the rear of the lot, empty. Fat Eddie's hadn't arrived yet. I couldn't see Smitty, José or Max anywhere.

Tamika had instructed me to sit on a park bench and wait for Eddie. The undercover cops landscaped nearby, giving no indication that they saw me. A few minutes passed, and Fat Eddie drove into the parking lot in his new Cadillac. I fought the urge to make eye contact with the undercovers.

Eddie drove toward me. He backed his car in facing the street with his rear bumper to the river, I guess for a quick getaway if need be. I stood up from the bench and faced the front of Eddie's Cadillac. I kept one eye on the undercover officers and one hand wrapped around the pepper spray in my pocket. Eddie stepped from the car with a sneer on his face. He shut the car door and lurched toward me.

"Jessica! You look so beautiful today!" he shouted over the leaf blower. "Come on, let's go for a ride. You can sit in the front seat with me this time. I'll be a gentleman. I promise I won't hold a gun on you."

Behind him, the Cadillac began to slowly roll backward down the slope toward the river. I wasn't sure if he was distracted by the sight of me or if he was just a bad driver, but he hadn't put the car in park. The leaf blower concealed the sound as it coasted down the hill. I tried to focus on Eddie, but my eyes shifted past him to the imminent demise of his second Cadillac. I bit the inside of my cheek and tried to hold it together.

"You and I will have so much fun together, Jessica," Eddie said, oblivious to the events happening behind him. "We'll get a drink, then go to my warehouse. I'll show you my catalytic converters operation. You know, the ones we stole from Vlad's garage. The guys use very dangerous chemicals to get the platinum out. You wouldn't want to get any on you. They leave very bad burns."

The undercover officers' heads slowly turned in unison as they watched the Cadillac take its last ride.

"Eddie, is it the same platinum Daniel Lakeland used to make his jewelry?"

"Yes. Daniel and I had a good thing going. Too bad about him."

I couldn't resist it anymore. "Hey, Eddie, turn around."

Fat Eddie turned in time to watch his replacement Cadillac gently dip into the river, ass end first, like a fat lady easing into a warm bubble bath.

"Son of a bitch!" he yelled, plodding down the hill toward the river in a vain attempt to save his car from the muck of the river bottom. By the time he reached the riverbank, the Cadillac was up to its windows, placidly drifting with the slow current. Seconds later the car sank, engulfed in the murky water.

"That goddam car with its freakin' stupid dial gear shifter. I hate that effing thing!" Fat Eddie screamed. He stomped around, red in the face. "That's the third time I put it in neutral instead of park."

"Tough break, Eddie."

Glaring, he lunged at me and I gave him a blast of the pepper spray.

Smitty stepped out from behind a tree, gun drawn, José right behind him. "Edward Nasato, you're under arrest. José, hook him up."

Max jogged stepped out from behind another tree, holstered his gun and stood beside me.

José cuffed Eddie behind his back. Eddie was still yelling about his Cadillac and didn't ask what the charge was.

"Hold on a second," I said. "Before you take him in, can you check his pockets for my car keys?"

José found my keys in Fat Eddie's right pocket. "He's got them."

"After we process your car for evidence, you can have it back. We'll have to check it for explosives and tow it," Smitty said. He walked Eddie back up the hill to a waiting squad car. Eddie was still screaming about the Cadillac. He was much more upset about the car than being arrested.

Tamika stepped out of the cruiser and put Eddie in the back. "Watch your head, dumbass," she said, slammed the door and drove off. The undercovers and Smitty walked to the pavilion to coordinate the search of my car.

An annoying whirring sound came from behind Max and me. We turned around, and Kenny Marshall, a reporter for *The Pottstown Post*, was coming in hot on his electric scooter. Kenny was a pain in the ass, never failing to hassle Mand and me for information about our cases.

"Hey guys, what's the scoop?" he said, and hopped off the scooter. He pulled his phone out of his pocket and stuck it my face. "Any comment on the police activity in the park? I heard it on my scanner and zipped right over."

"Well, you're late as usual, Kenny. And no, no comment," I said.

"There's a rumor on social that a car just sank in the river. What can you tell me about that?"

Max put his arm around me. "Why don't you jump in the water and find out for yourself."

"Sorry, Kenny, we can't talk about open police investigations," I said.

Kenny stuffed his phone back in his pocket. "Okey dokey, then. See you two at the station." He hopped back on his scooter. "Rats. No charge," he said, fiddling with buttons on the handlebars.

Max and I turned and walked back to Pottstown PD. The police processed Fat Eddie, and Max and I waited while the bomb squad checked my car for explosives and officers searched through it. Nothing had been stolen, but I knew I was going to have it professionally detailed after he sat in it. While we waited for the car to be released, Smitty brought Max and I some paperwork.

"As of now, you're both consulting with the department on the catalytic converter case," he said, after we signed the papers and handed them back to him. "Don't make me regret this."

Smitty asked Max and me to watch Fat Eddie's interview. The chief of police, Mike Fitzpatrick, stood in the observation room behind the one-way glass with us. Eddie was still riled up, but he calmed down a bit after an officer brought in some doughnuts and coffee. He was cuffed in front, awkwardly eating his doughnut with two hands in the interview room, his eyes still red from the pepper spray. Smitty and Tamika were seated across from Eddie with their backs to us.

Smitty started the interview. "Mr. Nasato, you're being charged with auto theft for stealing Jessica Byrne's car from her residence. Other charges will follow."

"First, I don't like the word *theft*. That's an ugly word. She destroyed my car, so I borrowed her car. Second, what other charges are you talking about? You cops got nothing on me. I'm an upstanding citizen. I give back to the community."

"Oh please," I said. Chief Fitzpatrick gave me the side-eye.

"Well, we got you on your side business," Tamika said.

Fat Eddie glared at Smitty. "What's this bitch talking about?" he asked.

Tamika leaned across the table, snatched the doughnut out of his hands, and made a basket with it in the corner trashcan without looking.

"I'm Detective Johnson, and that's how you will address me at all times. Detective Smits, would you inform Mr. Nasato about the additional charges he's facing?"

"Certainly, Detective Johnson. We're aware of your involvement with the catalytic converter thefts at Vladyslav

Boyko's garage. With that and the car theft, I could put you in the joint for a dime. Easy," Smitty said. "Add another twenty for the kidnapping of Jessica Byrne."

"And it's only a matter of time before we get you on Daniel Lakeland's murder," Tamika said.

"You got no proof of any of that. And I don't know this Boyko guy and I sure as hell didn't kill freakin' Daniel Lakeland. He was my business associate and a personal friend of mine." Fat Eddie sat back in his chair.

"Mm-hmm," Tamika said.

"Mr. Nasato, we have you on tape admitting to Ms. Byrne your involvement with the catalytic converter thefts right before your car took a swim in the river. Do you want us to play it for you?" Smitty asked.

"No I would not. You cops got it in for me."

"We know you aren't doing this work alone," Tamika said. "Who's working for you?"

"I ain't no rat, and I ain't talking anymore. I want my lawyer. Get Juan Epstein on the phone."

"Did he say his lawyer's name is Juan Epstein?" I asked Max.

"I heard him say that too," Chief Fitzpatrick said.

"Me too," Max said. "Like the guy on that old show *Welcome Back, Kotter*."

Chief Fitzpatrick knocked on the glass. Smitty and Tamika pushed back their chairs, stood up, and stepped into the observation room. I kept my eyes on Fat Eddie. He scowled at the one-way glass and muttered to himself about me, the Cadillac, and his trashcan doughnut.

"Get the paperwork done on Nasato and keep working the Lakeland case," the Chief said to Smitty and Tamika. "And get that car pulled from the river before the DEP shows up. Put it on Mr. Nasato's tab."

I turned to Chief Fitzpatrick. "Chief, is he going to get bail?"

"I wouldn't rule it out," he said, and left.

"I need to get my stuff and go back to my house," I said. "Mom and Harry will be home from Lancaster soon, and Fat Joey and Fat Vinnie are still out there. I need to make sure she's safe."

"Okay," Max said. "I'll call the company who did my security system and get them to send someone out to your place and install one today."

Smitty answered a phone call, then turned to me. "Your car's ready, Jess. It's in the side lot. You can ask for your keys at the front desk. We'll step up patrols in your neighborhood. Stay safe."

"Thank you. You guys are amazing," I said.

"We got you, girl," Tamika said. Smitty and Max shook hands.

We left the station and headed back to Max's house. Max called the security company, who said a technician would be at my house by two in the afternoon. Max and I ran upstairs, and I stuffed my clothes into my overnight bag, gathered up Bruce and his belongings, and lugged everything out to my car.

Max pulled me to him. "I liked having you here." He gazing down at me. "I always know what color panties you have on."

"Don't you enjoy the mystery of the unknown?"

"Not as much as I like having unlimited access," he said, kissing me. "Besides, when you're with me, I know you're safe."

"You don't have unlimited access yet, buddy. We're on a trial basis, remember?"

"You keep saying that."

Max followed me back into Pottstown. I kept my eyes peeled for the other Nasato brothers. I crossed the Hanover Street bridge as a crane truck backed down the boat ramp at Riverview Park. A couple guys in wetsuits stood at the water's edge, preparing to hook up the Cadillac and pull it from the muddy water. A crowd of gawkers formed close by.

Sam called. "It's all over social that you were tied up and naked in Fat Eddie's trunk when his car rolled into the river. I guess that's a lie?"

"I wasn't in Eddie's car today. But his Cadillac did roll backward into the river, and it was awesome."

"How in the hell did that happen?"

I explained to Sam how Eddie put the car in neutral and didn't hear it roll away since the cops were running a leaf blower.

"Huh. Some people really have trouble with those dial gear shifters," Sam said. "Not me. I can drive anything. I'm an excellent driver."

Sam makes a habit of driving with her knee while applying makeup in the rearview mirror and talking on the phone.

"Well, Eddie's steamed. He's up on multiple charges."

"I guess old Fat Eddie's not having good luck with his cars lately. He's got bad karma. Ha! See what I did there? Kar-ma."

"I get it, Sam. How's it going with you? Have you seen the two other Fat Brothers?"

"No. The coast has been clear. And if they know what's good for them, they won't be coming around Jalen's place. He's locked, loaded and highly motivated."

"Well, Eddie's in the pokey at Pottstown PD for now, but he'll get bailed out soon. He called his lawyer, Juan Epstein."

Sam got quiet for a moment. "How do I know that name? Juan Epstein...Juan Epstein," she repeated.

"Seventies TV reruns."

"That's it! I used to watch *Welcome Back, Kotter* on the oldies channel with my grandmom after school. That Horshack was hilarious."

"He was."

"Jess, I need to tell you something about Daniel."

"What?"

"I set up the Ouija board yesterday. I turned the lights down, lit some candles, played some Black Sabbath, and generally made it a ghost-friendly environment to summon Daniel's spirit."

"So how'd that go?" This ought to be good.

"Well, that all depends. Did Daniel like Mexican food?"

"I'm not sure. Why?"

"Because he spelled out 'nachos' on the Ouija board."

"Nachos? That's all Daniel said?"

"Yeah. Nachos. Does that mean anything to you?"

"Not really, but I'll think about it. Thanks." I knew who nachos meant something to, and it wasn't my dead client. "Sam, I have the eighties party with my mom tonight. Max will be there and the police are going to provide security in case Vinnie or Joey want to cause trouble, so I have to run. I have a few things to take care of at home. Stay safe."

"I will. Check you later."

We disconnected, and I turned onto Andrews Street. Mom's Corolla was in the driveway where she had left it, and Harry's Toyota Highlander was there too. I pulled into the driveway, and Max found a spot on the street.

"We have to act normal, okay, Max? I don't want Mom to know about the Nasato gang situation," I said, before we entered the house.

"Don't you think she'll pick up on the plainclothes cops milling around at the party?"

"I'm hoping at first she'll be too busy, and later on too buzzed to notice them."

We stepped inside, and I set the kitty carrier down and opened the hatch. Bruce burst out and scooted under the couch. Max carried my bags upstairs. I found Mom in the family room, humming and unpacking her suitcase. Harry sat on the couch watching a poker tournament on TV.

"Hi, Mom, hi, Harry. Did you have fun out in Lancaster County?" Mom turned around, and I gave her a kiss and a hug.

"We had a wonderful time. I love to see all the horses and buggies everywhere. One night, we ate dinner at the all-you-can-eat Olde Dutch buffet. I had bread pudding and Harry had shoofly pie."

"I love shoofly pie," Harry said, without breaking his gaze from the television.

"Your new quilt is up on your bed," Mom said.

"Thanks, Mom. Are you headed over to the Otter Club to set up for the party?"

"Yes, shortly. How were things around here?"

"Oh, you know, uneventful. Bruce missed you. And Max and I are back together. On a trial basis."

"You *are*? That's wonderful. Will you both be coming to the party tonight?"

"Yup. We wouldn't miss it. I can't wait to see your Lita Ford outfit."

"I'm Eddie Van Halen," Harry said.

Mom crossed herself. "May he rest in peace."

"Max is upstairs," I said. "I'll head over to the Otter Club with you when you're ready to leave." I headed to the kitchen, and Harry followed me out.

"Jessica," he whispered. "Is Charlie still on the loose?"

"One Charlie is in custody but may be released soon, and the two other Charlies are unaccounted for."

He patted his side. "I'm packing. And your mom doesn't suspect a thing. She really does love Amish Country. The mission is secure."

"It was an excellent idea to take her there, Harry. About tonight. A few officers in plain clothes will be at the party for security. Max will be there, and he'll be carrying too."

"Sounds like a plan." Harry said, and headed back to Mom.

I ran upstairs and searched my closet for an outfit to wear to the party. There wasn't a lot to choose from in terms of dresses that could pass as eighties fashion. My wardrobe was lacking in dresses period. I needed to do some shopping.

Max was stretched out on my bed with his eyes closed.

I nudged him. "So, what eighties attire did you bring to wear to the party?"

"I went with *Miami Vice* casual. Jeans, a suit jacket with a tee shirt, and my Stan Smiths. I can carry concealed under the jacket."

I yanked at dress hangers in my tiny walk-in closet. "I may have found a dress that could pass for an eighties dress. It's short and poofy."

"I love short and poofy," Max said, rolling on his side toward me. "Show me."

I pushed a few more hangers aside, found the dress, and held it up for him.

"Nice! And it looks like it will come off easy, too. Bonus."

"Glad you approve." I hunted until I found a pair of black heels I could run in if need be, fished around in my jewelry box for a pair of dangly earrings, and switched them with the small earrings I was wearing. I threw the dress and shoes in a bag and plopped down on the bed.

"I'll get dressed at the club after we're done setting up. I'm not parading around in a skimpy dress and heels all afternoon."

"Damn." Max snapped his fingers. "I'll stay here and handle the security system guy. After he's finished installing git, I'll change and catch up to you at the club. Will you be okay?"

"Yes. Harry's strapped, and I have a feeling he's not the only Otter Club member who is. But one thing is bugging me about Vlad's case, Max."

He sat up. "What's that, Red?"

"The cutters. The guys stealing the catalytic converters. We still don't know who they are."

"No, we don't."

"Maybe Fat Eddie would tell us."

"I doubt it. Eddie's not going to further implicate himself in a crime, and Juan Epstein probably won't let him talk to the police anymore."

"Right. We need to track the cutters down somehow."

"Agreed. Let's get through this party tonight and come up with a plan tomorrow."

Mom yelled up the steps that she and Harry were ready to go. I stood up and grabbed my dress and the bag. "I'll see you at the club later."

Max pulled me in and gave me a kiss. "Watch your back. Don't go anywhere alone."

"Don't worry. I'll be fine."

Eighteen

I tossed my stuff in the back of Harry's SUV and climbed into the back seat. We cruised downtown and found a spot right in front of the Otter Club. I scanned the street for Cadillacs, high-end vehicles, or other mob-type cars with tinted windows in the vicinity and didn't see any that set off alarm bells. We carted the party decorations into the vestibule. Jack McFarland said hello over the intercom and buzzed us in. I set my bag down and scoped out the downstairs. A few club regulars warmed stools at the bar, and some of the women on the party planning committee worked on food preparations in the kitchen. Smitty, Tamika, and the plainclothes officers would arrive around five in the afternoon.

I grabbed my bag and Mom, Harry and I hauled the decorations upstairs to the banquet hall and started the party preparations. Harry and I rearranged the tables to make room for dancing and general carousing, and Mom put the club's white linen tablecloths on the round tables and hung streamers. Harry blew up about a hundred neon-colored balloons with an electric pump, and we taped them all over the place. All we needed was the band, and the Otters would be ready to party.

At ten to four, the members of Flamethrower, four guys in their fifties and sixties, arrived to set up their equipment and warm up. Mom introduced herself to the band and showed them to the stage. The platinum blond lead singer wore head-to-toe spandex, and his tattoo sleeves consisted of faded dragons and skulls.

"Mrs. Byrne, I'm Chris, but everyone calls me Blade. We spoke on the phone."

"Hello, Blade, It's nice to meet you," Mom said, eyeing his tattoos. "This is my daughter, Jessica."

"Hi, there," I said. "I'm looking forward to the show."

"Thanks. This is an excellent concert venue. These old buildings have awesome acoustics. We're going to rock it hard tonight, right, boys?"

The boys agreed heartily with a lot of woo-hooing and high-fiving.

The guitarist had long black hair with gray roots, and his jeans were more holes than fabric. He stuck his hand out to Mom. "I'm Mike, and you can call me Mike. The guy in the Mr. Bubble T-shirt is Fletch." Mike began unpacking a red, flying V–style guitar from its case.

Fletch smiled. "I play bass. Leaky is our drummer. He's crazy, but most drummers are."

Leaky grinned and ran his hair through his Billy Idol buzz cut. He wore a Godzilla tee shirt and shorts and Converse Chuck Taylor low tops. A topless mermaid was tattooed on his calf and he held a forty-ounce soda cup in his hand. "Where's the bathroom?" he asked, and Mom and I pointed to the hallway.

"First door on your left," I said.

"Thanks," Leaky said, and power walked to the hallway.

Fletch pointed to a guy wearing a Warrant tee shirt, wheeling in amplifiers. "That's Doober. He's our roadie and pyrotechnics expert. Wave, Doober!"

Doober waved and set a Marshall stack amplifier on the floor. I was pretty certain Doober provided another service to the band.

Mom put her hands on her hips. "No pyrotechnics tonight, guys, but when you take your break, you can help yourself to the buffet."

"Good deal," Blade said. "Some places we play don't even give us a free soda. It's totally bogus, dude."

"So bogus," Fletch said.

The rest of Flamethrower agreed, and Mike strummed a power chord on the guitar. The band finished setting up their equipment and started their sound check.

Max entered the banquet room is his Sonny Crockett outfit. My knees buckled. Max looks great whatever he wears, and he looks even better naked.

"Hi, Red." He leaned down and gave me a kiss. "Nice decorations. Are we all good here?"

"Yes, we're good. So far, no Fat Brother sightings. But can you talk to the guy in the Warrant shirt? That's Doober the roadie, and I have a feeling he may be taking some, uh, smoke breaks. Tell him to make sure the side door stays locked. I'm going to get changed."

"Doober, huh? You got it." Max strolled over to meet the band, and I grabbed my bag.

The ladies' room at the Otter Club consists of two rooms. The first room has a huge mirror and a counter with seats to fix your makeup, two pink velvet couches and a chandelier. The second room is the actual bathroom. I took the last stall, stripped off my clothes and stepped into the little black dress. The top was fitted and strapless. I gambled and didn't try it on before the party. With some deep breathing and mild cursing, I sucked in my stomach and forced the zipper up. I'm a stress eater and I really needed to back off the muffins and doughnuts. I couldn't let Fat Eddie and his crew of morons make me gain weight.

I slid my feet into the heels and clicked out to the makeup room. The extent of what I know about eighties makeup is that there was a lot of it, so I went heavy on the blush and added a few extra coats of mascara, topping it off with hot pink lipstick. I fluffed up my hair, teased the front and shot it with some hairspray. Satisfied, I waltzed out to the banquet room. I tried to forget about the Nasato brothers situation. The police were on the lookout for them. It would be nice to relax and have a good time at the party, even if we were partying with the over fifty five crowd.

I passed Mom in the hallway as she headed into the ladies' room to transform into Lita Ford.

"Need any help, Mom?"

"I'll text you if I need help with the wig. You look nice. You should wear dresses more."

"Noted. Mom."

I entered the banquet room. Smitty had arrived, dressed in a Sonny Crockett outfit. He and Max were standing near the stage talking.

Max let out a low whistle. "Damn, you're fine."

"Thanks. It actually fits, technically." I turned to Smitty. "Looking good, Sonny."

"Max said I'd be out of place if I wasn't wearing eighties attire. I borrowed the pink tee shirt from my sister. Do I look dumb?"

"Nope. You nailed it," I said. "Did Fat Eddie get bonded out yet?"

"Not yet. But it could be anytime. He's locked up across the street. And man is he mad about the second Cadillac. He's blaming you for it rolling in the river."

"Figures." I wasn't happy he was only feet from my mom.

"We got plainclothes on the entrances, and you have Tamika, Max, and me in here," Smitty said. "Jack's will be checking people as they get buzzed in, to make sure no one slips in uninvited or brings a guest who's not on the list."

"Good," I said. "By the way, I can understand why you guys both chose Sonny Crockett for a costume. I mean, Don Johnson was an iconic eighties sex symbol."

Smitty muttered about needing to blend in and walked away.

Max gave me the up-down look. "I'll be Don Johnson if that's what you want. I can't wait to get you out of that poofy dress later."

Mom swept into the banquet room in head-to-toe vegan leather attire, high heels, and a platinum blond wig.

"Looking good, Mrs. B," Max said.

"Thank you, Max." She looked at me. "I can't believe that bitch Marjorie Butz didn't show up to help prepare for this party. She's the vice chairwoman of the party planning committee. She's on my shit list now."

Harry joined the three of us. His costume consisted of a long curly brown wig, a yellow blazer with black zebra stripes, a white tee shirt, and ripped jeans. He pulled it off pretty well.

Harry handed Mom a glass of rosé. "Remember, Valentina, no shit list."

"Cool jacket, Harry," Max said.

"Thanks. I'm Eddie Van Halen." He did a turn so we could admire his get-up. "I bought the jacket on eBay, and Valentina tailored it for me on her machine. I got the jeans at a secondhand store too, and the wig is, uh, one of your mom's. I like having hair again." He gave his new locks a flip.

I'd never seen my mom in a wig and I didn't want to know why she owned more than one. That was her and Harry's business. The less I knew about that the better.

At six o'clock the banquet hall steadily filled up with Otter Club members and their guests. Tamika appeared in the doorway, and I waved her over. Her long curly hair was down, not in the usual cop bun, and she wore an oversized black blazer, tight black leggings, and spike-heeled knee-high boots.

My mom studied her for a moment. "You make a beautiful Janet Jackson, Tamika."

"Thanks, Mrs. B.," she said. "I love her music."

"Me too," I said.

For about the twentieth time, Blade said, "Check, check, check," into the microphone. Jack jumped onto the stage and grabbed the mike from him. Jack was channeling Magnum, PI, with a red Aloha shirt, short-shorts and a big fake mustache.

"Good evening, Otters," he said. "Welcome to the club's annual winter party. Let's give a round of applause to the party planning committee for all their work! Nice job, ladies."

Everyone clapped, and Marjorie Butz appeared from nowhere dressed as Madonna and waved to the crowd. Mom looked ready to blow a gasket.

"Marjorie really is an asshole," I said.

Marjorie gave Mom the finger. Mom gave her the double fingers back.

"Max, not only do we have to worry about the Fat Brothers gang infiltrating the party, we're also going to have to keep Mom and Marjorie separated all night, or someone's going to lose a wig."

Max shook his head. "I'm not sure which is worse, the gangsters or those two."

Jack introduced Flamethrower, and Blade grabbed the mike back. The band started playing "Dr. Feelgood," and Blade marched around the stage dancing and gyrating to the beat.

"Nice," Max said. "The Crüe."

Mom invited Tamika and Smitty to join us.

"Who needs a drink?" Max asked before we sat down.

"Diet Coke for me," Tamika said.

"Red wine for me," I said. What I really wanted to do was drown my sorrows in a few shots of Jägermeister, but that was probably a bad idea. Max and Smitty made their way to the bar, dodging dancing Otters as they went.

Mom turned to Tamika. "Tamika, how come I never see you at the club? I didn't know you were a member."

"I'm not. I'm Joe's guest tonight. He joined a few weeks ago." That was a blatant lie. Smitty wasn't a club member either, but they needed a cover story for Mom.

"Would you excuse me for a moment? I forgot to tell Max to have the bartender put a lemon in my Coke." Tamika stood up and wove her way to the bar, no doubt to tell Smitty the story she manufactured. So far, Mom didn't have a clue about the undercover cops or the gangster situation. She'd been so caught up in decorating for the party and changing into Lita Ford, she hadn't noticed them.

Mom waited until Tamika was out of earshot. "Are Joe and Tamika dating? They make a lovely couple."

"I'm not sure, Mom, I'll have to ask Max." They did make a nice couple, and I honestly wasn't sure if they were dating. I hoped so, although the Chief might frown on partners fraternizing with each other.

I scanned the room. Otter Club members bring a lot of guests to their parties and there were many people in attendance I didn't know. Hopefully they wouldn't pose a threat to Mom or me. Another kind of threat was Marjorie Butz, the slacker, who was flouncing her big ass across the room toward us. Her Madonna outfit consisted of a short blond wig, a bustier barely containing her boobs, and black spandex shorts under a puffy lace tutu skirt. Her boobs and back fat blobbed over the top of the bustier, threatening to burst forth at any moment. A long-haired guy in his twenties in ripped jeans and a flannel shirt followed behind Marjorie. Just like Axl Rose, he'd wrapped a blue bandanna around his head. For a moment I thought they were going to visit our table and I prepared for battle. Mercifully, they stopped at the table next to ours. Disaster averted. For now.

Marjorie loudly introduced the Axl Rose guy to the people at the table. "This is my son, Jason." She extended her right hand out, flapping it around so everyone at the table could get a good look at her cocktail ring. "Jason gave me this new ring for my birthday. Do you love it? It has a two-carat sapphire *and* diamonds."

The people at the table murmured compliments to be polite. I glanced over at Jason as he chugged his beer. He set his empty bottle on their table, burped, and ambled over to the bar for another one. Marjorie flounced after him.

Mom drained her glass of rosé. "My ass Jason gave her that ring. He's a bum."

"Pace yourself, Val," Harry said. "Don't let that crazy ass bitch get to you."

Harry doesn't normally curse, and I grabbed a piece of bread from the basket and stuffed it in my mouth to keep from laughing. Max, Smitty, and Tamika returned with the drinks and their stories straight. Flamethrower started their version of "Back in Black," and more Otters crowded the dance floor, banging their heads to the beat.

"Nice," Max said, and handed me a glass of cabernet sauvignon. "AC/DC."

"I had no idea so many Otters were also Flamers,"
I said, sipping my wine.

Harry stood up. "Come on, Val. Let's dance." He took Mom's hand and led her out to the dance floor into the sea of Magnums, Sonny Crockets and Madonnas.

Tamika sat down next to me. "Heavy metal isn't my first choice when it comes to music options, but Flamethrower has a good sound. That Dr. Feelgood song is really catchy."

"It's a good song. Some hair bands are underrated," I said.

Flamethrower played a few more eighties metal hits as we people watched and chatted. Max wrapped his arm around my shoulders, tapping his foot to the beat.

Smitty's phone buzzed. He picked it up and read a text. "The chief says Fat Eddie just bonded out. He's waiting for his ride to show up." He leaned over and whispered to Max, then he and Tamika hurried downstairs to talk to the officers about Eddie.

Max turned to me. "Red, I need to tell you something. You're not going to like it."

I had just started to relax. "What is it now?"

"I don't want you to freak out."

"When you say that, it makes me feel like I'll freak out. Just tell me what it is."

"Well, when the police pulled Fat Eddie's car from the river, they found all of your underwear floating around inside of it."

It took me a moment to process that information. "Wait. You told Smitty the Nasato gang stole my underwear?"

"I may have mentioned it."

Great. That news was all over town by now. The Otters probably knew about it. I thought some of them had been giving me weird looks. I tried to suppress the image in my head of my underwear floating in brown river water inside Fat Eddie's car. I chugged the rest of my wine and plunked the glass down on the table. "I need another drink."

Max led me through the crowd to the bar. I caught the bartender's eye.

"What'll you have?"

"A shot of Jäger."

"Anything for you, sir?"

Max shook his head and the bartender left.

Max frowned. "Red, you know Jäger is not a good idea." He'd seen me under the influence of Jägermeister in college a few times and it was never a pretty sight. It usually involved unsightly dancing followed by consumption of gas station chili dogs at two AM. But the floating underwear situation had pushed me over the line and I was going for it.

The bartender returned, set the shot in front of me and I downed it. I was about to ask for another when Max stuffed a tip in the glass jar, put his arm around my waist and guided me back to the table. "I'm cutting you off," he said. "Jäger is not your friend."

After Flamethrower finished its rendition of "Pour Some Sugar on Me," Jack took the mike from Blade, announced the buffet was open, and stuck a disc in the CD player. Eighties top forty hits filled the room. Leaky stepped out from behind the drums, hopped off the stage, and made a beeline for the restrooms. Doober and the band headed over to the buffet, followed by a stampede of Otters and guests. Max and I took a place in line and heaped our plates full of salad, beef tenderloin, baked ziti, red bliss potatoes, grilled chicken kebabs, and meatballs.

Mom and Harry were at the table when we made our way back. We sat down and I picked at my food. Despite the shot of Jäger, the butterflies had started swarming in my stomach when Smitty said Fat Eddie was about to be released back into the wild.

Max leaned over and whispered in my ear, "Fat Eddie doesn't know you're across the street, and no one is getting past the officers downstairs. Try to eat something to soak up the alcohol."

"Okay." After a few bites of salad, I stuck my fork into a meatball and took a bite. It was amazing. Much better than a gas station hot dog. I finished them off and zeroed in on the chicken kebabs and ziti.

About halfway through our meal, Marjorie pranced by our table. A woman at another table called out to her, "Marjorie! Nice job on the party. We love the band!"

Marjorie cut a glance at Mom. "Thank you, Alice. Hiring Flamethrower was my idea. I adore heavy metal music. I worked very hard to pull this party together."

Mom gave Marjorie the death stare. Harry noticed and put his arm around Mom. "Take the high road, Val. Ignore her. She's trying to get to you." Harry's dated my mom for over twenty years, but sometimes it's as if he doesn't know her at all.

"Marjorie! Going back for thirds, you trough hog?" Mom yelled.

The Otters took a collective gasp, and a hush fell over the banquet hall. The buffet servers quit chatting and the bartender stopped mid-pour.

"You didn't lift a finger to organize this party, you lazy bitch," Mom yelled, "and you hate heavy metal!" Another gasp swept through the crowd.

Marjorie grabbed a dinner roll off a lady's plate and lobbed it at Mom. She missed our table by a five feet and the dinner roll bounced off Jeanette Arnold's head. Jeanette is my mom's friend from high school. Jeanette picked up the roll, dunked it in her beer mug, and whipped it at Marjorie, hitting her square in the face. Jason erupted in laughter, then burped loudly. Jack grabbed the bottle of whiskey from the bartender's hand, poured himself a shot, and tossed it back. The party was officially a shitshow.

Marjorie was reloading with another dinner roll when three loud bangs coming from outside drew everyone's attention from the cat fight to the street. Everyone got up and raced to the windows overlooking High Street.

Max pushed me back. "Everyone get down!" he yelled.

Me and the Otters hit the floor. Max put his back to the wall and slowly peeked his head around to get a look out the window. Another bang went off. From the floor, I prayed it wasn't gunfire courtesy of the Fat Brothers.

"We're clear," Max said. "Blade and the rest of Flamethrower are setting off fireworks in the plaza across the street."

I stood up. Doober was filming Blade, probably live streaming the fireworks show for fans. The Otters herded to the exit and tromped downstairs to watch the fireworks from the plaza. Max and I stayed behind. From the window, I checked the street for any signs of Fat Eddie or the other brothers. Parked two cars down from Harry's SUV was the tan pickup truck with the bashed-in tailgate.

"Max, that's the pickup truck Sam and I followed the other night."

I grabbed my phone, zoomed in on the tailgate, and snapped a photo.

"The dented pickup?"

"Yes!" I scrolled through my phone and found the picture I'd taken at Tracy and Daniel's house and showed it to him. "See? The damage is the same, Max. Let's go outside and get a better look at it."

"Are you sure? Fat Eddie may still be over at PD."

"Yes. I need to see it up close."

We raced downstairs and onto the sidewalk in time to watch Jason and Marjorie Butz get into the pickup and drive away.

Nineteen

"Jason Butz is a ninja," Max said, over the din of screaming bottle rockets.

"Yup. He's the one I followed from Vlad's garage to the warehouse the other night. And I saw that same pickup truck parked at Tracy and Daniel's house."

"So Jason Butz works for the Nasato brothers."

Doober sent up a series of Roman candles. The Otters gazed up at the sky, oohing and ahhing. Other Flamers gathered in the plaza to watch the show.

I turned to Max. "When I followed Tracy to Jason Butz's place last week, I took a photo of a guy leaving his house. I texted it to Daniel, and he told me it was his nephew Tony DiMario, Jason's roommate."

"So Tony DiMario is probably the other thief hired by Daniel. Tony probably brought Jason into the operation."

"It's a good theory."

From Borough Hall, a uniformed officer strode across the plaza toward Doober and the band members. Blade sent up another Roman candle. The officer pulled out a pad and began writing a citation. Undeterred, Doober continued filming the pyrotechnics show.

I texted Sam. *Jason Butz was at the party. He's one of the cutters.* I sent her a photo of him I snapped while he was on the dance floor.

Sam texted back, *No shit! Why is he dressed like Willie Nelson?*

I texted her, *He's Axl Rose.*

No he isn't. Also, I contacted Daniel on the Ouija board again. This time he spelled out Funyuns. I wasn't sure how to respond to that.

Max tilted his head toward the front steps of Borough Hall. "There's Fat Eddie,"

Fat Eddie plodded down the steps to a waiting Cadillac and eased himself into the passenger seat. He seemed unfazed by the fireworks display in the plaza, and was oblivious that Max and I were watching him from across the street. We ducked behind Harry's SUV and watched as the Cadillac made a right onto High Street, cruised past the plaza, and stopped at the red light. Blade sent up one last Roman candle as the cop finished writing the citation. Jimmy the Streaker came out of nowhere and ran naked through the plaza. Freezing weather doesn't deter Jimmy. The driver of a passing city bus, distracted by the commotion, rear-ended the Fat Brother's Cadillac. Eddie and Joey staggered out of the car, limping around and moaning about whiplash. Vinnie emerged from the backseat, covered in what looked like strawberry milkshake, still holding a burger in his hand. The officer left Flamethrower in the plaza and raced over to the accident. Doober and the band ran back into the Otter Club. Max, me, and the Otters followed the band back inside, and the party picked up where it left off.

Flamethrower kicked their second set off with "Rock You Like a Hurricane," and the dance floor filled with people swaying to the Scorpions. Blade dove of the stage into the dancing Otters and crowd-surfed. The rest of the Otters filled their plates with seconds at the buffet.

From the window, we watched as the officer handled the bus versus Cadillac accident. The Cadillac lost. Smitty and Tamika strolled over and had a brief talk with the Fat Brothers. A tow truck hooked up the demolished Cadillac. An ambulance arrived and packed up Fat Joey for his trip to the emergency room, followed by Juan Epstein in his Mercedes Benz. Fat Eddie and Fat Vinnie called an Uber and left, and the plainclothes officers returned to Borough Hall. Tamika and Smitty returned to the party and joined us back at the table.

"Those Fat Brothers really go through Cadillacs, don't they?" Tamika said, as the four of us sat down at the table.

Smitty nodded. "Two in one day has to be some sort of record."

An overwhelming sense of relief came over me. The Fat Brothers were temporarily out of my life. "What did you say to them?" I asked.

"Tamika and I briefly explained to the Nasatos what the consequences would be if anything happened to you, your mom, or your friends."

"The brothers are scared of you now, Jessica. They're convinced you have some special redhead juju powers and can wreck cars at will," Tamika said.

"She's got special powers alright," Max said.

"Oh for God's sake," I said. "I need more meatballs. And chicken on a stick."

Tamika stood up. "I hear that. Let's go."

The four of us navigated the buffet line a second time, filled our plates, and sat down to eat. Mom and Harry circulated around the room socializing with friends. Janine, another party planning committee lady, rolled out a dessert cart, and the Otters mobbed her. I managed to get a slice of chocolate cake, Max snagged chocolate chip cookies, and Tamika grabbed a red velvet cupcake before it all disappeared. Smitty skipped dessert and opted for another beer. Flamethrower played their last song, and Jack jumped up on the stage and stole the mike from Blade.

"Let's give a hand to Flamethrower for the great music and surprise fireworks display! Nice job, guys." Everyone was pretty sauced at this point, and Jack waved his arms around to stop the applause. "And now, I'll announce the winners of the costume contest." Leaky played a drumroll as Jack read out the awards. "The Totally Awesome Costume Award goes to Jim Edwards, who dressed as Nikki Sixx, and his wife, Jane, who dressed as a random groupie. The Most Bitchin' Costume Award goes to Val Byrne and Harry Miller, who came as Lita Ford and Eddie Van Halen."

Mom and Harry stood up and took a bow.

"The after-party is downstairs."

Blade tore his tank top off and threw it into the crowd. Leaky gave his number to a couple women, Fletch signed an autograph on a lady Otter's shirt, and Doober began packing up equipment. The house lights came up, and the Otters herded downstairs to continue partying at the bar.

Smitty and Tamika called it a night. Max and I spoke to Harry and Mom on our way out of the club.

"We're skipping the after-party," Harry said. "We've had enough for one night. We're heading to my place."

I gave each of them a hug and we watched them drive off. Max and I hopped in the Camaro. He cranked the engine and I watched him shift through the gears as he drove to my place. Watching him drive the Camaro is an instant turn-on for me. Mostly because I can't drive a stick shift car. So to me, it's a mysterious, sexy skill. My feelings may also have been brought on by the shot if Jägermeister. By the time we made it into the house, I was all over Max. He set the new alarm system as we kissed, and we continued kissing as we slowly made our way upstairs. I pulled Max's Don Johnson jacket off and dropped it on the floor in the hall. Max had my poofy dress off in seconds, and he pushed me gently back onto the bed.

"Leave the heels on, Red."

I watched him undress. He dove onto the bed, kissing me as he worked his way south. I took a deep breath and relaxed back into the pillows.

"Wait!" I sat up.

Max looked up at me. "What's up?"

"We're still on a trial basis, right?"

"Right."

"Okay, good. Keep going."

The next morning, after a soapy, mutual shower, Max and I reconvened downstairs in the kitchen. He stood at the stove making French toast, and I set our places at the table, admiring his ass in his faded jeans. Bruce was under the table waiting for the French toast.

"Jess, have you seen *The Pottstown Post* today?" He voice held a note of concern.

"No. What now?"

"I read a few stories while you were getting dressed. There's one you should probably see." He pulled his phone out of his back pocket and showed me a headline that read, *Cops Bust Man for Theft of PI's Car, Underwear*. A photo from my website of me smiling was next to the headline. The color drained from my face, and I slumped down in a chair at the table.

"Kenny Marshall has no respect for personal privacy," I said. "He better pray I don't see him on that stupid scooter of his."

"Smitty texted me. He needs you to come down and ID your underwear, so he can charge Fat Eddie with that too."

"Oh, this just gets better and better." My stomach dropped. My mother would have a conniption if she knew what was going on. I sent a text to Harry asking him to hide the newspaper from Mom. With the Otter gossip machine, this would be tough to conceal from her. I was so screwed.

Harry texted me back, *Already done, kid*, with a winky face emoji. I breathed a sigh of relief and tried to refocus on the murder case.

"Did you believe Fat Eddie when he said he didn't kill Daniel?" I asked Max, as I shook kitty kibbles into Bruce's bowl.

Max took the frying pan off the stove, turned to me, high-flipped a piece of French toast and caught it in the pan. "I don't believe a word that guy says, but I don't think Smitty has any solid evidence on him for the murder. Right now, the police's theory is that Vlad is the killer."

I poured us each a glass of orange juice. "Right. But Tracy had a motive to kill Daniel because if she killed him before the divorce was final, she stood to come into a lot more money. And she may have been involved with Jason Butz, but I haven't confirmed it."

"Vlad had a motive because somehow he determined Daniel and the Nasato brothers were stealing from him." Max piled all the French toast onto a plate and set it down on the table. He sat down across from me, and I forked three pieces onto my plate.

"I want to believe Anastasiya's theory about Vlad never leaving a good tool behind," I said, and drowned the French toast in butter and syrup. I stuffed a bite into my mouth and closed my eyes, savoring it. Sex, sleep, and a French toast breakfast. It did not get better than this.

Max chugged some juice. "I've been mulling over Daniel's insurance scam in my head. We know he sold jewelry made with the platinum sourced from the Nasato warehouse operation, and that he filed insurance claims stating the jewelry was stolen. If the Fat Brothers found out about the insurance claims, they would view that as Daniel stealing from them. They'd want a cut of the money from the claims."

"Probably a big cut. Ripping off gangsters will definitely shorten your lifespan." I re-syruped my French toast and added another blob of Mom's butter substitute. "You know what we need to do, Max?" I set my fork down and smiled at him. I turned the big green eyes on him.

"I know that look, Jess. Should I be afraid?"

"If we want to prove Vlad is innocent, we need some real evidence against Eddie or Tracy. Eddie's warehouse is off-limits to us since the police shut it down, but Tracy and Daniel's mansion isn't."

Max pointed his fork at me. "So you want to do a B and E on the Lakeland's place? In addition to being totally risky and completely illegal, it's also interfering with an active police investigation. Do you want to end up in the cell next to Vlad?"

"It's not technically interfering in a police investigation. Smitty and Tamika aren't investigating Tracy. And we're consultants to the police now, remember? Besides, their theory is that Vlad killed Daniel and the Fat Brothers were involved somehow. It's helping the police out, really."

"Red, you're walking on a razor's edge with that reasoning." Max drained his glass. "I'm not a fan of this idea."

"Well, I need to do this for Vlad and Anastasiya. I'll go by myself if I have to. I understand if you think it's too risky."

Max sighed and shook his head. "So, how are we going to pull this one off?"

"I have a good plan. Sam can be the mole while we're inside the mini mansion. She can go to the day spa when Tracy is there and make sure we're in the clear. If Tracy leaves, Sam can text us and tell us to vacate the mansion, in case she's headed back home."

"So you want to do a B and E in broad daylight?"

"Basically."

Max furrowed his brow. "How big is the house?"

"It's about five or six thousand square feet."

"Yup, that qualifies as a mini mansion. We'll need at least an hour. We don't know what we're searching for."

Max was right. We didn't, but I needed to give it a shot. The look on Anastasiya's face when we met at Dingle's was hard to forget.

I called Sam. "Can you come over to my place and talk to Max and me about a plan?"

"What type of plan are we talking about? More hiding in the weedy vermin field?"

"The type of plan we shouldn't discuss over the phone."

"So we're talking some James Bond shit. I'll be right over." Sam hung up.

Twenty minutes later, Sam and Sparkle burst through the door. Bruce flew up the steps to hide under my bed. Sam fished around in her oversized purse and pulled out a Kong chew toy.

"Can I borrow some peanut butter?" she asked.

"Sure. You know where it is," I said.

Sam opened the fridge, scooped some peanut butter into the hole in the Kong, and gave it to Sparkle. He wagged his giant tail, settled down at her feet, and started working on it with his oversized tongue.

"So what's the Bond mission you called me over here for?" Sam asked. "Do I have a big role? Am I the Bond girl?"

"We want to get inside Tracy and Daniel's mansion, and we need you to watch Tracy at the day spa while we're searching her house. If she leaves, you need to text us right away, in case she's headed our way," I said.

"So I'm your sleeper agent, activated for a day spa mission. This assignment is right up my alley, and I need a color update, anyway. Rita can work her magic on me again. I accept the mission as long as I can use the company credit card."

"Fine. Tracy normally gets into the spa around nine in the morning on weekdays," I said. "How about we get to the mini mansion right after she leaves for the day spa?"

"That would be the best time. Less people in the neighborhood in general during the workday," Max said. "But I hate this idea."

"Noted. Sam, how's tomorrow?"

"I'll make an appointment online." Sam pulled up the day spa's website on her phone. "Rita's first opening is at ten thirty tomorrow morning. Is that good?"

"That should leave us enough time. Book it," I said.

Sam punched a few buttons on her phone and a text came through, confirming the appointment.

"Wait a minute, Sam" I said. "How are you going to text us if you're in the middle of getting your nails done?"

"Good point. It'd be easier to call you on speed dial in case my nails are still wet. We need a code word. How about 'pachysandra'?"

"So you'll be sitting across from Rita getting your manicure, you tell her you need to make a phone call, and then you call me and say '*pachysandra*'? It's not normal sounding," I said.

Max paced around the room muttering about selling insurance if he lost his PI license.

"So what's your normal-sounding word?" Sam asked.

"If Tracy leaves the day spa, call me and just say, 'I'm running late.' It sounds totally normal, and no one would question it. Max and I will know Tracy may be on her way to the mini mansion."

"Fine. But a Bond girl would have used a code word."

Twenty

Sunday evening, Max went back to his place to mentally prepare for tomorrow's break-in. Around seven, Harry dropped Mom off at the house. I put the security code in the system and let Mom in the front door.

"What's this? We have an alarm now?" she asked. Shit. Think fast.

"Yes. Max recently had one installed at his house, and it was buy one system get another one free. He gave us the free one." When in doubt, lean into Mom's frugalness.

Mom dropped her overnight bag on the living room floor and plopped down into a chair, yawning.

"That's nice. I love a good BOGO deal. This past week has been a whirlwind. I'm totally exhausted."

I could relate. My eyelids were heavy and my feet hurt from the stupid heels.

"So was there any blowback at the Otter Club for the whole scene with Marjorie Butz? You know, when you bitched her out, she threw the dinner roll at you, and Jeanette retaliated."

"Oh, that. Yes, Jack said the three of us are on a week's suspension and Marjorie and I have to have a mediation. It was totally worth it, though. Marjorie's expression after she got hit with soggy roll was priceless."

I smiled. Mom was a bad ass.

I didn't mention to her that Jason Butz was a criminal with ties to the Nasato gang. That rumor didn't need to get out. I lugged Mom's bags into her bedroom, gave her a kiss, and said goodnight. Upstairs, I flopped face first onto my bed with my face in the pillows. Bruce popped out from beneath the bed, ready to nap. We were all snuggled in when Max called.

"Hey, Red. I talked to Smitty. He told me the medical examiner places Daniel's time of death on Sunday night or early Monday morning. He wanted to tell us at the eighties party, but it wasn't the right venue."

"We'll need to talk to Vlad about it when we visit him."

"Definitely."

"And how should I dress for tomorrow? We can't go in all black in the daytime."

"Wear khakis. We'll dress like salespeople doing an estimate for replacement windows or those rain gutter covers. Bring a clipboard. No one questions people carrying clipboards."

"Okay. Are you alright with the plan, Max?"

"No, but I understand your rationale, and you have compassion for Anastasiya. Your big heart is why I love you."

I froze for a millisecond, and my stomach flopped around. Max hadn't spoken those words to me in three years.

"You don't have to say it, Jess. I wanted you to know I never stopped."

"I never stopped either, Max." So much for the trial basis. It was going right down the shitter.

.

I rolled out of bed the next morning at seven thirty and showered and dressed while half asleep. Max showed up with warm beverages from Wawa. No residual weirdness lingered from our conversation with the L word the night before.

I test-sipped the hot chocolate. Still at burn level. I took the lid off and deposited the hot chocolate back into the cup. Max shook his head.

"How about I make some fake ID cards to help with our assumed identities?" I said.

"Wouldn't hurt."

We sat down in my office, and I dug around in my desk and found a clipboard and put some paper on it. I opened my laptop, found a generic geometric logo from the web. "What line of work are we in?" I asked.

"Let's go with the rain gutter cover salespeople."

"Hmm. How is 'Captain Gutter' for a name?"

"I like it. It's catchy. I always wanted to be a superhero."

I added the logo, picked a font, and added a phony phone number. "What do you want your name to be?" I asked Max.

"Let's see. How about Jim Rockford?"

"Nope. I like where you're going with the retro TV show, but no."

"Jean-Claude Van Damme?"

I rolled my eyes at him. "Be serious."

"Fine. I'll be Mike Smith."

"Great." I typed his fake name on his fake business card.

"What's your name?" Max asked.

"I'm Joan Jett."

"You get to be Joan Jett and I have to be Mike Smith?"

"*Fine*. I'll be Ann Shmoyer."

"Is Shmoyer a real last name?"

"It is now." I loaded the printer with perforated do-it-yourself business card paper left over from when I graduated from college. I hit Print and ran downstairs. Mom was at the kitchen table drinking coffee and reading *The Pottstown Post*.

"Good morning, Mom, how'd you sleep?"

"Great. I love Harry, but I don't miss the snoring when I'm home."

"I hear that, Mom. Hey, do you have any string? And can I borrow your laminator?" Mom bought a laminator a few years ago. She laminates whatever she can get her hands on. She laminates recipes, takeout menus, photos, you name it. I don't use the takeout menus. I order food online.

She gave me the hairy eyeball. "What do you need string and the laminator for?"

"Work stuff."

"If it's illegal, don't tell me about it. I'd rather not know." She got up from the table and returned a few minutes later with some red string and the laminator.

"Thanks, Mom." I took them from her and tore back upstairs before she could ask me another probing question. Max and I ran the business cards through the machine and cut them down to size. I punched holes in the top of each of our shiny, new fake ID cards and ran the string through them. We were good to go.

"I had no idea you were so skilled at the art of deception," Max said. "It's so Jim Rockford."

"It is. All I need is a Pontiac Firebird and a trailer on the beach." I sipped my hot chocolate and tried to relax. The butterflies were back, and they were multiplying. I'm nervous to do any illegal stuff, especially in the daylight.

Sam texted me at twenty after ten. *I'm outside the day spa and Tracy's Jag is here. I'm going in.*

I texted back, *OK. "I'll be there early" is your code phrase. Keep her in your sights.*

I'm on it. My Bond girl name is Coochie Bodacious.

"Sam's going into the day spa, Max. Tracy's there now." I didn't mention the part about Coochie Bodacious.

Max stood up. "Time to go."

I downed the rest of my hot chocolate, put my ID card around my neck, and stuffed the clipboard in my backpack. We shrugged on our jackets, and stepped onto the porch into the freezing cold. The gray sky threatened snow.

"Where's your car?" I asked.

"I rented a van last night. There's no way we're taking one of our cars on this op."

Max unlocked a white panel van on the curb and we got in. His backpack sat on the seat, which probably contained his security system bypass equipment. I didn't ask. We drove in silence over to Rosemont, and Max parked on the side street. We watched the Lakeland's house from the van for a few minutes and saw no signs of activity. The carriage house–style garage faced the side street, and the garage doors were down. The driveway was empty. Tall hedges around most of the backyard shielded the view from the neighbors. That made me feel a little better, but not much.

We moseyed up the Lakelands' brick driveway like we belonged there. Max handed me a tape measure from his backpack. "Pretend to take measurements in case someone is watching from somewhere."

He started disabling the security system.

"What should I measure?"

"I don't know. A window. Measure that window there."

I set my clipboard down on the patio and measured the window. For some reason, I wrote the measurement down on the paper on my clipboard. I took another fake measurement and jotted it down too.

"Alright, we're in." Max held the door open for me and we stepped inside the house.

"What if the house has security cameras on the inside?" I asked.

"Already disabled." He handed me a baseball cap, a neck gaiter, and latex gloves from his backpack. "Put these on."

"Just in case?"

"Yes."

I stuffed my hair underneath the cap and pulled the neck gaiter up over my nose. Max put on a cap and gaiter too. I shoved the clipboard into my backpack.

"Hello?" Max called out. We held our breath and waited for a response. None came. "We should split up to cover ground more quickly."

"Isn't that the number one horror movie mistake? People split up and they start dying. No way."

"To clarify, we're not in a horror film, Red. This is real life and we're breaking into someone's home. If we stay together, we have to move faster." He checked his watch. "Come on. It's ten forty-five. Let's look for an office or a study."

We had entered into a laundry room. We passed through it into the massive gourmet kitchen, with white marble everywhere and an island with plushy stools. The kitchen adjoined a great room with a stone fireplace. Beyond the kitchen, the dining room held a long table with fourteen chairs, a sideboard, and two china hutches. The immaculate house was professionally decorated, and I counted four crystal chandeliers since we entered the home.

We tiptoed to the front of the house and entered the formal living room. A grand piano stood in one corner. The furniture looked pricey, and the couches appeared as though no one ever sat on them. If they were mine, I wouldn't let anyone sit on them either.

Beyond the formal living room was a sitting room with comfy chairs and couches. No desk or computer. Sunlight shone through the bay window, and a door to the backyard was on the far wall.

We backtracked, entered the two-story foyer, and crept up the curving staircase to the second floor. A short hallway overlooked the foyer and the great room and connected the stairs to the enormous main bedroom. We entered through the double doors. A king-size bed sat on a riser, covered in silk duvet and throw pillows. A sitting area included couches, a fireplace, and a huge TV mounted on the wall. The walk-in closet was as big as my bedroom and had racks and backlit shelves that held shoes and clothes. A glass jewelry cabinet glittered with racks of earrings, bracelets, rings and necklaces. One wall in the closet was dedicated to Philadelphia sports team clothing and hats. We searched the nightstand drawers and came up empty. We retreated back to the hallway and found a study at the rear of the house.

The room held shelves stuffed with books that were probably never read. A mounted deer head observed us from above a fireplace, and a stuffed beaver crouched on the hearth. Max sat down in front of an open laptop at the mahogany desk. He touched the mouse pad, and the screen came alive. It was logged into Tracy's email. We both stared at the screen. Over the last few days, Tracy and Eddie Nasato had exchanged a lot of emails. Steamy ones.

Max snapped photos of a few of the racier emails. "Damn. Some of these get right to the point. *I can't wait to do you in the back of my new Cadillac.* Subtle."

"Eww. I sat in the back of one of Fat Eddie's Cadillacs."

"Block it out, Red," Max said. "Focus on the task at hand." He scrolled through the emails while I picked through the desk drawers in search of a journal or a diary.

"Do any emails mention getting rid of Daniel?" I asked.

"Not yet. I can't imagine they'd be stupid enough to discuss a murder over email."

"True. Criminals watch *Dateline* now." My phone buzzed in my pocket and I pulled it out.

"Yeah, Sam, what's up?"

"Pachysandra!" she hissed into my ear. "Pachysandra, pachysandra!"

"Sam, did Tracy leave the building?"

"Yes! And I'm not sure when! I had to go to the bathroom, and I was in there a while. I think it was my breakfast burrito that did it to me."

"Shit. Okay, thanks." We disconnected. "Max, we've got a major problem. Tracy left and Sam doesn't know when exactly. Sam was in the bathroom."

"She had one job!" He stood up from the desk and grabbed his backpack.

The low rumble of an engine made my heart skip a beat. I parted the heavy curtain an inch. Tracy's Jag pulled into the driveway. Moments later, the back door opened downstairs. My stomach plummeted into my boots.

"Hide, hide, hide," was all I could get out. My feet wouldn't move. I was in full-on deer in the headlights mode. Max yanked me into the closet and I scrunched my eyes closed in the darkness. If I couldn't see Tracy, maybe she couldn't see me. I prayed silently and made a deal with God that I would never do another B and E, I would volunteer in the community and eat fewer sweets. I'd try to curse less. I buried my head in Max's chest. He smoothed my hair as he tried to keep me from totally losing it.

Footsteps pounded up the staircase, and we heard Tracy's voice and a man's. That's it. we're dead. We're busted, and my life as I know it was over.

"I swear I set the alarm," Tracy said.

"Don't worry about it, babe, nobody's here. Just you and me, babe," the man said.

"I'm going to buy a dog. A papillon or a Yorkshire terrier. A good little watch dog I can carry around in a designer bag with me." Despite my intense fear, I rolled my eyes.

From the direction of the main bedroom, giggling carried down the hallway to our hideout in the closet. After a minute or two, the giggling stopped. I relaxed a tiny bit. Despite the horrifying thought of my impending arrest and public humiliation, snuggling up to Max felt nice. A thud-thud-thud sound started. The thud's cadence steadily increased. One of them moaned, and "*Oh babes*" and "*yesses*" accompanied the thudding. It sounded as though the bed was about to fall off the riser or the headboard was putting a hole in the wall. The thudding quickened, Tracy howled, and she and her gentleman companion grunted away like two wild boars at the height of mating season.

Max's body shook with silent laughter. I stuck my fingers in my ears and tried to hold it together. The wild animal mating sounds continued, and despite my disgust, I respected their complete commitment to the moment. But I hoped Max and I didn't sound like they did.

Apparently Tracy and the man were not post-coitus snugglers. From the closet, we heard muffled conversation. The bedroom door opened and footsteps approached the study. I held my breath, and Max's body tensed. Someone entered the study and sat down at the desk. The laptop keyboard clicked, and Tracy cursed under her breath. My heart was beating so hart I was sure Max could feel it.

The footsteps abruptly left the room. Tracy yelled, "Jason!"

"Down here, babe!" Tracy stomped down the staircase and yelled something about money not being in the account yet.

Max pressed his lips against my ear and whispered, "We need to get out of here, now."

I stood on my toes and smooshed my mouth up to his ear. "Can't we wait for them to leave?"

I felt his lips on my ear again. "Too risky."

"We need a distraction," I whispered, and pulled my phone from my pocket. I texted Sam, showing Max before I hit send. It read: *Bring a pizza to Tracy's house and ring the bell.* I sent her the address.

Sam texted back, *Are you hungry?*

No. We're trapped in a closet. I need you to do a fake pizza delivery as a diversion.

Okay, got it. Coochie's on it.

Max reached for the closet doorknob, opened it a crack, and we listened. Downstairs, Tracy and Jason were chatting about taking a trip to the Bahamas. Max pushed the closet door open and stepped out into the room. He took my hand, pulled me after him, and we moved silently to the doorway.

Giggling floated up to the study. A few moments later thudding started, followed by more moaning. It sounded like they were having kitchen table sex, but thankfully, we didn't have a visual on it. The grunting started, followed again by the "*oh babes*" and the "*yesses.*" Tracy and Jason were about to reach another crescendo down in the kitchen. We stepped out into the hallway.

The doorbell rang, and the action stopped. "Who the hell is that?" Jason yelled.

"Get off of me," Tracy said. After a minute, she stomped to the front door, and we ducked back into the study. The doorbell rang again, and we heard Tracy yank the door open.

"What do you want?" she yelled.

"Is this 6420 Brookdale Drive?" Sam asked.

"No."

"It's not? Oh, well, do you want a pizza? I can't find the house this is supposed to go to. Must have been a crank call. It's my first day delivering pizzas."

"Jason!" Tracy yelled. "Do you want a pizza?"

"What's on it?" he yelled back.

"What's on it?" Tracy asked.

"Uh...it's half bacon, half mushrooms."

"Half bacon, half mushrooms!" Tracy yelled.

Jason was clearly mulling it over. "Uh, yeah, but I'm not eating the mushrooms."

"I'll eat the damn mushrooms!" Tracy grabbed the pizza, slammed the door in Sam's face, and stomped back to the kitchen.

My stomach growled loudly. Max pulled me back into the hallway to the top of the staircase. In full stealth mode, we gingerly tiptoed downstairs as plates banged and drawers opened in the kitchen. Tracy giggled, and soon the "*oh babes*" and "*yesses*" started all over again, this time with "*mmmms.*" They may have been mixing sex with pizza. I had to will my stomach not to growl as the aroma of mozzarella cheese wafted in the air. We reached the first floor and stopped. The kitchen table banged rhythmically against the hardwood floor.

Max pointed through the living room to the sitting room. I nodded. He put his hand up and did a count of three with his fingers. On three, he yanked me through the foyer and the formal living room into the sitting room. He opened the door, and we slipped outside. We raced through the neighbor's backyard, crashing through high priced landscaping. Two doors down we turned right, sprinted through another backyard, scaled a fence, dodged an angry labradoodle, and ended up on the sidewalk a block away from Tracy's mini mansion. I doubled over, laughing and gasping for breath. The sounds of Tracy and Jason having sex were burned into my brain, probably forever. Max watched me, trying to suppress a smile.

"Come on, Red, pull it together. We need to get back to the van."

We took the gaiters off and tried to act casual. A woman pushing a pricey stroller power walked by us. She gave us a wide berth and the side-eye as she passed.

"Okay, okay. But I have a stitch in my side."

My phone buzzed on my hip, and I answered on speaker. "Did you pachysandra the hell out of there?" Sam yelled.

"Yes. Thanks for the fake pizza delivery. It helped distract them. That and Tracy kept banging Jason all over the house."

"You're lucky she's a nympho," Sam said. "And she needs some etiquette training. She didn't offer to pay for the pizza or say thank you. That's no way to treat Coochie Bodacious."

"What the hell happened at the day spa, Sam?" Max asked. "How did you miss Tracy leaving?"

"On the way to the spa, I stopped at the Gas 'n Git and ate a breakfast burrito with jalapeños, and I guess it didn't agree with me. I had a code brown emergency right in the middle of my manicure."

I stopped walking and crossed one leg over the other. The adrenaline surge, the porn show, and Sam's code brown situation was too much for me to handle. "I'm going to pee myself right here on the sidewalk. I can't move."

Max had seen me in this state before. "Take a few deep breaths, Red. You're not going to pee. Sam, we'll call you back later."

"I understand," Sam said. "She's having a code yellow emergency. I get them too."

Twenty-one

The thought of being arrested by Smitty and Tamika for breaking into Tracy's house helped me regain what was left of my composure. Max and I turned onto the side street and hoofed it to the rental van. Tracy's Jag was in the driveway and no cops were there. Somehow we'd escaped the mini mansion undetected. We jumped in the van and took off.

"Where to, Red?"

"How about Pottstown PD? Smitty asked me to identify my underwear and I haven't done it yet."

"Right. First, I need to return the van to Beater Rentals."

In a half hour, Max drove us to the police department in the 4Runner. He waited while I made a positive ID on my underwear, which was one of the more humiliating things I've had to do lately.

Afterward, I stomped back to the 4Runner and heaved myself in. Max cranked the engine, and my stomach growled long and loud. Max gave me a look.

"Come on, Red. Let's get some takeout before you turn hangry." He drove to my office, parked and we stepped into Tito's Tacos. Manny appeared from the kitchen looking hot as ever.

Max approached the bar and eyed Manny like he was a potential bust. "Manny," he said.

Manny eyed him right back. "Max."

"Well, now that we got that out of the way," I said. "How are you?"

Manny turned his gaze to me and smiled. "I'm well, Jessica. What'll you have?"

I gave him our standard order and he disappeared into the kitchen. Ten minutes later he returned with our takeout bags, and Max and I headed up the steps to my office. Sam was at her desk, scrolling on her phone.

"Sparkle's at home," she said. "I couldn't take him on today's mission. Is that Tito's food I smell?"

"Yup. I got you the usual."

"Excellent. Delivering that pizza made me hungry. What Tracy doesn't know is, I ate a piece in the car on the way to her house and I smooshed it back together to hide the piece I took. And she can't call and complain because she doesn't know where it came from."

"Where'd you get the pizza?" Max asked.

"Uncle Geno's. I told them I had a pizza emergency, that my brother just woke up from a coma and was asking for a half bacon half mushroom. They moved pretty quick after I said that."

Max rolled his eyes. "Good cover story,"

"It's what a Bond girl would have done," she said. "So Tracy and Jason are doing it, huh? How old is he, anyway?"

"He's younger than us," I said, and stuffed some fries into my mouth. "He's probably around twenty-three or twenty-four."

"Jason's got to be half Tracy's age. She's a cougar," Sam said.

"Jess and I established she's also hot and heavy with Fat Eddie too. Her laptop had some X-rated emails on it."

"Damn, Tracy's a freaky cougar," Sam said. She wasn't wrong.

I chomped a burrito and washed it down with a slurp of fountain Sprite. "I know having an affair doesn't make you a murderer, but it doesn't make her look any less guilty." I burped involuntarily and fizz came out of my nose. Sam and Max ignored it. They were used to it.

I wiped my nose. "Pardon."

"On another topic," Max said, "we need to confirm our visit today with Vlad."

"You guys are lucky," Sam said. "I've always wanted to visit someone in jail."

"We'll tell Vlad you said hi," Max said.

I pulled my phone out of my bag and called the jail. They confirmed Max and I were on Vlad's visitor list and scheduled in the afternoon.

"We're good to go for two thirty. Let's stop at my house so I can change clothes. I can't ever wear this outfit again. It feels dirty."

Max and I arrived at the county jail at quarter after two. After we passed through security, an officer led us to the visiting area. We sat at a counter divided by a plexiglass partition, with telephones for communicating with inmates. A few minutes passed, and heavy doors clanged open and closed. Vlad appeared in the doorway, followed by a short, stocky guard. Smiling broadly, Vlad sat down at the counter and picked up the phone. The guard stood expressionless in the corner. I picked up the receiver and held it so Max and I could both hear.

"Jessica, my lady detective," Vlad said. "I see you brought a friend."

"Hi, Vlad, this is Max. He's a PI too, and he's an ex-cop." Vlad didn't appear to remember Max from his prior involvement with law enforcement.

"Hello, Max. Anastasiya said you'd come, Jessica."

"Yes, Max and I met her at Dingle's Donuts on Friday morning."

"Yes. Mr. Dingle is a good man," Vlad said. "Best doughnuts in town."

"No doubt," I said. "How are you doing in here?"

"American prison is like a country club. American criminals are soft with their TV, cards games, and exercise time. But the food is terrible." He shook his head. "Only the pudding tastes good."

"Right. Pudding is hard to mess up," I said.

Max gave me the side eye and cleared his throat. "Vlad. The evidence the police have against you for Daniel Lakeland's murder is compelling. They found a screwdriver on the body with your fingerprint on it."

"That's what my lawyer Jamie told me. The first time I am robbed, I tell the police the *zlodiyi* also break into my garage. They steal my father's toolbox. Made in Ukraine. Not like cheap tools made in China. And I don't know this man they say I've killed, this Daniel Lakeland."

"Daniel was doing business with local gangsters, and his crew stole the catalytic converters from your car lot," I said.

"Yeah. The police told me this when they questioned me. But I haven't met this Lakeland man. Or these bastard gangsters."

"Vlad, last week I followed the thieves from your business back to a warehouse in Pottstown. The warehouse is owned by the Nasato gang. It's the same warehouse I got kidnapped from."

"They're lucky I'm in this cushy country club jail." Vlad pounded his fist on the counter, and the guard glanced over and told him to settle down. Vlad muttered to himself about lazy American prison guards.

"Vlad, what were you doing last Sunday night?" Max asked.

"Sunday night Anastasiya and I watch the Eagles play the Dallas Cowboys. Aleksander and Vasyl, my mechanics, come over to watch but they left in the third quarter."

"So after the third quarter, say around ten o'clock, Anastasiya is your alibi," I said.

"Yes. After the Eagles beat the Cowboys, Anastasiya and I go to bed. Eleven o'clock. I wake up at five in the morning for work. I do not take Monday off like typical lazy football fans."

"What can you tell us about the thefts, Vlad? Do you have any information linking back to the Nasato brothers?"

Vlad shook his head. "No. I have never met these fat Nasato brothers." The guard said Vlad's time was up. Vlad directed his gaze to me. "Jessica, I don't do this crime. Remember what I told you Tuesday when you visit my office." He hung the phone up, turned, and disappeared through the doorway.

I hung up the phone. Max and I passed through security and out into the cold. The sun made a halfhearted attempt to break through the clouds. I zipped my coat up as far as it would go and shoved my hands in my pockets.

"What did Vlad mean about what he told you on Tuesday?" Max asked when we were back in the car.

"I'm not sure." I cranked up the heat and ran through our conversation in my head, when Vlad admitted to me that he blew up Eddie's Cadillac.

"Vlad said after he blew up the car, he waited to make sure I escaped from the building. He said he left because blowing someone's car up is a parole violation," I said. "Maybe what Vlad meant is that if he killed Daniel the night before, he wouldn't be worried about violating his parole with the explosion."

"Right. If Vlad had killed Daniel the night before, he'd be lying low, not chasing gangsters around and blowing up cars."

"We need to figure out who stole Vlad's tools," I said. "And you're not going to like my next suggestion."

"*I* have a suggestion. Let's stop at HappyCart, pick up some whipped cream, and go home and take your clothes off. You looked hot talking on the jail phone. I pretended the roles were reversed and you were the naughty prisoner and Vlad was your parole officer."

"Oh my God, Max, would you focus? We need to get inside Jason Butz's house."

"No. Absolutely not, Red. No more break-ins. That's a trash box idea."

"I know it's a trash box idea, but it's necessary if we're going to help Vlad."

"Have you forgotten about this morning already? We nearly got busted at Tracy's. Do you know what that would mean for both of us if we were arrested?"

"I agree this morning was bad. It was also disturbing and icky. But we established that Tracy and Jason are romantically involved, and we learned that she's also doing Fat Eddie from the dirty emails. We didn't leave the mini mansion with no intel."

Max shifted around in his seat and drummed his fingers on the steering wheel. Minutes passed as we dodged potholes, clunking along the highway in silence. He took a deep breath and blew it out.

"*Fine*. We'll do it. But it's my op and we do it *my way*."

"*Fine*. You're such a control freak."

"And Red, this time you're going to owe me again. We're talking sexy lingerie, *two* cans of whipped cream, some light spanking, and some tasteful porn. All night."

"If you insist, Max, but I'm going to come out alright on that deal."

"No doubt."

We arrived at OIC. In Max's office, I settled into a leather chair in front of his desk while he checked his emails.

"Jess, I have a new email from my client, Daniel's insurance company. It's a copy of another insurance claim. It must be the last one he filed before he was murdered. It contains photos of the jewelry Daniel claimed was stolen."

I scooted around to Max's side of the desk and looked over his shoulder. He slowly scrolled through the claim forms, which showed losses of at least a thousand dollars per ring, some as much as five thousand dollars. All the bands described in the claim were platinum. Most stones were emeralds, sapphires, or diamonds, and all were over a carat in weight.

"Wait! I know that ring!" I yelled. Max stopped scrolling on a photo of a two-carat sapphire ring with diamond baguettes. "We've both seen it. That's Marjorie Butz's cocktail ring! She waved it around at the Otter Club brunch and the eighties party. She said Jason gave it to her."

"I don't remember the ring specifically, but I remember when your mom threw the pancake at Marjorie. She didn't see that coming," Max said, chuckling. "Are you positive it's the same ring?"

"Yes, I'm positive. That's Marjorie's ring." I jabbed my finger at the screen, and my stomach growled. Max opened the top desk drawer and handed me a fun size Snickers bar.

"Remind me to keep healthy snacks here for you. I don't want to contribute to your sugar addiction. You have a real problem."

I tossed the Snickers bar in my mouth. "I can stop anytime."

"Right. So, we've established Daniel filed fraudulent theft claims with the insurance company on rings he actually sold, and they were made with the platinum from the catalytic converters stolen from Vlad's garage by the Nasato gang's cutters."

"And Marjorie Butz is walking around flashing one of those rings," I said. "No wonder Daniel could afford a house at the Jersey shore."

Max pushed his chair back from the desk. "Red, you're right. We need to get into Jason's house."

"I've staked it out a couple times when I followed Tracy. Jason's house is on Earl Street, near Memorial Park. The houses on Earl are close together and right on the street. No front yard and skinny backyards with a rear alley."

Max rummaged around in one of his desk drawers. "Let's go do some recon." He pulled something out of the drawer and stuffed it in his backpack.

"Can we stop for dinner first?"

"Definitely."

Twenty-two

Romeo's Delight has excellent pizza, but what's even better is the array of delicious dessert items you can take to go, including all types of cookies, cakes, and gelato. When we finished the pizza, we bought a bag of gourmet chocolate chip cookies for the road. I pulled two oversized cookies from the bag and handed one to Max. I bit into my cookie and closed my eyes.

"Oh my God, it's incredible," I groaned. "The chips are melty."

Max bit into his cookie and gave me a wink. "I hope I have a similar effect on you, Red."

"It's a tie. You're going to have to work a little harder to beat this cookie."

"That's not a problem."

Max turned down Earl Street and parked a half a block up from Jason's house. Lights shone from the first floor, and Jason's pickup truck was in its usual spot on the curb by his front door. Traffic on the street was light but steady. Every so often, a person walking a dog passed by.

"Now that Fat Eddie has been arrested and the cops busted the warehouse, do you think that's the end of the catalytic converter theft ring?" I asked.

"Probably not. The brothers have too much invested. This operation is bigger than Pottstown. It reaches from Reading to Philly, at least."

"So the cutters' services are still needed."

"If the cutters deliver, the Nasato gang has no reason to eliminate them."

We observed the house for a few more minutes. A Great Pyrenees yanked a lady down the sidewalk past us.

"When we do this, we'll approach the house from the alley. There's too much activity on the street," Max said.

"We're going to need Sam on this op. I'll tell her no gas station burritos this time."

"Fine. But she better stay on task." A blue Mazda pulled up and stopped behind Jason's pickup. "Do you know that car?"

"I haven't seen it before, but the guy resembles Daniel's nephew, Tony DiMario. I saw him here with Tracy last week." Tony unlocked the front door and entered the house.

"So two people total live in the house?"

"I think so. And obviously Tracy stops by. I don't know if Jason has other girlfriends or if Tony has a significant other. Marjorie gave Jason the house, so she may pop in too." Stupid Marjorie.

"When we do this, we'll have to be extremely cautious. I'd like to avoid a run-in with the cutters or the police. We're pushing our luck." I could tell Max had reservations.

"I'm sorry, Max. I keep talking you into B and Es. I don't want to be the reason you break the law."

"Red, that ship has sailed on this case."

"What if I go in the house alone, and you watch the street? We'll stay in communication, and you can let me know when my time is up and I need to leave. I'd feel better if you were keeping an eye out."

"Fine. I'll watch the alley and Sam can watch Earl Street." He grabbed his backpack. "Wait here."

Max left the 4Runner, crossed the street, and strode toward Jason's pickup. He bent down, and I lost sight of him. A second later, he popped up, jogged back to the SUV, and jumped in. Max put the car in gear, and hit the gas.

"Did you just put a tracker on Jason's pickup?" I asked.

"Yes I did, Red."

"How illegal is that?"

"How illegal is it to do B and Es?"

Good point.

Max took me back to my house. He pulled me close and kissed me until I was dizzy and lightheaded, which didn't take that long. I wanted to go back to his place with him, but it would need to wait for another time. We said goodbye, I stepped inside the house, and watched as his car pulled away.

I chatted with Mom for a while, keeping it surface level. Then headed into to the living room. I had one problem that needed to be addressed. I'd been borrowing my mom's underwear since Fat Eddie stole mine, and I was becoming traumatized by wearing her cotton briefs. *Do you want to go shopping at what's left of the mall?*

Sam answered immediately. *Sure. Boyles is having a sale right now. Coochie needs some new clothes. Be over in twenty.*

I relaxed on the couch and waited for Sam to arrive. She rolled up and we took my car over to the mall, which consisted of about four stores. We entered Boyles, a department store that carries some decent name brands plus a lot of clothes for the AARP crowd. I made a beeline to the Ladies' Intimates department. Sam followed me, and we wove our way through racks of bras and shapewear until we got to the underwear section.

"Do you need some sexy underwear since you and Max are back together? Do you need to upgrade your granny panties?"

"Just because I don't wear thongs doesn't mean I wear granny panties." I dug around in a pile of bikini underwear on a table. "I sort of lost all my underwear."

"What do you mean you *lost* all your underwear? That only happens at the laundromat when some pervert raids your dryer when you're not looking. And you don't go to the laundromat, so what happened?"

"You didn't see the headline in *The Pottstown Post*?"

"No. You know I don't pay much attention to the mainstream media."

"Well, when Fat Eddie took my car, he also broke into my house and stole some stuff." I tilted my head down toward the table full of underwear.

"Oh, hell no," Sam yelled. "Fat Eddie the fake mobster did not steal your panties!" An elderly saleslady glared at us, shook her head, and went back to pricing push-up bras.

"It gets worse. He robbed me of every last pair in the drawer, and when the cops pulled his Cadillac from the river, my underwear were floating around inside the car. Smitty and Tamika, the divers, and the tow truck guy all saw my underwear. And stupid Kenny Marshall wrote a story in the newspaper about my stolen underwear, with my picture. It was humiliating."

Sam crouched down on the floor, laughing. "Code yellow, code yellow!" Tears streamed down her face.

"It's not funny, Sam. How would you like it if a psycho stole *all* your underwear, a bunch of people saw them, and then some jerk put it all over social media?"

Squatted down, Sam laughed uncontrollably, and the saleslady looked like she was about to call security. I hustled Sam out of Ladies' Intimates, and we rode the escalator upstairs to the restroom.

"I peed a little before we made it to the bathroom," Sam said from her stall.

"Well, it serves you right." I started laughing too. Then I had a code yellow and ran into the stall next to hers.

"So what if some people saw your underwear?" Sam said. "You should be proud of it. At least you wear them. Some people don't have the decency to even wear underwear. And remember low-rise jeans? A lot of ass crack was on display back in those days. You've got nothing to be ashamed of."

A woman entered the bathroom, talking loudly on her cell phone, and Sam and I fell silent. She took the stall on the other side of Sam's and slammed the door closed.

"I'm at Boyles, and I bought a new Dooney and Bourke handbag and a Michael Kors winter coat fifty percent off," the woman bragged. "I don't usually shop sales, but this was fun."

I rolled my eyes. It was the unmistakable voice of Tracy Lakeland. I texted Sam. *Tracy is next to you.*

She texted back, *I knew I recognized her voice. That bitch owes me for a pizza.*

DO NOT say anything to her, I texted.

Tracy said "no" a few times to the person on the other end of the line. After a pause she said, "Ed, I didn't know about the insurance claims. If I did, I would've told you about them. He must have put the money into a separate account." She flushed the toilet, and we heard her zip up.

I texted Max, *In the bathroom with Tracy at Boyles*. He texted me a question mark, a toilet emoji, and a laughing face. I texted him that I'd call him later. Tracy said "uh-huh" a few times, washed and dried her hands, gathered up her bags, and left. Sam and I flushed, left the stalls, and washed our hands at the sink.

"I don't understand people who talk on the phone while going to the bathroom," Sam said. "That's a major etiquette breach. Why the hell does she think people on the other end of the phone want to hear her biological functions? And what the hell was she talking about with the insurance?"

I brought Sam up to speed on Daniel's insurance claims for the jewelry he made with the stolen platinum as we headed back to the escalator.

"No wonder he drove around in a Mercedes and lived in a mansion. He probably had a house at the shore too. And Tracy's saying she didn't know about the fraud. I'm not sure I believe all that," Sam said.

"Right. I wonder if she figured it out. I should call Max and tell him, but I didn't accomplish my primary objective yet, which is to replace the underwear Fat Eddie the gangster stole."

"That's not a sentence you hear every day. Let's do this."

We took the escalator back downstairs to Ladies' Intimates, and I picked up a dozen pairs of bikini underwear in various materials and colors. Sam bought some shapewear and a minimizer bra. It was nice to do something normal for a change, that didn't involve me or someone I know breaking the law or getting shot at. Objective completed, Sam and I cruised around the store and browsed. We didn't spot Tracy, which was fine with me. I'd had enough of her to last me a lifetime. I bought Sam a couple boxes of fudge at the candy counter to make up for the pizza Tracy stole from her, and a box for Mom and me to share, and we left. As we headed back to my place, I told Sam about the planned break-in at Jason Butz's house and how we needed her help.

"So you need Coochie Bodacious back on the case?"

"I need you to cover Earl Street and tell me if someone comes home or if the cops show up."

"Coochie can do that."

Max called when I got home. "What have you been up to, Red? What was with Tracy in the bathroom at Boyles?"

"Sam and I went to the mall to restock my panty drawer. Sam almost peed her pants when I told her about what happened to my underwear."

"Figures. But you didn't need to replace them. I liked your underwear drawer empty."

"Well, sorry to disappoint, but commando is really not my scene. Anyway, when Sam and I were in the restroom stalls, Tracy came in. She was on the phone and oblivious to me and Sam."

"Did she say anything linking her to the murder?"

"Not exactly. She was talking to someone named Ed and told him she didn't know about the insurance claims and that Daniel must have put the money in a secret account she didn't have access to."

"Interesting. It's hard to know if she's telling the truth."

"Agreed. But if she is, Daniel hid money from her *and* the Nasato gang," I said.

"Right. So when do I get to view the new undies?"

"I'll let you know." You have to keep them guessing a little. With men, it's all about the chase.

"When do you want to do the op at Jason's house, Red?" Max asked.

"Tuesday seems to be the cutters' night to go out and steal stuff. How's tomorrow night?"

"That works. Tomorrow I'm going to meet with my insurance company client and bring them up to speed on Daniel's case. I'll be busy most of the day with that."

"The cutters are active around eleven p.m."

"Alright. Let's meet at my office at ten."

"We'll be there."

We said goodnight, and I headed downstairs. I found Mom in the family room on the couch laying into the fudge. She handed me a piece, and I settled down next to her. Bruce hopped up and stuffed himself in between us.

"When is your suspension over with at the Otter Club?" I asked.

"Well, it went into effect immediately after the party, so I'm allowed back in the club next Sunday morning. We can go to brunch."

"Definitely."

"How's it going with you and Max?"

"Good, but I'm trying to take it slow with him." Trying and failing.

"Don't take it too slow or your eggs are going to dry up in there."

"*Mom.* I'm only twenty-nine. My eggs are fine. And Max and I aren't even engaged."

"Oh phoo," she said. "You don't need a ring to make a baby."

> I could not believe what I was hearing. "Mom! I don't want to have a love child with Max." "There are worse things."

I have nothing against having a love child. In fact, it's sort of romantic. But the idea of a kid right now scared the hell out of me. Bruce was the most responsibility I could handle at the moment, and Mom helped me out with cat care duties.

"Max and I agreed we're going to take it slow. I love you and I'm going to bed."

I gave her a kiss, trotted upstairs, flopped on my bed and sent a text to Max. *Mom wants us to have a love child soon.* A few seconds later he texted back, *We need way more practice.*

Twenty-three

S am and I met Max at his office at ten on Tuesday night. Sam brought coffees for herself and Max and a hot chocolate for me. Max ordered hoagies for us, and the three of us sat down at his conference table and dug in.

"Fill up now, because there's no snacking during this op," Max said. He was in full ex-cop mode. "You focus on the job. No Ring Dings, Devil Dogs or Doritos. And hit the bathroom before we leave. No snackies, no potty breaks, and no texting or talking on the phone unless it's to each other."

"Damn, Max, no need to be a hard ass about it," Sam said. "One bad burrito and you never live it down."

He gave her a look. "We don't need Jessica going to jail."

"Nobody's going to jail," she muttered.

"Stop saying jail, you guys."

I bit into my turkey hoagie and a mayonnaise blob and a tomato slice squished out the bottom of it and landed on the conference table. Max tossed me a napkin, and I cleaned up the mayo and shoved the tomato back in my hoagie. Max gave me look and I shrugged. My hunger surprised me because a whole herd of butterflies were partying in my stomach.

"Max, how long should I be inside Jason's house?"

"I want you out of there in twenty minutes. The longer you're in there, the greater the risk of getting busted. Are your phones charged up?"

Sam and I checked and said yes.

"Who made you the boss of this op? Jess and I do just fine without you," Sam said.

"If by fine you mean Jessica getting kidnapped by the Nasato brothers, I would have to disagree with you."

"I didn't stop for a damn Krimpet," Sam said. "That was all Jess."

"It wasn't a Krimpet. It was the chocolate cupcake with the white stripe," I said.

"Guys. Not now. We need to focus. It's almost time to go."

We finished up, hit the restrooms, and regrouped in Max's parking lot. I wore all black and my lock kit and flashlight were stowed in my backpack. My hair was pulled back in a ponytail and I had on a black baseball cap. I handed my binoculars to Sam.

"The plan is, Jess rides over with me and she enters the house from the rear alley," Max said. "Assuming no one comes home while you're inside the house, you'll exit from the rear and I'll be there waiting. While you're inside searching, I'll keep an eye on Jason's truck on the tracking app on my phone. Sam, your only job is to watch the street and report any movement near the house to me on my cell. My cell phone will be on speaker so Jess can hear it. Got it?"

"Yup, report any movement on the street. Got it. Coochie Bodacious can handle it."

Max gave her a puzzled look.

"I'll explain it to you later," I said.

"Jess, you'll be talking to me on this." Max handed me a burner phone with a hands-free earbud. "Stay in communication with me the entire time you're in the house.

I'll keep you informed on what's happening outside. You tell me what you see inside and if you get jammed up for some reason."

I nodded. My mouth had gone dry. I shoved the fear way down into my gut and told myself I was on a mission for Vlad and Anastasiya. I wasn't going to let him go to prison for a murder I was sure he didn't commit. And I was hell-bent on catching Daniel's real killer.

"Okay, let's do this," I said.

Max and I jumped in his 4Runner, and Sam followed behind in the Mustang. When we reached Hanover Street, Sam peeled off and turned right onto Earl Street. We pulled over to the curb and stopped. Max called Sam on his cell phone and put the phone on speaker. She answered on the first ring.

"This is Coochie. Over."

"Are you in place?" Max asked.

"That's affirmative. The street is pretty full of parked cars, but I got a spot about a block up from the Butz house. Over."

"Good," he said.

"Sam, is the dented pickup on the street?" I asked.

"That's affirm. The ninja truck is right in front of Jason's house. And there's lights on in the house. Over."

"Sam, you don't have to say *over*, you're on a cell phone," Max said.

"Roger that," she said.

"Maybe they aren't going out cutting tonight," I said.

Max pushed back in the seat. "Let's give it twenty minutes. If there's no movement, we'll leave."

"How's the street, Sam, is it quiet?" I asked.

"Yeah. The people who live on this street must be the early riser go-getter types. It's quiet and most houses are dark. No bogies."

We fell silent, waiting. The minutes dragged on and the butterflies in my stomach were having a rave. I hoped I didn't get the nervous scoots. I didn't want to waste time in the bathroom during a break-in.

"Guys," Sam said. "I have bogies at eleven o'clock, repeat, bogies at eleven o'clock."

"Who?" I asked.

"It's Jason and another guy. Over."

"Are they getting in the truck?" Max asked.

"Yes, and they're dressed in ninja black, as usual. They put some tools in the truck and are leaving. They're driving down the street away from me. Over."

"Is the house dark now?" I asked.

"One light is still on downstairs." Crap.

Max checked the tracker app to make sure it was working. He drove a half block farther and turned right onto the rutted alley behind Jason Butz's house. He pulled over and turned to me.

"Okay, Red, it's all you." He pulled a burner phone out of his backpack, powered it up, and dialed my burner phone. I put the earbud in my ear and answered the call.

"Can you hear me?"

"Yes." I stuffed the phone in my pocket.

"You good, Red?"

I gave Max the thumbs up. My mouth was completely dry and my heart was beating too fast. I took a deep breath.

"I'm good." I definitely wasn't good. The butterflies were gone and had left behind a knot in my stomach. I grabbed my backpack and took out my lock kit and my flashlight.

"Relax and stay calm," Max said. "Keep your mind on the job." He handed me latex gloves, and I tugged them over my sweaty palms. Max checked the tracker app. "The ninjas have stopped. They're about two miles away. I'll be watching them."

I started to pit out. I was a mess, but I wasn't going to let Max see it.

"Sam, Jess is going in."

"Copy that."

"What if Jason has a security system?" I asked.

"Let me know and I'll come help you get inside. Don't panic."

I pulled my gaiter up over my nose, stepped out of the SUV and on wobbly legs, sneaked up the concrete walk through the narrow yard to Jason's back door.

"No security cameras or keypads," I whispered.

"Good," Max's voice in my ear reassured me. "You're doing great."

Hyped up on pure adrenaline, my hands shook as I opened my kit. I picked the lock on the back door and slipped inside the house. I stepped into the dark kitchen and froze, listening for signs of life. Something brushed my leg. I flinched, my heart shipping a beat. I clicked on my flashlight and shined it around the room. A fluffy gray cat with a big poofy tail rubbed himself up against my calf. The tag on his blue collar read *Burt*.

I resisted the urge to bend down and pet Burt, even though I really wanted to. First I needed to make sure I was alone in the house. I tiptoed through the kitchen and peeked around the corner into the living room. My heart had crawled up into my throat. A single lamp lit the room, which was furnished with worn pink plaid couches and a pink rocking chair. Probably Marjorie's old stuff from a million years ago. The flat screen TV on the wall was turned off, and the curtains on the picture window next to the front door were drawn.

"All clear downstairs. There's a cat. I'm going upstairs now," I whispered.

"Okay, Red. I'm clear in the alley. Sam, what's going on?" I couldn't make out her response. "Sam says we're good on Earl Street," Max said in my ear.

The stairwell leading to the second floor was pitch black, and I prayed no one was upstairs preparing to kill me. The steps creaked as I slowly ascended, and I renewed my deal with God that I'd never to do another B and E. Burt darted past me to the landing, turned, and waited for me.

After an eternity, I reached the second floor landing. "I'm upstairs," I whispered. Burt rubbed himself up against my leg.

"Good job, Jess. Sam, check in." A moment later Max's voice was in my ear. "Jess, Earl Street is still clear, but the tracker shows that the ninjas are on the move. They're out in Upper Pottsgrove right now."

"Okay, tell me when I need to bolt." My voice was barely audible.

In front of me was a bathroom. To the right was a bedroom, and to the left was the primary bedroom and a smaller bedroom. My flashlight shook in my hand as I entered the bathroom. I stared at the shower curtain, positive that someone was lurking behind it, ready to jump out and stab me. I held my breath and yanked the shower curtain back. Empty. I breathed again. No one hiding in the bathtub with a butcher knife. I replaced the curtain and whispered, "Bathroom clear."

"Okay, Red."

I cleared the bedroom to the right. It held a twin bed, an empty dresser, and a set of dumbbells, which I almost tripped over. The smaller bedroom on the left appeared to be Tony's room, according to papers on the desk, and was a disgusting, smelly mess with dirty clothes, grimy dishes, and miscellaneous crap strewn about. I'd never find anything in that shit heap.

I closed the door. "Tony's room is clear, just a disaster area."

"Good job. The ninjas are still moving away from us. You're good, Jess."

I entered Jason's bedroom. His room wasn't much better than Tony's. I shined the flashlight around the room, and the lump of covers on the bed nearly sent me screaming for the nearest window to jump out of. I froze, praying someone wasn't asleep under there. Or dead. I hadn't come this far to bail out now. Wide-eyed, I held my breath and inched toward the bed. I raised my trembling hand, poked the lump with my flashlight and jumped backwards. The lump didn't stir. My knees knocked together. I leaned over and poked it again. It was just a bunched-up comforter on an unmade bed. This was definitely my last B and E. I couldn't handle this level of terror. Burt jumped on the bed and settled onto the pile of covers, kneading it with his little paws.

"Jess, what's your twenty?" Max's voice was tense.

"I'm in Jason's bedroom. I thought I saw a dead body but it was only a pile of blankets," I whispered. Although I was pretty sure no one was home, it seemed wrong to speak at a conversational volume.

"Stop freaking yourself out, Jess. Sam, are we clear on the street?"

"All quiet. Over."

I started with Jason's closet, shined the flashlight inside, and searched through all his crap. Boots and sneakers covered the floor, and the shelves above the rack of clothes contained folded sweatshirts and blankets. Nothing incriminating. I shut the closet door and moved on to a battered trunk at the foot of the bed. I pushed dirty clothes off of it, opened it and rifled through the contents, which included old porno DVDs, a baseball card collection, his weed stash, and some more clothes. Burt jumped into the trunk, and I shooed him out. An engine revved on the street and my heart skipped a beat.

"Are we good, Max? I hear a car."

Max asked Sam for a report. "Sam said someone parked down the block and went into their house. We're good on Earl Street. But the ninjas moved. They're over in West Pottsgrove now. Maybe at Vlad's, maybe not."

"Alright. I need more time in here. I haven't found any clues yet."

I reminded myself to breathe, knelt down, and peeked under the bed. I pushed some clothes and boxes aside and that's when I saw it. A beat-up old red toolbox shoved far under the bed. A little voice inside my head said, *Time's up, better leave.* I ignored it. I set the flashlight down, crawled halfway under the bed, and dragged the toolbox out. Burt appeared beside me and watched, purring. I stuck the flashlight in my mouth and opened the toolbox. The set contained six screwdrivers, with one empty space where another screwdriver should have been. I photographed the open toolbox, shut it, and took another picture. I stuffed it back underneath the bed and replaced the clothes and blankets. I gave Burt a scritch behind his ear and stood up.

"I found some evidence, Max." I headed to the bedroom door.

Sam yelled so loudly on the speakerphone I heard her clearly on my call with Max.

"Pachysandra! Pachysandra! We have bogies at eleven o'clock. The ninjas are back!"

"Get out of there, Red," Max's voice was loud in my ear. "Get out now. Sam, where are they?"

"They just pulled up to the house. Hurry! They're heading inside. Dammit."

I heard Sam's car door open and her yell, "Yoo-hoo! Excuse me. I'm lost. My phone died and I keep driving around in circles. Can you give me directions to the movie theater by the dead mall?"

Uh-oh. Sam was off book, trying to buy me time with a distraction. Panicked, I raced down the creaky steps, trying not to trip over Burt. I zoomed past the front door and through the living room. Keys jingled. I made it into the kitchen as the front door banged opened. I slipped out the back door, and Burt ran outside with me. I stuffed him back in the house and sprinted down the walk to Max's SUV. He reached over, pushed the passenger door open, and I jumped inside. Max stomped the gas, and the 4Runner lurched and bumped over the alley's potholes. When we hit Hanover Street, he flicked the headlights on and floored it through two yellow lights, over the bridge, and out of the borough.

The line was open with Sam, and we heard her Mustang accelerate as she sped away.

"Jessica! Did you pachysandra the hell out of the house? Those ninjas came out of nowhere."

"I'm okay, Sam. We're headed to Max's house. Thanks for covering my ass. Are you good?"

"Yeah, I'm good. But I'm going to stop at Wendy's on the way home and get a Frosty first. They have a calming effect on me."

I could relate.

Twenty-four

"What happened to the stupid GPS tracker?" I yelled, as we barreled down the back roads to Max's house.

"I don't know, Jess. The app showed Jason going to two locations. Assuming they were out cutting catalytic converters, the first location may have been another place they robbed. After that, I lost the signal. Either they found the tracker and got rid of it or it fell off when they drove over a pothole or the railroad tracks." Max looked over at me. "Did they see you?"

"I'm pretty sure I escaped without being spotted, but it was really close. Burt tried to leave with me."

"Wait. Who's Burt?"

"The cat. The cat is Burt. He ran outside with me, and I had to shoo him back inside the house. I didn't know if he's an outdoor cat and I didn't want him to get lost. Burt was super friendly." My heart felt like it was trying to exit my body through my throat.

"That's nice of you to care about the cat, Jess, but not worth getting shot or arrested or both." He checked his rearview mirror to see if we were being followed, then looked over at me and smiled. "You did good, Red. You'd make a great thief."

"Well, at least I know I have a fallback career as a criminal if I lose my PI license."

We pulled into Max's driveway, and he put the 4Runner in the garage next to the Camaro. He disarmed the security system, and we entered his house. Max poured me a glass of cabernet, and grabbed a beer for himself, booting the refrigerator door closed with his foot.

"So what's the evidence you found?" he asked.

"Right!" In the sheer terror of nearly being caught, I'd forgotten about what I'd found.

"I think I found Vlad's missing toolbox under Jason's bed. I took photos." I fished my cell phone out of my backpack and showed him the toolbox photos. "See, one screwdriver is missing from the set." I sipped my wine and tried to relax.

"Nice work, Red. The missing screwdriver could be the one from Daniel's forehead."

"That's a revolting thought, but yes, that's my guess too. Let's visit Anastasiya tomorrow morning and ask her if she can identify the toolbox."

"Definitely. It doesn't prove Vlad didn't kill Daniel, but it's a step in the right direction."

I drained the wine glass. "I'm beat. I need sleep."

"You have enough energy for one last activity?"

"You're going to have to convince me."

"Not a problem."

Sunlight streamed through the windows, informing me that I'd overslept. My phone read five after nine. I sent a text to Mom and let her know I was at Max's working a case together so she wouldn't worry. She didn't need to know the gory details of the break in at Jason Butz's house. Next I sent a text to Anastasiya about meeting up. Max walked into the bedroom, leaned down and gave me a lingering kiss.

"I just reached out to Anastasiya about meeting this morning," I said.

My phone buzzed. A text from Anastasiya read, *I don't talk on the phone. You come to Vlad's garage please. One hour.* I texted back, *See you then.*

> "We have a meeting with her in an hour at Vlad's garage. I need a shower badly."

> Max pulled his sweatshirt and tee shirt off at the same time. "I'll join you."

After an extended, soapy shower, Max and I headed over to Boyko Motors. Max pulled the 4Runner to the curb, and we entered the office. Anastasiya was talking on the phone, and she motioned for us to sit down on the couch. She rushed the person off the phone and hit the button to unlock Vlad's office. "You come in Vlad's office with me."

Anastasiya sat down at Vlad's desk, and Max and I sat in the worn leather chairs. The capped vodka bottle sat on the desk, waiting for Vlad's return. I pulled up the toolbox pictures on my phone and handed it to Anastasiya.

"Do these photos look like Vlad's toolbox and screwdrivers?" I asked.

She took the phone from me and swiped through them. "Yes, I think so. Where do you find this?"

"Jessica found it inside the home of one of the men who robbed you," Max said. "A man named Jason Butz."

"Wait one minute. I get Aleksander from garage. I want him to have a look." She left Vlad's office and returned a moment later with a tall man with work muscles, heavy arm

tattoos and a Jason Statham buzzcut. Anastasiya spoke to him in Ukrainian. Aleksander took a look at the photos on my phone.

"Vlad's?" I asked him.

He nodded. "*Tak, tak.* Yes, is Vlad's." He whispered to Anastasiya in Ukrainian and returned to the garage.

I forwarded the photos to her phone. "Anastasiya, would you be able to confirm that with Vlad?" I asked.

"Yes. I have a video call with him in one hour. I show him the photos and text you."

As we stood up to leave, she said, "I know Vlad does not do this. I tame him after we married. He is a good man now. Like a big pussycat."

Max and I said goodbye to her and we rolled to my office. Sam sat at her desk, and Sparkle had stuffed himself under the coffee table and was chewing on a hot dog squeaky toy. Thankfully, Sparkle killed the squeaker a while ago. He slapped his tail on the floor when he saw Max and me. We both gave him some pets, and he went back to slobbering on his hot dog.

"Hey, Jess, tell me what happened after you got out of Jason's house. After I asked for directions and stalled them," Sam said.

"Thanks for that. You saved my ass again."

"Coochie has your back. She can think on her feet."

I caught Sam up on the toolbox and Burt.

"It's official, you're a cat burglar," Sam said.

"Burt was super friendly, and he followed me around the whole time. I think he was trying to keep me calm. He was gray with stripes and kind of chonky."

"Burt's a good name for a cat like that," Sam said. "I love a chonky fat cat."

"Me too."

"Okay chonkies," Max said. "We have GPS locations we need to check from last night. One location could be the new base of operation where the catalytic converters are processed for the platinum."

"Right. Max and I visited Anastasiya this morning to show her the photos I took." I told Sam that Aleksander and Anastasiya positively identified the toolbox as Vlad's and that she would show Vlad the photos this morning.

"So what's the next move? Do you need Coochie's help on another mission?"

"After we talk to Anastasiya, our next move is to go to the police with what we have," Max said. "And what's with the Coochie, Sam?"

"Coochie Bodacious is my Bond girl name. I use it when we're on a mission."

"Good to know."

"So what are you two going to tell Smitty and Tamika? That Jess broke into the cutters' house?"

"I haven't worked that part out yet. We may have to wing it," Max said.

My phone buzzed with a text from Anastasiya. It read, *Vlad said that's his tato's toolbox. Missing since November.* I read the text to Max and Sam. Sam Googled what *tato* meant in Ukrainian.

Sam shook her head. "The ninjas stole his daddy's tools from him. That's low. Those ninjas have no respect for the working man."

"Let's go visit Smitty and Tamika," I said. I wasn't looking forward to speaking to them about the B and E. To prove Vlad was truly innocent, I needed to put my fears aside.

Fifteen minutes later, Max and I marched into Pottstown PD and asked to speak with Detectives Smits and Johnson. After a short wait, Smitty emerged from his cubicle and ushered us upstairs to the conference room. Tamika sat at the table with a legal pad in front of her. Max and I sat down.

"What did you two want to see us about this time?" Tamika asked.

I paused and took a deep breath. "I'd like to make an anonymous tip." With my peripheral vision, I saw Max give me the side-eye. My armpits started to sweat.

Smitty looked confused. "But you're sitting right here. How is it supposed to be anonymous?"

"Pretend you can't see me."

Tamika put her elbows on the table and leaned forward. "Are you sure you want to make an *anonymous* tip? Because if it's about the Lakeland case, Tracy put up a twenty-thousand-dollar reward for information leading to an arrest for Daniel's murder."

I kicked Max under the table.

"So any information pertinent to the case, regardless of how we obtained it?" Max asked.

"I know you didn't interfere in an active police investigation," Tamika said.

"You better tell us what you have, and we'll make a determination on that later," Smitty said.

I swallowed hard. "Well, I can prove Jason Butz is in possession of the toolbox that contained the screwdriver that killed Daniel Lakeland."

Smitty kept a poker face. "Go on."

I set my phone on the table. "I may have taken photos from inside Jason Butz's house last night."

"Mm-hmm," Tamika said. "And how did you manage to get inside Jason's house? I suppose he invited you in?"

I felt lightheaded, and the butterflies were partying in my stomach again. Tamika pushed the bowl of Hershey's Kisses over to me. "They're fresh. Valentine's Day is coming up."

I unwrapped the pink wrapper on a Kiss, shoved it in my mouth, and balled up the foil as sweat trickled down my arm. "I may have picked the lock on the back door." I spilled my guts. It felt good to get it all out. "I found the toolbox upstairs stuffed under his bed. I took photos." My armpits stopped sweating.

"I'm going to need those photos," Smitty said. I texted them to him. Tamika looked at them on my phone.

"Vlad's wife, Anastasiya, spoke with Vlad today, and he confirmed they are his tools. The ones that went missing back in November," Max said. "And I drove Jessica to Jason's house and was the lookout. She didn't do this alone. I was part of it." He left out Sam's role as lookout.

Smitty sat back in his chair and crossed his arms. "We like Vlad for this murder, that's why he's in jail. What else do you know? What made you decide to go to Jason's house?"

Max told Smitty and Tamika about his client's email that contained the insurance claim form with the photo of the cocktail ring Marjorie wore to the Otter Club and he explained the insurance scam Daniel had been running.

"The Nasato brothers sold Daniel the platinum from stolen catalytic converters at a discount compared to what he would've paid wholesale. Daniel made jewelry with it and sold it in his shops," Max said.

"When we searched Daniel's shop in Lower Pottsgrove, we found business receipts from Diamond Goods Inc. They looked legit, but we were focused on Vlad," Smitty said.

Max nodded. "Daniel got greedier and filed false insurance claims on the jewelry, reporting it as stolen. But he didn't have legitimate receipts for all of his claims and his insurance company, my client, got suspicious."

"So the Nasato brothers used Daniel to buy the precious metals, and in return, they get laundered money," Smitty said.

"Right. And if the Nasato Brothers found out about Daniel's insurance claims, Max and I think they would have wanted a cut of that money too." I popped another Kiss into my mouth. "Oh, and Fat Eddie is doing Tracy Lakeland, and so is Jason Butz."

Smitty and Tamika looked at each other and grimaced. "Gross."

"Do we want to know how you obtained this information?" Tamika asked.

"Probably not," I said. Max shifted around in his seat and cracked his knuckles.

"I don't think the Nasato brothers would farm out a hit to Jason Butz," Tamika said. "They would want that feather in their cap. We should invite Fat Eddie in for another conversation."

"If Tamika and I can get Eddie to roll on Jason for the catalytic converter thefts, that will get us inside Jason's house."

"What about Vlad?" I asked.

Smitty shook his head. "He stays put until we get this sorted out."

Max stood up to leave. I grabbed a few more Kisses from the bowl for the road. "Are we in trouble?" I asked.

"Of course you are," Smitty said. "But since you provided us with valuable information and helped us establish the connection between Diamond Goods, the Nasato brothers, and Daniel Lakeland, we'll overlook the fact that some of your information was obtained without regard for the law."

"Mm-hmm," Tamika said. "Now get out of here before we change our minds."

Twenty-five

"So Tracy putting the reward money up helps her look less guilty," I said, when we were back in the 4Runner.

"Sure does. And that kind of money is chump change to her."

"Must be nice. What are the chances of us getting the reward money based on the info we gave Smitty and Tamika?"

"I guess it depends on whether Tracy is actually involved in the murder or not. Right now, that's a big if."

I messaged Anastasiya to meet me at my office, and she texted back that she would be right over. We drove around the block to my office, headed upstairs and plopped onto the couch in reception.

Sam looked up from her laptop. "How'd it go with the five-o? How many charges are you up on?"

"None so far," I said. "The police were fairly receptive to what we told them. Anastasiya is coming over now so we can fill her in. And there's a reward."

"Say what now?"

"Tracy put up a twenty-thousand-dollar reward for information about Daniel's murder," Max said.

"You gave the cops a bunch of information," Sam said. "Where's your check? And where's my cut?"

"Our information has to lead to an arrest that doesn't include Tracy," Max said. "If she goes to jail, we can forget the reward."

"We risked our lives last night. You can never tell what a ninja might do, they're unpredictable," Sam said. She wasn't wrong about that.

We heard footsteps on the stairs, and Anastasiya appeared in the doorway.

I stood up. "Hi, Anastasiya. Please come in and sit down." I offered her water, and she took off her sunglasses and sat down on the couch.

She pulled a tissue from her purse. "What did the police say?"

"We told them about the evidence we found last night, and that Vlad confirmed that the toolbox in the photos was the one stolen in November."

She dabbed her nose. "Yes. Vlad was happy you broke into their house."

I smiled. It was worth the heart palpitations.

"The police are going to question a man named Eddie, Jason's boss, the guy who was stealing from you," Max said. "They hope to get information from Eddie that they can use to search Jason's house."

"We're making progress," I said. "We have another lead we need to follow up on, and we'll let you know what happens when the police question Eddie. In the meantime, try to stay strong for Vlad."

Anastasiya dabbed at her eyes. "Thank you all. I need to get back to the shop." We said goodbye, and she put her sunglasses on and left.

"She's a real nice lady," Sam said. "We need to help her and get Vlad released from the clink before he gets shanked or joins a gang."

"Or starts a gang," Max said. "Jess, let's go check those two locations from the GPS tracker."

"Okay, but I need lunch first." My stomach was empty and hangriness was fast approaching.

"Does anyone want food from the Purple Panda?" Sam asked.

The Purple Panda is an Asian restaurant downtown. Its old, brick exterior contrasts with the modern, open concept, long bar, and upscale feel. Max and I were both down for Purple Panda food. Sam put our orders in on their website, and fifteen minutes later Max left to pick up the food.

While Max was gone, Sam and I chatted. I told her about my mom being in favor of Max and I having a love child.

"Is your mom a hippie? Or is she getting impatient for grandkids? Or both?"

"She's definitely not a hippie and I don't think she's putting grandkid pressure on me. She wants Max and me to get back together for good, settle down, and she doesn't care if the baby comes before the engagement. I guess she thinks if all that happens, she can stop worrying about me."

"Your mom has a modern, up-to-date perspective on relationships. Are you ready to settle down with Max?"

"No way. Not anytime soon. We're still on a trial basis, and I like it that way."

"Trial my ass."

The truth is, the trial basis situation felt safe to me. I wasn't ready for anything permanent and I didn't have baby fever like some of my other friends. I changed the subject. "How are you and Jalen?"

"We're solid. That man is so hot I ovulate every time he walks in the room." I could relate. Jalen is hot.

Max bounded up the stairs and set the takeout bags on the coffee table. Sam and Max had ordered spicy noodles with beef, and I got chicken fried rice. I was ravenous, ate too fast, and spilled rice and peas on the floor. Sam called Sparkle over to clean it up. He searched out the rice and peas, hoovered them up, shoved himself under the coffee table, and started snoring.

After we finished our lunch, we said goodbye to Sam and Sparkle and headed out to check the locations Max picked up on the tracker on Tuesday night. The first place was a small used car lot in Upper Pottsgrove Township.

"This could be definitely be one of the places the cutters hit," I said, as Max slowed the car. "Look how those cars in the back don't have for sale signs on them. Maybe they're missing catalytic converters."

"Not much lighting here, either. Low security. It's an easy target for thieves."

I checked the second GPS location on Max's phone.

"Next we're headed to a place off of Shuman Road, in the commercial area near Walmart."

I put the address into Max's GPS and he took the highway south back toward the borough. Max made the right onto Shuman Road, and we drove past a string of one-story buildings. We made another turn, passed by more ugly, flat buildings, and after about a quarter mile, the street dead-ended at a dilapidated warehouse. The building's faded white paint had nearly peeled off, and the parking lot was more potholes than asphalt. The few windows were small and cruddy. Railroad tracks ran behind the warehouse and parked in front were a blue Mazda hatchback and Jason Butz's bashed-in tan pickup truck.

"Here's the Fat Brothers' new Pottstown base of operations," Max said.

"I guess it didn't take much time for them to set up. And it's a perfect location. There are no neighbors, and it's surrounded by trees and scrubby woods."

The two garage doors were raised up about six inches each, probably for ventilation from the harsh chemicals used during the extraction process. I pulled out my phone and snapped a few photos. Max's phone rang.

"Hey, Smitty. Jess is here with me."

"Hey, Jess. Eddie Nasato is coming in to talk in a half hour. I want you two to come in listen in on what he says."

"Got it. Be there soon," Max said, turning the car around and heading away from the industrial park. We rolled to the police department and met Tamika at the front desk.

"Before you ask, Jess, we have doughnuts in the break room. Don't take them all. Leave some for others."

"Great. Max, do you want one?"

"I'll pass this time."

I hurried to the breakroom and inspected the box of doughnuts sitting by the coffee maker. An officer I didn't know was seated at a table having a Boston cream and a cup of coffee. I said hi, and he looked up from his phone.

"Are you the one who let Fat Eddie Nasato's car roll into the river?"

"That's me."

"Nice job."

"Thanks. It was all him, though."

"A pair of your underwear is making the rounds through the department. The officers are calling you PI Panties. I thought you might want to know."

I resisted the urge to scream and managed to mumble thanks. I grabbed a cream-filled doughnut with chocolate frosting and sprinkles and got the hell out of there. I passed two officers who gave me the up-down look and grinned. Gritting my teeth, I found Max talking to Smitty and Tamika outside the interview room.

I narrowed my eyes at Smitty. "PI Panties? When were you going to tell me?"

"Tell you what?"

"About my underwear."

"I thought you knew Fat Eddie had your underwear in his car."

"I *know* Fat Eddie had my underwear. What I wasn't aware of is that a pair is being passed around the department. Aren't they supposed to be in the evidence locker?" I took a bite of doughnut and cream squirted out and landed on my boob.

"Can I help you with that?" Max asked, as he swiped the cream off of my chest with his finger and ate it. Tamika and Smitty watched us, smirking.

Smitty cleared his throat. "How would you like me to address the situation?"

"I want you to locate my underwear and return them to me. There's no way that pair is evidence if it's gone around the whole department."

"I'll make an announcement at the morning meeting tomorrow. I was unaware of the situation."

I glared at Max as he suppressed a smile. "So you're okay with other men handling my underwear and whatever else guys do with ladies panties?"

The smile disappeared. "I am not." He looked at Smitty. "Dude, get her underpants back."

Fat Eddie's voice carried down the hallway, and Smitty ushered us into the observation room. A few moments later, Tamika and Chief Fitzpatrick joined us. The chief blushed when he saw me. I doubted I would ever live this PI Panties situation down with the police.

Through the one-way glass we watched as Fat Eddie was led into the room by an officer. Smitty entered a few minutes later and sat down at the table across from Eddie.

"Thanks for coming in, Mr. Nasato. Will your attorney be joining us today?" Smitty asked.

"Juan's running late. He'll be here."

"Are you comfortable speaking without him being present?"

"Yeah, sure. I ain't confessing to nothing. And I got nothing to hide."

"Mr. Nasato, the district attorney may be willing to drop the auto theft charge you received for stealing Jessica Byrne's car in exchange for some information."

"She destroyed three of my Cadillacs," he said, and jabbed his finger on the table. "When is she gonna get charged with destruction of a Cadillac? My first Cadillac got blown up because of *her*. And the only reason my brother's Cadillac got rear-ended by the city bus is because my second

Cadillac rolled in the river. Because of *her*. She's prejudiced against Cadillacs." Fat Eddie was red in the face.

"Your second Cadillac ended up in the river because you failed to put it in park. We could add a charge of careless driving if you like. And you were at Riverfront Park on the premise of returning Jessica's stolen car to her. However, we have reason to believe you planned to kidnap her that day. For the second time."

"Kidnap is an ugly word. I don't care for that word. Jessica and I were going to spend some quality time together." I threw up in my mouth a little.

"Regardless, the DA is willing to drop the burglary charge regarding Ms. Byrne's underwear if you tell us about Jason Butz."

"What's to tell? Jason Butz is my employee. He does...odd jobs for me," Fat Eddie shifted around in his seat.

"You're going to have to do better than that, Mr. Nasato."

"And you'll drop the burglary charge?"

"That depends on what you give me." Fat Eddie glared at the one-way mirror, then refocused on Smitty.

"Jason may have assisted me with my catalytic converter enterprise which you people recently shut down. You cost me a lot of money."

I knocked on the one-way glass, and Max, Tamika, and the chief looked at me. Smitty stood up and came into the observation room and closed the door.

"His Pottstown operation isn't shut down," I said.

"The Fat Brothers moved their *enterprise* to Roberts Street, over by Walmart," Max said. "Jess and I drove by the new warehouse today. It's operational."

"Keep that under your hat, Smits. We can use that later," Chief Fitzpatrick said. He looked at Tamika. "Go see what more you can get out of him."

"Yes, sir." Tamika strode into the interview room. She dropped her legal pad onto the table and sat down.

"I know Jason didn't work alone. Give me a name."

"I gave you Jason."

"Well, that's not enough. We need his partner too."

Eddie sighed and leaned forward, lowering his voice. "Daniel brought his nephew in. The nephew brought in Jason. If you ask me, neither one of those kids are too bright."

"The name."

"Tony DiMario. Him and Jason are roommates or whatever."

Juan Epstein burst into the interview room. "Shut up, Eddie. Why do you like to talk to the police without me?"

"Because you're always friggin' late, that's why," Eddie said. "I don't want to be here all day."

Juan glared at Tamika. "Is he under arrest?"

Tamika glared back. "Not yet."

"Then my client is done here. Eddie, let's go." Juan jerked his thumb to the exit.

"Well, it's perfect timing because we're done with him. We got what we needed," Tamika said. Smitty walked back into the interrogation the room and told Juan about the deal they made with Eddie.

Juan frowned. "Have the ADA send me the paperwork."

"And Mr. Nasato, one piece of advice before you leave," Smitty said. "Stay far, far away from Jessica Byrne and her family. Don't think you can intimidate witnesses in my town."

"I don't want nothing to do with her. She's a Cadillac killer."

Juan hustled Eddie out the door, and we could hear Eddie arguing with him about legal fees as they made a hasty exit. Tamika and Smitty returned to the observation room.

"Tell the DA to drop the burglary charges based on what Fat Eddie told us. When the time is right, we'll bust him on the second warehouse location on Roberts Street," Chief Fitzpatrick said. "Get a warrant to search Jason Butz's house. Now. And you two"—the chief pointed his finger at Max and me—"I don't want to hear that you're anywhere near the Roberts Street location." He looked at me, blushed, and stomped down the hall.

Tamika gave me a look. "Girl, I think he saw your underwear."

Twenty-six

T amika turned to Smitty. "I'll get started on the warrant for Jason's house. Check you guys later."

"I'll let you know when we serve the warrant," Smitty said. "And guys, stay out of trouble please."

"Thanks, brother," Max said.

Max and I left Pottstown PD, jumped in the 4Runner, and drove to my house.

I cranked the heat up to full blast. "Are we really going to stay away from the Nasato gang's new warehouse?"

"That doesn't sound like us. But we need a compelling reason to go. We've narrowly avoided charges already, and I don't want to push our luck."

Max had a point. It was a bad idea to further jeopardize our relationship with the police. He pulled in behind Harry's SUV and we headed inside the house. Bruce raced down the steps and wove around my legs. I picked him up, gave him a kiss, and set him down on the couch. He flopped over on his back and put his feet in the air, which is one of his happiness indicators. Mom came out from the kitchen, wiping her hands on a dish towel.

"Hi, you two. I'm making a pot roast. Why don't you both have dinner with Harry and me?"

"Sounds good, Mrs. B. I love your pot roast."

"I'll set two more plates." She smiled and disappeared into the kitchen.

Harry strolled into the living room. "Hi, guys. What's the Charlie update?"

"Charges have been filed, but the perps are still at large. I'd keep your piece on you and stay alert," Max said.

"I saw in the paper that charges were filed against Eddie Nasato and his brothers for the catalytic converter operation in town. Is that who we're dealing with? Mob guys?" Harry asked.

"They're mob adjacent and very dangerous. Max and I are working with the police to put some more puzzle pieces together."

"Your mom read the article too, but she doesn't suspect anything," Harry said. He patted his hip and returned to the kitchen.

"Harry's cool," Max said.

We headed upstairs to my office. As much as I wanted to take a power nap, we needed to focus on the case. I sat down at my desk and swiveled around to face Max, who took a seat on my pink exercise ball. He slowly bobbed up and down on it.

"What if Jason killed Daniel and the Nasato gang had nothing to do with it?" I said.

"What's Jason's motive? Tracy? She and Daniel were in the middle of a divorce. Jason could have waited that out if he was really into her."

"Okay, so if the murder wasn't for love, we need to follow the money. What if Jason killed Daniel for business reasons? Jason Butz and Tony DiMario were only acting as the Nasato gang's low-level cutters. They stole the catalytic converters, and they knew how to extract the platinum and rhodium, which from what I've read is a dirty, dangerous process."

"If the cutters wanted a bigger piece of the action, getting rid of Daniel would be the first step. It's a theory, Jess. One we should run down."

Mom yelled up the steps that dinner was ready. We headed downstairs and joined her and Harry at the kitchen table. Everyone served themselves a hunk of pot roast and dumped potatoes and carrots on their plate. I drowned my plate in gravy, and Mom and Harry poured themselves a glass of red wine. A glass would have been nice with dinner, but between it and the pot roast, it would mean lights out for me on the couch.

"So, Mom, how's your Otter Club suspension going?" I poured myself a glass of iced tea with caffeine.

She sipped her wine. "I'm keeping busy. The other ladies from the party planning committee and I are meeting tomorrow to start organizing the St. Patrick's Day festivities. We aren't meeting at the club, so I'm not breaking any rules of my suspension."

"That's good, Mom. I vote for a U2 cover band and all you can eat shepherd's pie."

"I'll make a note of it."

We finished up the meal, and I loaded the plates into the dishwasher. Mom set an Entenmann's chocolate fudge cake on the table, and the four of us laid into it.

Max's phone buzzed with a text, and he took a break from destroying the cake and read it. He looked at Mom and me.

"Mrs. B., the dinner was excellent, but Jess and I have some more work on our case we have to attend to."

I forked the last chunk of cake into my mouth and stood up. "Thanks for dinner, Mom. See you, Harry." Harry winked at me, and Max and I hurried back upstairs to my office.

"Smitty and Tamika are serving the search warrant at Jason Butz's house in a half hour," Max said. "Let's go sit on the Roberts Street warehouse and see what goes down."

I dressed in layers and pulled a black beanie on my head so my ears wouldn't freeze. Max and I took the 4Runner through town and stopped for hot beverages to-go. Wintertime surveillance is less terrible if you have hot chocolate. We drove to the commercial district on Shuman Street, left the car behind at the Quicky Motel, and followed the train tracks north until we were behind the Nasato's crappy warehouse on Roberts Street. We made our way through the woods and stopped at the edge. From our hiding spot, we had views of the warehouse's garage doors on the side of the building and the entrance on the front of the building. The parking lot was poorly illuminated by a few light affixed to the building. One garage door was open a few feet and Jason's pickup was parked in the lot. Max and I crouched down in the scrubby pine trees and peered through binoculars at the garage doors.

"We're going to bide our time and watch. Okay, Red?"

"Yup. Got it. Do you think Jason knows the warrant is being served right now?"

"We—I mean the police—typically have to notify someone in the house that they have a search warrant. If Tony's at the house, Jason might not be aware of it," Max said. "Cell phones may have been on the warrant."

"So Jason may be oblivious to what's happening at his house."

Max lowered his binoculars. "It's entirely possible."

Through the trees, headlights appeared on Roberts Street and moved toward the warehouse. We ducked farther back into the woods. Tracy's Jaguar purred into the parking lot. She tossed her cigarette butt onto the driveway and strutted through the front door. It clicked shut behind her, and a minute later the Jag's headlights went out. We crept back to the edge of the woods. I sipped my hot chocolate, removed a pinecone from under my ass, and rested my back up against a tree trunk.

Max sipped his coffee and checked his phone. "Smitty texted me. Tony answered the door. The police located the toolbox under Jason's bed."

"That's a relief. I was afraid Jason would pawn it or sell it on eBay, and that evidence would be gone."

The garage door opened and Jason Butz exited the warehouse carrying a five-gallon bucket. He wore rubber gloves, safety goggles, and a bandanna over his nose and mouth. He lugged the bucket behind the warehouse to the railroad tracks and dumped the contents of it in the woods. He returned to the warehouse, and Tracy met him inside the garage door. Jason dropped the bucket and removed his goggles. She pulled his bandanna down to his neck and they kissed. When they finished, Jason grabbed the bucket, and he and Tracy disappeared into the building.

Another set of headlights moved down Roberts Street, and Fat Eddie's electric Cadillac silently pulled beside Tracy's Jaguar. He got out, looked at the car as though he was checking to make sure it wouldn't roll away, and entered the front door.

My body was nearly frozen from the waist down. I wasn't going to last out here much longer. Time to take Fat Eddie down. "Hold my hot chocolate." I shoved the cup into Max's hand, raced to the warehouse and plastered myself up against the wall.

A few seconds later Max sprinted over to me. "What the hell are you doing, Jessica? This is not the plan. Are you trying to get shot?" Max doesn't like to divert from the plan. Ever.

"I wanted to get a better look. Maybe we can hear them talking from here. And I'm freezing. I need to move around and get my heart rate up or I'm going to turn into a damn icicle."

Max shook his head and moved in front of me, and we snuck along the north wall toward the open garage door. We strained to hear the voices inside the building. Coming from the woods behind us, we clearly heard, "Ca-*caw*, ca-*caw*."

"Max, did you hear that?"

"Yes. Who the hell is that?" The phony bird call came again, and a figure appeared at the tree line. Sam jogged over and mashed herself up against the wall next to Max and me.

"How in the hell did you know we were here?" I hissed at her.

"After your dumb ass got kidnapped by the stupid Nasato gang last week, I put a tracking app on your phone. Coochie Bodacious can't have her sidekick getting kidnapped another time. I have an image to maintain."

"Wait, how am I *your* sidekick? You know what? Forget it." Sidekick my ass.

Max shushed us. The three of us fell silent and listened to the voices inside the warehouse.

Gravel crunched behind us, and we all jumped and whipped around. Fat Eddie leveled a .44 at us.

"I know that's not a gun pointed at me," Sam said, more annoyed than scared.

"It is a gun. A big one," Fat Eddie said, his voice angry and unhinged. "You just won't leave it alone, will you, Jessica? You must really want to end up in the river. Move. All of you." He motioned with the gun and marched the three of us through the garage door into the warehouse.

Shit. Abducted by the Nasato brothers again, and Vlad was locked up and could help save us. Still at the wrong end of the .44, Fat Eddie forced us into a room full of fifty-five gallon drums. It had the same stinky chemical smell as the shop building in Norristown. About fifty catalytic converters were piled up against one wall. Jason, Tracy, Fat Vinnie, and Fat Joey stood in a half-circle, staring at us. Joey leveled his pistol at us and Vinnie pulled out a Glock. In his other hand he held a milkshake.

I smiled at Eddie. "I saw you pull in, Eddie. Did you get another new Cadillac?" I couldn't help myself.

"Yes I did, Jessica. This one is red, and you won't have time to destroy it, since you and your friends are going inside those barrels soon."

The light bulb flickered on in Tracy's head. She glared at me. "I know you. You and your friend there visited my day spa last week. Sheree said you chew your nails. That's a disgusting habit. And your friend stunk up my bathroom."

Sam laughed as I gave Tracy the finger with my stumpy but painted nail.

Fat Eddie pointed his gun at Max and me. "These two are private investigators, Tracy." He flicked the gun toward Max. "And this one here is an ex-cop."

Fat Joey looked at Max. "Gimme your piece. Now."

Max pulled his Glock from the back of his pants, set it on the ground and pushed it over to him. Double shit. Now we were really screwed. Maybe I should buy a gun. A little one.

"I'm actually not a PI," Sam said. "I'm a paranormal investigator." Everyone looked at Sam for a moment, then back to Fat Eddie.

"The police are searching Jason's house right now," Max said. "And do you know what they've already found?"

Jason looked like he was going to pee his pants or pass out.

"What's that?" Fat Vinnie asked.

"They found Vlad Boyko's toolbox. That toolbox was stolen from Vlad's business back in November, two months before the murder," Max said.

"In it was screwdriver that Jason used it to kill my client, Daniel Lakeland," I said, my voice shaking.

The Fat Brothers looked at each other, stunned. Eddie took the gun off of us and aimed it at Jason. "*You* killed Daniel? You *idiot*. We were making so much money. Why would you do that?"

Jason held his hands up and began pleading with Fat Eddie. Tracy looked confused.

"And what's more," I said, "Tracy's two-timing both of you." That took a minute to sink in with Fat Eddie and Jason.

Jason looked at Tracy. "Babe, it's not true. She's lying."

Tracy screamed at me that I was liar and started bawling.

"Stop crying, you skeevy ho," Sam yelled. "And I want my pizza money! $12.99!"

An explosion outside rocked the warehouse, and everyone hit the floor. Max jumped up first, pulled a gun from his ankle holster and pointed it at the brothers. "Drop your weapons! Face down and put your hands behind your head." Max was back in full ex-cop mode.

"And shut up," I added.

Jason tried to make a run for it through the garage door, and Sam gave him a krav maga kick to the groin. Groaning, he fell face down with a thud, and she straddled his back with her knee in his spine. Max kept his gun on the Fat Brothers, and I kicked their guns away as they lay cursing on the floor. Sirens wailed in the distance. Max winked at me.

As the sirens drew closer, Jalen and Harry stepped through the garage door, guns drawn. Jalen pointed a Sig Sauer at Jason. Sam stood up.

Harry trained his .357 Magnum on the Nasatos. He looked at me and grinned. "Your mother and I bought a police scanner at Costco yesterday. I heard the call on the radio about an explosion. I had a hunch, so I rallied the troops to come check it out." Behind him about twenty Otter Club members, all graying retirees, stood with their guns pointed at the gangsters. I recognized one woman gripping a .22 from the party planning committee.

A voice from somewhere in the crowd of Otters said, "Hi, Jessica, tell your mother hello."

The explosion caught the warehouse on fire, and smoke began to fill the room. Max, Jalen, and the Otters quickly marched the Fat Brothers, Jason, and Tracy out to the parking lot, and Sam and I followed. Fire trucks and police cars tore down Roberts Street, lights on and sirens blaring. Fat Eddie's new red Cadillac and Tracy's Jaguar were two heaps of flaming, twisted metal. Jason's pickup was undamaged. We watched from a safe distance as the warehouse burned out of control. Smaller explosions inside the building lit up the night. Officers arrested Jason, Tracy, and the brothers and stuffed them into separate police cars. A cruiser screeched to a halt at the end of Roberts Street and Smitty and Tamika jumped out.

Air horns blaring, fire trucks pulled up and firefighters piled out, hooked into a hydrant, and blasted water at what was left of the cars and warehouse. Emergency vehicles and ambulances pulled up and joined the mayhem. Harry and the other Otters stood in a group, talking to two police officers.

"Is everyone okay?" Smitty asked, the fire's glow flickering across his face.

I nodded. "We're all good."

"Was that a Cadillac?" Tamika asked, pointing to the hunks of metal. "Did it blow up?"

"Yes," I said. "So did a Jaguar."

"That's a damn shame."

Smitty stared directly at Max. "Who blew up the Cadillac this time?"

"It wasn't me," Max said. "Talk to the Otters. Maybe one of them did it."

"Some other dude did it. Mm-hmm," Tamika said.

Smitty scanned the scene, running his hand through his hair. "I'd say good job to you guys, but I have to assess the damage first. This is a total disaster."

An Uber pulled up to the curb, and Kenny Marshall hopped out and scurried over to us.

"Hey, guys. Heard about the fire on my scanner. What's the dealy?" He pulled his phone out and started taking video.

I lunged toward Kenny, and Max caught me by the waist. "It'd be worth the night in jail to punch him right in the throat." I wriggled out of Max's grasp. "He deserves it for the underwear story."

"Get behind the tape, Kenny," Tamika warned him. "We'll give you a statement later." Jimmy retreated to the crowd of gawkers forming across the street.

Smitty motioned to Tamika. "Let's get started. This is going to be a crap ton of paperwork. It's going to be a long night."

"You guys better get out of here before the chief arrives," Tamika said over her shoulder. "Him seeing Jessica's underwear isn't enough to make up for all this mess."

I turned to Sam and Jalen. "Max's car is at the Quicky Motel. Where's yours?"

"I parked next to you and walked up the train tracks," Sam said. She turned to Jalen. "How in the hell did you know I was here?"

"After you told me about the Nasato brothers last week, I put a tracking app on your phone. You weren't going missing on my watch."

"Can we please stop GPS tracking each other now? It's highly invasive," I said.

Max shifted his weight from one foot to the other. "Let's talk about it later."

Sam, Jalen, Max, and I slogged through the fire hose–drenched parking lot toward the railroad tracks. When we reached the edge of the woods, Aleksander stepped out from behind tree, and I almost had a heart attack.

"Vlad and I are cousins. We serve in the Ukrainian Army together," he said quietly. "In the army, I drive a tank. I teach Vlad to drive the tank. Vlad blow up stuff in the army. He teach me to blow up stuff. Last Tuesday night, I follow Jason Butz back here. I watch what goes on." He paused. In the fire's glow a smile flickered across his face. "Tonight, I blow that Cadillac fifty feet in the air." He stepped back into the woods and disappeared into the darkness.

Twenty-seven

The four of us trudged down the train tracks back to the Quicky Motel, processing what happened.

"How about Aleksander coming through in the clutch? Vlad and Aleksander bailed us out twice," I said, as we crunched along the railroad ballast. "Who knows what would have happened if Aleksander hadn't blown up Eddie's new Cadillac."

"That was a fortunate turn of events," Max said. "It gave me a chance to grab my backup piece."

I looked at Max. "I didn't know you carried an extra gun with you."

"I got another piece too, Red. Want to see it?"

It was too dark for him to see the look I gave him. "Not helpful."

"And how about those Otters? They're homegrown vigilantes," Sam said. "They're real law and order types. The mayor should give them a citation for their courage and bravery in helping bring down the Fat Brothers."

Jalen put his arm around Sam. "Half of those Otters probably couldn't see what they were aiming at."

"That's an inappropriate, ageist comment. Coochie doesn't agree with that." Jalen gave Sam a quizzical look.

"But it's probably true. We're lucky we weren't shot by friendly fire," Max said.

I hopped from one railroad tie to the next. "Well, the Fat Brothers didn't know the Otters are visually impaired."

"Fat Eddie should consider buying an economy car," Sam said. "I could picture him in a Kia Rio or a Chevy Spark. He's got no luck with high end electric cars."

Jalen laughed. "Gangsters don't drive economy cars. Especially ones that are trying to be like the Mafia. He should probably stick to Uber for a while."

"Eddie's not going to have to worry about a ride for at least a decade. The state's going to be his chauffer," Max said. "Jason, Vinnie, and Joey too."

> We stepped off the train tracks and hiked down
> the hill to the Quicky Motel parking lot.

My stomach growled loud enough for all to hear. "I'm hungry. I need food, stat. And a warm beverage."

"And I need a Frosty to calm my nerves," Sam said.

I turned to Sam and Jalen. "Thanks for having our backs."

"I'm sorry I called you a dumbass earlier, Jess. That was uncalled for. It wasn't your fault fat gangsters kidnapped you. It could've happened to anyone."

"That's okay, Sam. I'll see you guys later."

Max and I hopped into the 4Runner, and I cranked the heat all the way up. I was frozen from the ears down. I waved as Jalen and Sam drove off.

"Where to, Red?"

"How about Fred's Bar for some takeout?" Fred's is a corner bar on the east side of Pottstown that's been around forever. It's two blocks from my house. Harry and Mom go to Fred's for a change of pace from the Otter Club, and I love it for the cheap beer and fried food.

"It's a date." Max hit the gas and we headed down Shuman Road.

A half an hour later we were drinking beer and feasting on burgers and fries on the couch in my living room. We set up on the coffee table and waited for the ten o'clock local news to begin. Bruce was stretched out on the floor napping, and Harry and Mom were in the kitchen drinking coffee.

When the news started, Mom stuck her head into the living room. "I stopped by Maryanne's Moist Muffins and More today and I have a fresh box of assorted cupcakes in the kitchen after you're finished eating." She scrunched up her nose, stepped toward Max and me, and sniffed my hair. "You two smell like smoke. Harry smells like smoke. Do the three of you want to tell me what's going on?" She narrowed her eyes and crossed her arms over her chest.

Shit. We're busted.

Harry appeared in the living room doorway, his eyes wide with fright. He wasn't afraid of many things, but my mom pissed was one of them.

"Mom, Max and I have been working on two related cases. Max was investigating my divorce client for fraud, but then he was murdered."

Mom sank down into the recliner across from us. Harry disappeared from the doorway and returned a moment later with a bottle of rosé and a wine glass. He poured Mom a glass, handed it to her, and she took a big gulp.

"And who was your client?" she asked. Her tone was mildly pissed.

I sipped my beer. "Mom, my client was Daniel Lakeland."

"The man who owns the jewelry store chain? Daniel Lakeland is a multi-millionaire. He's a big deal in this town. Why is he involved with criminals?"

"He *was* a big deal. Mom. He was in business with the Nasato gang. They sold him platinum from their stolen catalytic converter operation for his jewelry stores."

"And you were mixed up in this, Jessica?"

"My other client, Vlad Boyko, was arrested for the murder, so I had to investigate, Mom. Vlad hired me to find out who was stealing his catalytic converters."

"Oh my God." Mom drained half her glass of wine.

"We're not sure how Daniel ended up in business with the Nasato gang," I said. "But he also committed insurance fraud on some of his jewelry, and that's where Max came into it."

"Daniel's insurance company hired me to investigate him for business fraud," Max said. "But these mob wannabes, the Nasato brothers, kidnapped Jess in an electric Cadillac."

"Kidnapped?" Mom took another gulp of rosé and shook her head. She held the wine glass in a death grip.

"But Vlad blew up the Cadillac right before the Nasato brothers had a chance to break my kneecaps and throw me in the river," I said. It felt really good to unburden myself. "And Max had put a GPS tracker on my phone, so he knew where I was. He kicked the door in and cut the zip ties off me and we got away."

"You were *zip-tied*?" Mom asked.

"Yes, to a chair on a sheet of plastic in a smelly old building in Norristown." Mom stuck her wine glass out and Harry refilled it.

"That's why you and I hurried off to Amish Country," Harry said. "Jess was afraid the gangsters were going to kidnap you next."

"So you really didn't have a coupon for the Amish Feast buffet?" Mom seemed genuinely disappointed.

"I had a coupon, Val, but it wasn't about to expire." Mom slowly nodded as she took it all in. Thankfully, the wine was kicking in.

"One gangster, Fat Eddie, stole my car, but I got it back from him at the park but his car rolled into the river." I couldn't stop talking. I hated hiding stuff from my mother. "So, Fat Eddie broke into our house, stole my underwear and left them in his Cadillac. When they pulled the car from the river, all the cops saw my underwear. And one cop took a pair and passed it around the whole department. It was in the newspaper."

Mom stuck her glass out and Harry filled it halfway.

"That was the day I said someone stole the newspaper, Val," he said. "I'm sorry I lied to you. It's okay now. Everyone is safe."

"The police arrested Fat Eddie, but he bonded out of jail the night of the eighties party. When he was leaving town, his brother's car got rear-ended by a bus," Max said.

"Yes, I remember that happened when Flamethrower was setting off the illegal fireworks display in the plaza. But you haven't explained to me why you all smell smoky," Mom said. "Do I want to know?"

"Jess and I have been following one of Daniel's murder suspects," Max took a gulp of his beer. "While we were hiding outside Fat Eddie's new warehouse tonight, he found us and took us inside at gunpoint."

Harry retrieved the box of cupcakes, and we all dove in. I took a bite and washed it down with beer. Surprisingly, it wasn't a bad flavor combination.

"Sam was there too," I said. Mom loves Sam, and I hoped that might score some points with her. "We were inside the warehouse and Fat Eddie was getting ready to shoot us and dissolve us in some barrels of chemicals, but Vlad's friend Aleksander blew up Fat Eddie's new Cadillac."

"In the confusion I was able to pull out my spare piece," Max said. "And we got the guns away from the Nasato brothers. Harry and the Otters showed up right after that. They were heavily armed."

Mom took a gulp of wine and snatched a second cupcake from the box.

Mom looked at Harry. "Is that where you went? I thought you went to Wawa to buy a lottery ticket. I wondered what was taking you so long."

"Val, I heard about the explosion on the new police scanner. I knew who Jessica and Max were dealing with, and I put two and two together. I sent out a group text to the Otters. We beat the cops to the warehouse by a couple minutes," he said proudly.

"Oh, and the warehouse caught fire," I said, snarfing down another chocolate frosted cupcake.

"About three fire and ambulance companies showed up, and Smitty, Tamika, and most of Pottstown PD arrived on scene. We left right after that," Max said. He handed me a napkin and pointed to my nose. I wiped icing off the tip of my nose with my finger and ate it. Max shook his head with a slight smile.

Mom stood up, a little unsteady on her feet. "I need an aspirin. We'll discuss this more in the morning."

"Goodnight, guys," Harry said. He put his arm around Mom and walked her back to the bedroom.

"How long is your mom going to be upset about this?" Max asked, when they were out of earshot.

"Not that long. Harry has a way of smoothing stuff over with her."

Max pulled me to him and gave me a kiss. "Want to come over? We can scrub the smoke smell off each other."

The thought of a steamy shower in Max's spa-like bathroom followed by a night of sexual depravity was enticing, but I was beyond exhausted.

"Rain check. I'm in no condition to give you my A-game tonight."

He leaned down and gave me one of his dizzying kisses. "I enjoy your B-game too.

I pushed him out the door and locked it behind him.

When I woke up the next morning, I still smelled like a bonfire. The sun poured through the window, but it was just another sunny, frigid January day. Bruce lay at the foot of the bed making biscuits and purring to himself. I fought the urge to hibernate, crawled out from beneath my new Amish quilt, stuffed my feet into slippers, and shuffled to the bathroom. With the Fat Brothers off of me, I felt as though I lost a hundred pounds. More like eight hundred to nine hundred pounds, if you added the three of them up.

I took a shower, dressed in jeans, boots, and a warm sweater, added a little lipstick, and fluffed my hair into something resembling a style. Downstairs, Mom sat at the kitchen table drinking coffee and working on a crossword puzzle. Harry was nowhere to be seen. Great, I had no buffer. I was screwed.

"Hi, Mom," I said sunnily.

"Good morning, Jess." She looked up from her crossword puzzle. "Harry talked me out of being angry at you today. He said you're an adult and you love being a private investigator and I need to support that, even if it's not my first choice for you as a career."

"Thank you, Mom. I'm not sure if I love being a PI, or if I'm even any good at it. But I want to see where it takes me. And I promise to be more careful. When I can tell you information about my cases, I will."

"You kids do things differently than we did at your age. And I won't bother to ask you if you want to go back to working at a law firm. I know what your answer is." She pushed back from the kitchen table. "Do you want some French toast?"

"More than you can imagine." I was starving. I helped Mom make breakfast, and we sat down together at the kitchen table to eat. I filled her in on more details from the past two weeks but held back a few parts, like Fat Eddie's torture tools and the break-ins, including impersonating door-to-door salespeople to get inside Daniel's mini mansion.

"Sounds like Jason Butz is up to his neck in trouble," Mom said. "Marjorie has been covering for that kid's screw-ups for years. I don't think she can fix this one."

"Me either, Mom. He's going upstate."

Max texted me. *Smitty wants us to come downtown. Pick you up at 10:45.* I texted back, *Great. See you then.* I cleaned up the dishes while Mom worked on her sewing machine in the family room. The machine's sound has been a constant part of my life and it makes me feel safe and happy. I sat on the couch while she worked, listening to the motor and dreading the interview with the police. Smitty was going to read me and Max the riot act.

Max rolled up at quarter to eleven and knocked on the door. I gave Mom a smooch, grabbed my jacket, and we jumped in the Camaro. Before he pulled away from the curb, he leaned in and gave me a kiss, and my unit ignited momentarily.

"Good morning, Red."

"Hi, Max. Are we in trouble with the cops again?"

"We're about to find out." He gave me a wink, chirped the tires, and headed for Industrial Parkway.

Twenty-eight

Smitty was waiting for us at the front desk, and he ushered us upstairs to the conference room. A few officers avoided eye contact with me as we passed by. The three of us sat down and Tamika joined us a moment later, carrying a box of Dingle's doughnuts with her. Snacks were a good sign.

"Were my underwear recovered?" I asked. "I saw some guilty-looking cops downstairs. And they better stop calling me PI Panties."

Max gave me the side eye. Smitty cleared his throat and stared down at the table.

"Your underwear were anonymously placed in the lost and found box," Tamika said. "I put latex gloves on, picked them up with a plastic fork, and threw them in the incinerator in the basement."

It goes without saying that I never wanted to see that pair of underwear again. "Thanks, Tamika, I owe you one."

"Yes, you do." She smiled and pushed the doughnut box toward me.

I selected a cream-filled chocolate doughnut and bit into it. I looked down at my shirt, lap, and the table. No blobs of cream filling anywhere. My luck must be changing.

"Tamika and I wanted to tell you both that this morning, we charged Jason Butz with the murder of Daniel Lakeland," Smitty said. "Not only was he in possession of Vlad's tools, like you said, Jessica, but we found Daniel's engraved Rolex in a safe in Jason's basement. A presumptive test indicated blood on the watch. Jason's work boots are also being tested for blood."

"We assume it's Daniel's blood, but we'll confirm that when the lab results come back. I think that dumbass planned to keep the Rolex," Tamika said.

"After we informed Jason that we found Daniel's Rolex, he sang like a canary," Smitty said. "He spilled his guts on the whole operation. He cried for his mom, and snot was going everywhere. We almost called in the custodian to clean it up."

Tamika grimaced. "It was awkward."

I was glad I missed that scene. "So what was Jason's motive for killing Daniel? Max and I didn't think it was over Tracy."

"No, the murder wasn't about his relationship with Tracy," Tamika said. "Jason wanted to get rid of Daniel for another reason. Jason found another buyer for the precious metals. Someone who was willing to give him kickbacks on the jewelry that was made from the platinum. Jason wanted to cut Daniel from the picture and bring his guy to Fat Eddie. Jason wanted to play a bigger role in the operation than simply a catalytic converter thief."

"What about Daniel's nephew, Tony DiMario?" I asked. "Was he in on the murder plot?"

"Tony passed the polygraph," Smitty said. "He claims to know nothing about the plot to murder his uncle. He said he felt horrible because he brought Jason into the operation."

"And the Fat Brothers? How do they factor into Daniel's murder?" Max asked.

"Tamika and I weren't able to make any direct connection between the Nasato brothers and the murder of Daniel Lakeland. Jason didn't implicate them. We have circumstantial evidence from their business dealings, but no physical evidence. Fat Eddie denied involvement and offered to take a poly. But Juan Epstein advised him against it."

"Fat Eddie and his brothers are going to prison for a long time, between the catalytic converter ring and your kidnapping," Tamika said. "But Fat Eddie's going to skate on another murder charge."

I shoved the rest of the doughnut in my mouth before the cream could plop out. Tamika slid a bottle of water across the table at me.

I took a sip. This was going better than I thought it would. "What about Tracy? Was she involved in the murder?"

"Tracy also took a poly this morning and passed. Jason didn't implicate her either," Smitty said.

"She's just a rich skank," Tamika said.

Smitty tapping his pen on the table and giving us both a hard look. "As for you two, we could bring trespassing charges against you. We also feel certain you both participated in a break-in in Rosemont recently, but we can't prove it. You're narrowly escaping breaking and entering charges too."

"And the two of you wouldn't know anything about Fat Eddie's Cadillac exploding in Norristown, would you?" Tamika asked.

Max shifted around in his seat and drummed his fingers on the conference table. We both shook our heads no. There was no way we were giving up Vlad after he helped save my life. I reached for the doughnut box, and Tamika snatched it away and closed the lid.

"Uh-uh," she said. "No more doughnuts for you. You're holding out on us."

"Regardless, we appreciate the contributions you both made to help solve the murder of Daniel Lakeland. But we better not see or hear from you in a professional capacity for a while," Smitty said.

Max stood up. "Got it. We'll fly under the radar. Let's go, Jess."

Max and I grabbed our jackets and headed for the door.

"Wait," I said, turning to Smitty and Tamika. "What's going to happen to Vlad?"

"The DA dropped the murder charges against Vlad earlier this morning," Smitty said. He glanced at his watch. "He should be out of jail by lunchtime."

I smiled, and a tear welled up in my eye. No crying in front of the cops. I nodded and shut the conference door behind me.

Max reopened the door and stuck his head in. "One more thing. What about the reward money?"

"We'll talk to Tracy," Smitty said. "For now, get lost."

Max and I left Pottstown PD and jumped back in the Camaro. Max cranked up the heat and put the car in gear. "Now that the case is solved, want to go back to my place and get naked, Red?"

He pulled me to him and kissed me deeply. I leaned in and let the kiss go where it wanted too, thoroughly enjoying the slight oxygen deprivation. All the fear and anxiety from the past two weeks melted away in his arms.

"Come on, Jess, let's get out of here" Max's right hand was on the gear shift, and his eyes were focused intently on mine. My stomach growled loud and long. This is not the first time my stomach has undermined my sex life.

"You *just* ate a doughnut, not a half an hour ago."

"It wasn't enough. Can we stop for lunch first?"

"Sure, I could eat. How about Fred's again?"

"How about it?"

Max hit the gas, and we cruised down the parkway. We parked out front, took seats at the bar and gazed up at the TV. A Flyers game was on, we were up by one in the first period, and Gritty was dancing in the stands. Fred ambled over to us, and Max ordered beers while I perused the menu. I felt like turning over a new leaf, so I ordered a salad with grilled chicken.

"Look at you with the leafy greens," Max said. He handed the menus back to Fred. "I'll have the same. And an order of fries." Nice.

Fred returned with the beer, and Max and I were about to make a toast when the door to the bar burst open. Everyone turned to see who entered. Vlad, Anastasiya and Aleksander approached us.

"There's my lady detective and her ex-policeman partner." Vlad's voice boomed over the game.

"Vlad! You're out!" I hopped off my stool.

Before I knew it, Vlad grabbed me and hugged me, lifting me up off the floor in the process. "You forget to take the GPS tracker off your car. I've come to say thank you."

He set me back down, and I gave Anastasiya a hug. She was smiling from ear to ear. Vlad shook Max's hand and pounded him on the back. A few people at the bar moved down, and the three of them sat next to us.

Fred reappeared. "What'll you have, Vlad?"

"Ginger ale for my wife, two shots of vodka for my cousin and I, and a round for the house." Everyone in the bar cheered. Fred pulled down a bottle of vodka from the shelf, poured the shots and set them in front of us.

Vlad plunked down a wad of cash. "Leave the bottle on the bar." Fred rang the bell and Vlad raised his glass. "To my brave lady detective, Jessica, who set me free today. And to my beautiful wife, Anastasiya, and to our baby boy." He kissed her belly, we downed the shots, and everyone in the bar cheered again.

Max put his arm around me and clinked his bottle of beer to mine.

"To us, Jess."

"To us. Trial basis, though, right?"

"Right."

I hope you enjoyed the first book in the Jessica
Byrne, P.I. mystery series. If you would like to join my
newsletter to learn about upcoming books in the series,
please visit https://www.kristenandrews.com
Or
You can use this special link to join and receive a preview of
the first two chapters of Book 2:
https://dl.bookfunnel.com/2duuf03esv
In addition to news about books,
you'll also receive photos of my pets, snack food items,
and critters that live in my backyard.

• • • •

If you know someone who might enjoy
reading about Jessica and her crew,
please let them know and leave a review.
Thank you.

• • • •

Facebook: @kristenandrewsauthor[1]
Amazon Author Page:
https://www.amazon.com/author/kristenandrewsbooks

Author's Acknowledgement

• • • •

MANY THANKS GO OUT to those who have supported and encouraged me (instead of laughing) when I began writing the Jessica Byrne, P.I. series. Who knew something I loved so much could bring feelings of fear and doubt that made me want to hide under the bed? If not for the cheering on of friends who read chapters as I finished them, and my husband John's unwavering support and love, Jessica may not have ever solved her first case.

• • • •

JUST AS MY FAVORITE writers have done for me, this book was written to entertain, make readers laugh and provide a place for your imagination to take over. I thank each of you for spending your time reading my book and I hope it did what I set out to do. Or at least got you to listen to some heavy metal.

• • • •

Rock on, my friends.
Kristen